# More Than We Bargained For

## Timber Falls, Volume 4

Fiona West

Published by Tempest and Kite, 2020.

MORE THAN WE BARGAINED FOR

**First edition. October 13, 2020.**

Copyright © 2020 Fiona West.

ISBN: 978-1952172113

Written by Fiona West.

To the victims of the Oregon fires. May you dream again sooner than you thought.

# PROLOGUE

*THUMP.* The strange noise startled Starla as she finished off her Valentine's Day consolation wine over the kitchen sink. She still wasn't used to being alone in an apartment since the divorce . . . it wasn't even final yet, she reminded herself. Soon. It had only been two months since she'd packed up and left Charlie. It was a bit squishy with the four of them here at her friend Ainsley's, even with two bedrooms. *Thump, thump.* It was coming from the front door. Cautiously, she padded over to the peephole and looked out. Her soon-to-be ex-husband stood there, holding their sleeping six-year-old daughter in his arms. He appeared to be trying to get his phone out of his pocket . . . probably to call her to open the door for him. Starla twisted the deadbolt and opened the door.

"Hi," he whispered. His black suit fit him perfectly, complementing his broad shoulders and brown hair; he looked the very definition of tall, dark and handsome. He even had a pink rosebud in his lapel to match Em's dress. As always, his good looks made her stomach flip flop, but it soured immediately. She hated that she could still be attracted to him. She felt like a slob in her pajamas, wondering if she still had flour on her nose from baking with Aiden.

"Hi," she whispered back.

"Our princess partied a little too hard tonight. Hit the cupcake table a couple of times, took one spin around the dance floor, and then pooped out on me."

"Okay." She held out her arms to take her; good thing Emily was built like she was at the same age, or she didn't think her back could take it. His face fell.

"I can't tuck her in?"

She'd promised herself that he wouldn't set foot in this apartment except when it was absolutely necessary. This didn't seem like one of those moments. Sure, Em would probably wake up during the transfer, but then they could say goodnight, and that'd be that. No drawing things out. No hanging around. But his face was so sad, and she didn't want to ruin their special father-daughter night together. At least he still took his responsibilities as a father seriously.

She sighed. "All right. Just tuck her in and go."

Charlie smiled as he ducked inside, giving her a peck on the cheek on the way by. "Thanks, honey."

She shook her head, exasperated, and squeezed her eyes shut. *I'm not your honey. Not anymore.*

She closed the door behind him and crossed the living room. Ainsley was out, and for once, Starla was a bit sorry. Usually she relished the quiet and having one less body in the small apartment, but it was Valentine's Day. Ainsley and Kyle were having dinner at his house . . . his big, empty farmhouse. All those rooms, all to themselves. At least she wasn't the only one not having sex tonight; they were waiting until their wedding, just a few months away now. She tried to set aside her envy over being alone and went to the overstuffed chair where her book was waiting. She could see Charlie down the hall, tucking Emily into the big bed, carefully taking off her shiny black shoes. It was the kind of sweetness that had inspired her to stay all those years. He kissed Emily's head, tucking the quilt up under her chin.

He checked on Aiden, too, ruffling the boy's hair gently, not even waking him; that kid always slept like the dead. Which was good, since she was sharing a bed with both of them right now. Ainsley had offered to let her share her room, but that would mean sharing her bed, and it felt a little weird to be taking Ainsley's space like that, even when she was invited to do so. They were good friends and had been since middle school, but it was already too much that she was letting them crash with her. Starla would need to find something more permanent soon. Ainsley and Kyle were engaged, but they weren't getting married until June, since Ainsley was a teacher. Starla couldn't wait that long for her to vacate the apartment and leave it to them. Her parents had offered for her and the kids to stay with them, of course, but their retirement home was pretty small; she was their only kid in the area so they didn't usually need room for kids and grandkids to stay with them. Plus, they'd been really weird about her separation from Charlie. Her siblings were all single by choice, an option that was looking better to her all the time. Love was for suckers; she wasn't going back down that path ever again. Been there, bought the T-shirt, had to pawn the T-shirt to pay her legal bills.

Charlie quietly closed the bedroom door and came back down the hall.

"Thanks for taking her tonight."

"Oh, my pleasure. We really had a good time."

"Good."

"I wish you could've been there, too, though."

"Why?" The word came out harsh. She didn't mind. She had every reason to be skeptical where Charlie was concerned. There was no room left in her heart to trust him; it was jam-packed with lies, deceit, and downright deception that he'd attempted over the years. It was full up.

"So I could dance with you," he said, almost sheepishly, hands in his pockets. He really did look handsome tonight. It was still annoying.

"We don't dance together anymore, Charlie." *That's how I got into this mess. I should've listened to my mother when she told me that
sophomores shouldn't go to senior prom.*

"Why not? Aren't we still friends?"

"Of course. We parent together, we'll be interacting, I'm sure."

"Interacting? That's cold, Star. That's not you." He held out his
hand. "Come on. One dance."

She wanted to slap his hand down and run, but she didn't. For
the kids, she told herself; they'd both noticed the tension between
them. For the sake of peace. One dance.

"You smell amazing," he said as he drew her close.

"It's just vanilla extract. Aiden and I made a Valentine's Day
cake."

"Heart-shaped?"

"Of course. There's no other way on a holiday, is there?"

"Not for you, no," he chuckled, leaning in closer. He was warm
and strong, and it felt really, really good to be held. She hadn't realized that being divorced was going to mean she was so solitary. It
wasn't just that there was no one to share your bed with; it was that
there was no one to share your day with. She missed the sense of calm
in the evening, snuggling with someone. Being held. Being close. She
hooked her arms up over his shoulders, and his hands slid to her hips.

"How do we know when one dance is over if there's no music?"
she asked.

"I'll let you know," he murmured. That glass of red wine she'd had
earlier had clearly gone straight to the 'good decisions' part of her
brain, robbed it blind and taken up its boozy residence.

"Do you ever miss me, Starla?" Charlie's voice was low. She liked
it when he used that register. He smelled good tonight, too; he'd
used that cologne she liked, the one that smelled like seawater on a
summer day.

"Yeah. Sometimes." She swallowed. Ainsley would blow her stack if she were here. *Maybe she'll come home early, and then she can yell at me for being an idiot.* But the front door stayed firmly shut, no matter how she stared at it over Charlie's shoulder. "Do you miss me?"

"Every day, beautiful. I wish you'd come home. We can still tear up those papers. Nothing's finalized yet." His hands were moving soothingly over her back.

"You cheated on me, Charlie."

"It was a one-time thing, baby. I'll never do it again, I swear. All I want is for you and the kids to come home." He kissed her neck. *Home.* God, she missed her house. Her kitchen window overlooking the Santiam River every day. The big yard for the kids to play in out front. Her big four-poster bed. He kissed her neck again, and again. It wasn't that she forgot that he wasn't allowed; she was just so stinking lonely. She was tired of making other people happy. Her kids were so clingy and needy lately . . . she couldn't blame them, this was a weird situation, and they wanted to go home, too. They cried, and her heart broke that they didn't understand why this was necessary. They cried, and they just wanted her to make them feel better. Maybe that's why she'd been baking so much lately. Right now, her mind was firmly focused on the idea that Charlie would make *her* feel better, and then he could leave. She hadn't given him any notice before she moved out. This would be it; a Valentine's Day 'screw you' to her soon-to-be ex. She turned her head to kiss his lips, and he squeezed her gently as her tongue slid against his.

"This is the last time," she whispered.

"Oh, baby," he groaned. "You're killing me. Don't say that. Please, honey. You don't mean that."

"Yes, I do. This time, I do." It was on the tip of her tongue to apologize, but she held it back. She wasn't the one who'd done wrong.

"Just come home, Starla. I miss you too much. I miss this body so much . . . I haven't touched anybody else since you've been gone. I've been so good." She wanted to believe him. He did seem a tad desperate tonight; the gentlest touch of her fingers over his skin had him panting. She relished the way he was reacting to her; it felt good to be wanted again. And Charlie was good in the bed; they'd always been good together that way.

"You're it for me, baby. You always have been. I love you so much." She kissed him hard. That was enough talking. If he kept talking, feeding her such obvious lies, she was going to lose her nerve and send him away and wind up crying herself to sleep. She was sick to death of that.

"Got a condom?" she asked. He didn't miss a beat.

"Of course, honey," he murmured, his gaze heated, as he took off her glasses.

She'd deal with the emotional consequences later.

# CHAPTER ONE

*MARCH*

There were a few things Starla Miller knew for sure: if she forgot her coat, it would rain. If she let her daughter play with her jewelry, it would disappear. And if it was Thursday, she'd find an anonymous package by the back door of the library and see Sawyer Devereaux. He wouldn't be there until the afternoon, but he'd be there. Always was. But since it was only 8:20 a.m., he wasn't one of the irritated patrons waiting outside the library—she was late again. Starla sighed as she dragged herself up to the front doors, a bag of heavy books over her shoulder.

"Sorry, everyone. Rough morning." She turned to Mrs. Foster. She had a cozy mystery tucked under her arm, a new genre to Mrs. Foster; she'd checked it out to her just yesterday. "You didn't DNF it already, did you?"

"DNF?"

"It just means you marked in your 'to be read' list as Did Not Finish," Starla clarified as she unlocked the front doors.

The older woman blushed. "Oh, no. Quite the opposite. I stayed up all night reading it. We have the next one in the series, don't we?"

Starla gave herself a mental high five that she'd correctly recommended a book that Mrs. Foster would love. "Yes, we do. And I think someone just returned it."

Mrs. Foster shrugged her shoulders in obvious delight, a shy smile stretched across her face.

"Can I get my holds? I really need to get to work. Some of us can't be late," Mr. Kirschbaum complained, and it made the joy in her heart wither. She didn't know why it was so hard to get out of bed lately, and that troubled her, too.

"Yes, of course. Sorry about that," Starla said, leading the way inside, flipping on the lights. "Just the two, right?"

"Yes, it was two."

A flash of a striped tail in the back corner had Starla muttering under her breath. She wouldn't mind having a library cat . . . if the cat were actually allowed to be here. Based on his tag, his name was Taylor. She didn't believe in giving animals people names, so in her head, she called him Sir Poops-a-Lot. She'd mentioned him at a town meeting once, but no one confessed to owning him. She was this close to just buying a litter box and giving up; until then, she'd go looking for whatever presents he'd left her in a few minutes. Maybe she'd print out more signage once the early crowd cleared out: *This is Taylor. Taylor loves the library. Taylor does not belong in the library. Please don't let Taylor in the library.* She hurried to the back door to let Sir Poops-a-Lot outside, and sure enough, there was the box of books. It was big today; she'd need the hand truck to get it inside. Infuriating.

She tried to shake off her annoyance, even though Mr. Kirschbaum was still glaring at her.

"Got your card?" Starla asked cheerfully, and he patted his pockets, then grimaced.

"I think I left it at home."

"That's okay," she said, waving away his concerned look. "I got you covered."

"You can look it up?"

"Of course," she smiled, keeping her gaze on the computer screen.

Once she worked through all the patron needs, she got up to check in the returns and re-shelve them. Starla brushed her fingers along the books in the children's section, looking for the Roald Dahl books to reshelve *James and the Giant Peach*. She'd convinced another reluctant reader to try his work . . . *Matilda* was her personal favorite, but she'd usually start them on *Boy* or *The BFG;* they seemed to have more mass appeal. She'd seen a video once in which Roald Dahl had detailed his writing routine. It had convinced her to never try writing a novel, no matter the circumstances. Writers were all clearly at least a little bit unstable.

Her own son, of course, would have none of her book recommendations. Aiden had staunchly decided about six months ago that he was only going to read *City of Ember* for the foreseeable future, and he'd stuck to the decision. He had to be bored with it by now. He *had* to. But he was his father's son in many ways, and when Charlie put his mind to something, he rarely changed it. It would've been nice if he'd managed to apply the same commitment to their marriage. Eleven years down the drain; eleven years wasted with him, just waiting for him to change. She'd known that he'd been seeing other girls when they were dating. She just thought he'd stop when they got engaged, and while there had been too much evidence to the contrary to let her mind rest, there had never been enough to convict him of cheating. He'd stayed just out of her reach all this time, being careful to sneak around when he wouldn't get caught. It didn't help that he worked in another city . . . she wondered now if they'd decided to put the dealership in Stayton just to stay out of Timber Falls. Not Jason; Charlie's brother was guilty of nothing, she was sure of it. He adored his wife Lacey and their baby, even if he wasn't able to be very reliable when it came to helping out. Lacey would call her occasionally, needing to vent a little, and Starla always listened with a sympathetic ear. But she didn't complain about Charlie; she didn't feel like she could. She'd known how he was, and she'd married him anyway, for Aiden's sake. And then Em had come along, and well, it had just made sense to stay.

Until That Day.

"Starla?"

She turned to see who it was and grinned at Hattie. "Hello, Mayor," she said. "You here for book club?" The Mind Readers met here weekly, and they were the only ones allowed to bring hot drinks into the library. Really, they didn't spill any less than any other group, but Starla had a soft spot for kickass older ladies, and all these gals fit that description to a T. Mildred Wilson and Tansy Draper were right behind her.

"I keep telling you, I'm not the mayor any more than you are."

"You can say it all you want. I know you're pulling strings in this town all the time."

Hattie set her coffee on the low book shelf and began pulling chairs into a circle by the front windows. "You make me out to be some kind of puppet master, but I'm just an old lady who likes her horses and her books. That's all."

"Mmm," Starla said, hoping her skeptical tone was coming through. "If you say so. Don't forget your sweets on your list of likes," Starla added, reshelving a copy of *Harriet the Spy*.

"Yes, those, too," Hattie smirked, rubbing her belly. "Thank you for reminding me, Ms. Moore." Hearing her maiden name used again was strange; she felt like it should make her happy, but instead, it made her frown, just thinking about all the ways she'd changed since she'd last used it. She glanced at Hattie and found her wearing a matching frown.

"Your book fairy stop by lately?" her friend asked.

"Last night," she said with a sigh. "It's always Wednesday night."

Hattie laughed. "It really vexes you, doesn't it?"

"You know it, lady. That dumb fairy leaves easily more than $300 worth of books on my doorstep every month, and never leaves a trace to lead back to their identity. No receipts, no address on the box, nothing. Every book still has a price tag from Powell's on it; the City of Books has been busy on this person's behalf for months now."

"I think it's nice," Hattie soothed, and Starla glared at her.

"I hate a mystery."

The older woman strolled closer to her, lowering her voice as she drew her away from the others. "How's the divorce going?"

"Almost done. Our court date's in a month. It should be straight-forward; he says he wants to be agreeable."

"Yes, he's always been agreeable on the outside. But I bought a car from him once. He's always got an agenda."

"True." Starla knew that all too well; he was a master manipula-tor. It was easier to see now that she didn't love him.

"Just watch yourself, all right? You've got a good lawyer?"

Starla nodded. "My cousin Peg. She's great; she specializes in this kind of law."

"Good." Hattie patted her hand. "You'll need it going up against Mr. Goldberg." The Miller family's lawyer was on retainer for a rea-son. No one in Linn County wanted to mess with him. He'd some-how gotten Chase Carpenter's drug charges dropped the first time, and the second time, he'd gotten off with rehab instead of jail time. She was trusting Charlie that he wasn't going to try anything weird with their divorce. If anything, he seemed sort of apathetic about the terms. She didn't understand it, but she couldn't be sorry about it.

The rest of the Mind Readers were coming in, chatting, as they basked in the sunshine streaming in through the front windows. Starla moved off quietly to give them some space . . . and also, the smell of their coffee was doing weird things to her stomach. She usu-ally loved it, but she hadn't been able to touch it lately. Odd, real-ly. Oh well; she could get a marionberry scone or a ginger cookie at Riverside on her break instead of a coffee.

The morning raced by; she did the toddler story time and vacuumed afterward, and by the time she finished cataloging the new books, complete with plastic covers, barcodes, and labeling, it was time to take a break. Hands in her pockets, she crossed the street to the coffee shop . . . but that smell. It was still getting to her. What little breakfast she'd had was threatening to make an appearance right on their checkered floor. It was so confusing; she must have picked up a bug somewhere. She covered her nose with her sleeve and tried to breathe slowly, but her stomach was lurching around inside her like a drunkard. She shuffled forward in line and tried to smile at the large, freckled blonde woman behind the counter. "Hey Paige."

"Hey Starla," she smiled. "What can I get for you?"

"Just a ginger tea, I think."

"Yeah, you look a little green around the gills." Starla blinked at her, feeling self-conscious. She forced a smile.

"Oh, no. I'm fine." It was troubling to think that other people could see she was unwell; she'd have to try harder to act normal.

Paige lifted an eyebrow, but said nothing as she poured fresh ginger tea from the carafe.

"Can I get a little honey and lemon juice with it, too?"

"Of course. Anything else?"

"No, that'll do it," she said passing her a five dollar bill. "Keep the change."

"Thanks, hon. Have a great day."

Starla pushed her way out of the coffee shop, forcing down a gag. She sat down on the metal bench and took a sip of the tea . . . it soothed her throat and her nerves. Where could she have gotten sick? Neither of the kids had even been sniffly lately. Maybe it was a stomach flu . . . but it wasn't usually going around this late into the year. She took a longer drink of the tea and took some deep breaths. She would be fine. Just fine. She'd march back to the library, sanitize everything within an inch of its usefulness, and get back to work.

The kids were going to Charlie's tonight; she could go to bed early. Yes, she'd do that. She wouldn't even read, just go straight to bed. Surely that would help.

That afternoon, her kids hadn't shown up yet when Sawyer came into the library. His gaze was downcast as usual, avoiding the other patrons, striding up the walk in that white and blue flannel shirt, the one that brought out his eyes. *You have no right to think about his eyes.* Through the window, she saw him do the same thing he always did: he dropped his three books into the return outside, came inside, and went straight to her desk. "Hey. Got my holds?"

"I sent you an email to that effect, I believe," she replied evenly, not looking up from her computer. She didn't know why she was messing with him; with any other patron, she'd already have their holds waiting on the desk when she saw them coming. It's not like she was trying to draw out their interactions, but she wasn't trying to shorten them, either . . .

"Yeah, I got it. That's why I'm here."

"No," she said with a smile, lowering her glasses to look at him over the top of the frames, "you're here because it's Thursday."

"That, too." He smiled back. Shaking her head, she reached behind her desk and grabbed his holds, three more books, rubber-banded together.

"Let's see what you've got," she said, turning the spines so she could see them, and she saw him cross his arms in her peripheral vision. She already knew he'd gotten the first three books in the Stephanie Plum series by Janet Evanovich; she just liked ruffling his feathers from time to time. Especially when he wore that shirt.

"Can I just have my books, please?" That light southern accent; it reminded her of Harry Connick Jr., though his looks had more of a flannel-loving-hermit-bachelor-thing happening. She'd never seen him come into the library in anything but jeans. A ratty baseball cap covered his longish blond hair and shadowed his eyes. She already knew they were a crystalline blue, like Crater Lake.

"A mystery, a mystery, and . . . a mystery." She gave him her best deadpan stare. "Way to change it up, Devereaux."

He uncrossed his arms and put his hands on his hips. "Well, I did get some written by a woman this time."

Starla blinked; she'd teased him last week about only reading books by dead white guys. She didn't think he'd even heard her. Hope fluttered in her heart that maybe he'd finally cave.

"If you're looking to mix it up, I could recommend something you'd—"

"Nope."

Why was he being so difficult? Mrs. Graves was approaching the desk, and Starla hurried to get his compliance, knowing he would clam up as soon as other people were around.

"Come on," she hissed, "you never let me pick a book for you. I'm great at picking books." She was too late; she saw Sawyer stiffen as he heard someone else coming. He held his hand out flat, and, grumpily, she handed the books over.

"You're missing out."

"See you next week." He tipped his hat to her politely, then went over to say hi to her kids, who had just walked in and were taking off coats and backpacks, finding their spots to wait for her to finish work. She was still staring after him, trying to make sense of why he was so hot and cold, when Mrs. Graves cleared her throat.

"Sorry, Margie," she blushed. "What can I do for you?"

# CHAPTER TWO

ON FRIDAY AFTERNOON, Sawyer pulled into a close spot in the parking lot of Miller Motors in Stayton and hopped out of his truck, print-out in hand. Jason Miller was a nice guy, but he'd learned to bring a written list of what he wanted or he often left without half the things he'd come for. Sawyer headed straight back to the garage, bypassing the front office, knowing Starla's ex, Charlie, was probably working up there. He made Sawyer want to take a shower afterward; there was just something slimy about the man. It was better that they not cross paths, for both of them. He'd only interacted with him a handful of times, all of them unpleasant.

When he came around the corner to the open garage door, he saw a familiar pair of children squatting in the gravel driveway, looking at something in the dirt.

"It's still alive, Aiden. Leave it alone," Emily said, holding her brother back with one hand.

"It's gonna sting somebody. We should squish it."

"No," Emily insisted, "it's not hurting anyone. It's endangered."

*Where on earth did she learn that?* Sawyer couldn't help but be impressed. Then again, her mama was smart as a whip, so clearly, the apple didn't fall far from the tree. If they were here, maybe Starla was, too. That made his heart rate pick up a little bit, and he adjusted his T-shirt self-consciously.

"What're we looking at?" he asked quietly, leaning over with the kids.

"It's a bee," said Aiden, still staring down the insect. "We're going to smash it."

"No, we're *not*," Emily said loudly, and Sawyer shushed her a little.

"Listen, it's not worth your time. Let nature take its course. If he can recover, that means more honey for us. If not, that's life. Let the bug be."

"I think you mean death," Aiden quipped, and Sawyer cocked an eyebrow at him.

"Yes, I suppose so. Your uncle Jason around?"

The kids pointed into the darkened garage, then went back to their speculative observation. Sawyer strode into the garage, following the sound of two voices speaking in muted tones. He paused when he got close enough to hear what they were saying.

"I really appreciate this, Jase," said Starla.

"It's not a problem."

"No, really. Having testimony from his own brother will help my case."

"Well, I want you to know that I tried to stop him, plenty of times." Sawyer could hear Jason picking up tools and putting them down, clanking around. The man was always in motion. "Talked to him about it a bunch of times," Jason continued, "but it just went in one ear and out the other. I don't think there's anything you could've done differently."

"Still hurts," she said softly, and the way her voice cracked had Sawyer's own heart feeling bruised. "And it hurts to think I'm losing you and Lacey and Iris, too . . ."

"Hey. You're not losing us. That's not happening." Jason was an intense guy, and all his sincerity was coming through just fine.

"You don't have to say that," Starla said, her voice so wobbly and watery, Sawyer felt tears spring to his eyes.

"I'm not just saying it, I mean it. We're related. Period. You're gonna come over for dinner, we're gonna meet at the park, all that stuff. Lacey feels the same way. Seriously."

"Okay," Starla said, in a way that showed she wasn't sure if she believed him. Sawyer felt he should've announced his presence earlier, so he quietly backtracked, then let his boots slap the concrete floor loudly as he approached.

"Hello? Anybody here?"

Jason's tattooed arms were still wrapped around Starla, and he didn't let go when Sawyer stopped in the doorway of the back office.

"Hey, man," Jason greeted. "Just a sec."

"Sure."

He let Starla go, but he held her momentarily by the shoulders. "I meant everything I said. Say you believe me."

She nodded, and he squeezed her lightly before he let her go completely.

"You two know each other?" he asked, glancing between Starla and Sawyer.

"Oh, yeah," Starla said, wiping her eyes. "Sawyer's one of my regulars at the library."

"Of course you'd be into books, Devereaux," Jason snickered. "You're so boring, man."

"At least I didn't flip my ATV and shatter my collar bone."

"That only happened twice," Jason said, pointing at him, and Sawyer just shook his head, smiling.

"You got those parts for me?"

"Oh, right. No, not yet." He turned to the computer as if to look them up, but Sawyer cleared his throat and held out the printed list.

"You're learning my ways," Jason grinned. "I'll be right back. Make yourself comfortable."

Sawyer glanced at Starla, who had recovered enough to be interested in his shirt, apparently. Then she seemed to snap out of whatever she'd been thinking about, because she called after Jason.

"Wait, you didn't sign my . . ." She trailed off, throwing Sawyer a chagrined look.

"Is this a bad time? I can come back."

Starla sighed. "No, no. Don't blame yourself. Jason is . . ."

"Distractible," Sawyer finished, and Starla nodded with a tired smile.

"Exactly. If it wasn't you, it would've been something else."

They stood there in silence. Sawyer wasn't uncomfortable, but he glanced at her and caught her staring at him. He grinned to himself when she looked away quickly, her cheeks reddening. When she peeked at him again, he pretended to be fascinated by a magazine on a mountain of papers on the desk.

"One time," he said, not looking up, "he left me waiting here for an hour while he went to lunch and ran some errands. Completely forgot about me."

"That's nothing," said Starla, pushing her hair back from her face distractedly. "He forgot his own wife's birthday *during the party*."

Sawyer's mouth fell open as he looked at her. "He did not."

"Did too," she said, turning to face him. "We sent him to the store for candles for the cake, and he came back two hours later with a ham, a quesadilla maker, and a case of beer. He'd run into an old friend and spent an hour talking before he even got inside." She paused. "We don't send him to the store anymore."

Sawyer chuckled. "I can see why."

"Do you have a car in the shop?" Starla asked, shoving her glasses up her nose.

"Uh, no, I'm just buying some parts off of him. We work on the same kind of machines."

"I see." She sat down on the far end of the couch, nodding toward the close end, and he accepted her invitation gratefully. "Are you enjoying the Stephanie Plum books?"

"Haven't started them yet." He cleared his throat nervously. "What're you reading?" He shouldn't ask that, really. It was just asking for trouble. If it wasn't what he wanted to hear, it was just going to annoy him. And if it was . . .

"We just got some new historical fiction in," she said, picking at a loose thread on one of the couch cushions, and he couldn't resist pressing her a little bit.

"Historical fiction or historical romance?" he asked, letting a hint of a grin through so she'd know he was teasing.

Starla lifted her chin defiantly. "Historical romance *is* historical fiction."

"Uh-huh. Was this a book fairy donation?"

"As a matter of fact, it was." He schooled his features into a careful mask, lest she look at him and see how much that delighted him. He wondered if she'd gone for the Lisa Kleypas or the Courtney Milan. He was pretty sure she'd love both of them . . . but he didn't get much feedback on his choices. It was one of many flaws in his system.

"You still stewing over those donations?"

"I will stew over it forever," she said adamantly, but she gave him a shy smile that made him wish there wasn't so much in the way of him getting to know her better. Even if she was getting divorced, she'd never be interested in him . . . but there she was, staring at him again.

"Do I have broccoli between my teeth or something?" he asked, slicking his tongue over his top row of teeth.

"I should go find Jason," Starla said, standing up quickly, snatching some paperwork off the top of a filing cabinet. "You want to come?"

"Sure," he said, and he reached to open the door for her. Their hands collided on the handle, and he felt the warmth of her skin for the briefest moment before they both pulled back quickly. "Sorry," he blurted, "I was trying to . . ."

"No, it's my fault," she said, shaking her head, but her head slowed as he caught her gaze and held it. This was why he kept his visits to the library brief and at busy times; whenever he looked into her eyes, he felt something he couldn't put his finger on. Something he didn't want to look away from, but couldn't name. Not breaking eye contact, he reached out and opened the door for her, and she darted through it. He ambled out behind her into the garage, lagging behind to give her a little space. Seeing her from behind was no hardship, either; she was often sitting down when she was at the library. If he was really lucky, she was reshelving; he routinely had to bite the inside of his cheek on those days. He heard Jason's voice before he saw him crouching with his niece and nephew in the dirt.

"I don't think it's a centipede," Jason announced. "Not enough legs." He glanced up to see the two of them approaching, and he smiled. "Oops. Busted. I gotta get back to work, kids. I'm coming," he called out, jogging over empty-handed. Jason signed whatever Starla had for him (Sawyer made a point of not looking at it—he'd been too much in her business already today), then Sawyer pulled a second copy of his list out of his pocket and handed it over.

"Yeah, you're learning," Jason said, ambling back into the garage, whistling as he went.

"Good to see you," Sawyer called after Starla as she gathered her kids, and she gave him another shy smile.

Was it Thursday yet? He'd return those books even if he hadn't read them yet.

# CHAPTER THREE

ON SATURDAY AFTERNOON, Starla was asleep when she heard the kids thundering up the steps outside the apartment. Groggy, she looked around, finding sleep as hard to push off as the heavy quilt over her lap. Her book had fallen to the carpet at some point, but apparently the noise of that hadn't disturbed her. She picked it up and set it on the arm of the couch . . . was that where she'd stopped? She couldn't remember. She glanced down at the page: who was the Duke of Arningham, anyway? Maybe she should skip back a few chapters to see if anything rang a bell. She'd been *so* exhausted lately; right around three o'clock every day she could barely keep her eyes open. And that was exceptionally poor timing, because that's right when the kids came in and wanted to chat about their days and get a snack and needed their homework reading logs signed and . . . *and right when Sawyer comes in.* She was bounced out of the thought when the front door banged open.

"Dad took us to the zoo!" The kids bounded into the apartment; their arms were full of exotic stuffed animals, T-shirts, books, and puzzles, and based on how fast their mouths were running, their bellies were clearly full of elephant ears, tiger dogs, and whatever other animal-themed treats they'd conned out of Charlie. He didn't usually have a problem saying no to them

. . . but then again, it was spring break. There wasn't any harm in them cutting loose for once, she supposed.

"Sorry," Charlie said, looking like he meant it. "There was a mix-up at the dealership, and Tracy just kept buying them stuff while I was distracted. I don't think she knew what else to do with them."

"Tracy?" Her arms crossed automatically over her stomach.

"Yeah. You know. Tracy."

"No," she said, barbed. "I don't know Tracy. Who is this person?"

"She's the one you . . ." His gaze dropped to the side. "Saw me with. That one day." That's how he was going to describe finding him undressing a beautiful blonde on her favorite sofa? *That one day?* I mean, it was exceptional in that it was the only time she actually caught him. But still. She felt like it should at least be capitalized. That One Day. It had given her what she needed to end it. Suddenly, the sugar rush and the excess of gifts felt a lot less forgivable.

"What was she doing there?"

"I brought her along to help. She's working the front desk at the dealership, and she likes kids."

"Uh-huh." Her gaze slid to the kids. "Em, no shoes on the couch." Emily turned and knocked her book off the couch. One shoe flew to the middle of the room, and the other flew behind the couch.

"Anyway, we all had a great time." He paused, fidgeting with the bill of the University of Oregon hat he was holding. "You three going to do anything special this week?"

Starla decided she would not be outdone. "Yes. We're going hiking."

"Oh. That sounds like fun."

"It will be," she confirmed, nodding, as if that confirmed it. She would make it fun, through sheer force of will. She would shake off this fatigue and make an effort. Plus, it was free. That was right in her budget right now.

"Well, if you guys run out of stuff to do, Tracy said she's happy to take them another day this week, let them hang around at the office."

"I don't think that'll be necessary."

Charlie gave her a pitying smile. "You think they'll be happy hanging around the library all week?"

"Thank you, but we'll be just fine." *Tracy can watch them over my dead body.*

"Okay. Well, I'll see you next Saturday, then. Unless you need anything . . ."

"Nope," Starla said firmly.

"Okay, I'll be off then." He seemed to be lingering. Why was he lingering?

"Goodbye, Charlie," she said, opening the front door. He gave her a knowing smirk, then sauntered out. When she shut the door and turned back toward the living room, Aiden was waiting there, scowling, tablet in hand.

"Where's Dad?"

She resisted the urge to cross her arms over her stomach. "He left."

"I was going to show him something in Minecraft! I finally got my nether portal to work!" His muscles tensed, and she could tell he wanted to throw the tablet in his hand, but didn't dare.

"He had to g-go," Starla stammered, angry with herself for being intimidated by her own son. "He doesn't live here, Aiden."

"You always send him home right away! Why can't he hang out here with us?"

*You were there. You know why.* She still hadn't really talked to Aiden about that day. They'd walked in, seen Charlie on the couch on top of another woman, and walked right back out. She'd taken Aiden to Annie's and bought him a burger and a milkshake while she went outside and called Ainsley, crying, watching her son through the restaurant window. When Annie went over and sat with him, Starla had let herself crumple to the ground, the way she'd wanted to since the first moment, behind the brick restaurant.

"You spent all day with Dad. Don't you want some Mom time?" she asked, reaching out to ruffle his hair, but he moved away before she could touch him, storming down the hall to their shared room and slamming the door behind him. She hadn't expected teenage angst this early; he'd just turned nine a few months ago.

"What *are* we going to do next week?" Emily asked, looking up from where she was reading to her dolls. Charlie was constantly trying to shove STEM toys, doctor kits, or experiment kits into her hands, but she just put them in her closet and went back to her dolls.

"We're going hiking."

"What day?"

"How about Friday?"

Emily smoothed her doll's very chaotic hair. "Okay. What about the other days?"

Guilt gnawed at her. She could've taken some vacation this week, but it was a busy time at the library. "The other days, Mom has to work. You guys will hang out at the library with me."

Emily mumbled something under her breath, then collected up her dolls and went to Ainsley's door and knocked. At least her kids were polite to other people . . .

# CHAPTER FOUR

THE FOLLOWING WEEK dragged by like a two-legged dog. The kids were snippy with her, bored to tears (in Emily's case, quite literally), and impossible to placate with baked goods. This resulted in a lot of sweets that Starla ate herself, and she couldn't bring herself to regret that part; cinnamon-sugar donuts were amazing, and whatever her stomach's deal was, they seemed to settle it. It was cheaper than going to a doctor; she didn't think she was still on Charlie's insurance. She should probably work on that. Sometime.

"You guys headed out?" Ainsley asked, pausing the movie she and Kyle were watching.

"Yeah, we thought we'd go hiking," Starla said, trying to seem excited by the idea. She was out of donuts, and her stomach was growling and gurgling again. And yet, her jeans felt a little tight. It was truly odd. Must be bloated or something from all that sugar.

"*You* thought we'd go hiking," Aiden corrected. "I think I'll stay here."

Kyle shot him a look that said, 'I think not,' and Starla covered her laughter behind a cough.

"Nice try, kid. Get your shoes on. Let's get out of Kyle and Ainsley's hair, let them have some privacy." Kyle looked visibly relieved, even as Ainsley grinned at her.

"You know where you're going yet?"

"I was just going to go to the falls."

"Oh, don't do that; it'll be packed with people at this time of day, too many tourists," said Ainsley. "You should head up the hill on the other side of the freeway . . . it's Forest Service Road 533, I think? There's a nice little trailhead up there. Very level, nice creek running that way, and there's a hot spring around there, somewhere, too. Take your swimsuits and see if you can find it."

"It'll be like a hot tub!" Emily bubbled, and Aiden nodded.

"Only it won't smell like the one at Grandma and Grandpa's."

They took off down the hall, still plotting, and she went over to see the map Ainsley was pulling up on her phone. It didn't look too far away, and the loop wasn't too long. Also, since it was off a Forest Service Road, that meant no parking fee . . . and if there was anything Starla was a fan of, it was freebies. Especially since she'd gotten the first bill for her lawyer and almost passed out; Ainsley had made her sit down on a bar stool, concerned about how white she'd gone. She packed up the backpack with drinks, snacks, and a map of the area, determined to show her kids a good time. Of course, she'd hated this when her dad used to take her. And her mom hadn't ever seemed too keen on it, but she'd never complained, she thought, as she slathered them with sunscreen. But hey, it was good for them to be outside, she thought as she sprayed them with DEET. They spent far too much time looking at screens, thinking about screens, talking about screens . . . this was good. This was better. Starla look around as they piled into the car; it was a beautiful Oregon spring day, with the exception of a small bank of dark clouds that were visible just over the rise of the hill. That didn't seem too likely to cause trouble. She kept her eye on it as she wound down Highway 22, chatting with the kids, who'd mostly reformed their attitudes. In fact, she was so busy chatting, she almost missed the forest service road that Ainsley had indicated.

The kids were in good spirits as they start into the woods down the narrow trail. Chickadees and nuthatches cheeped at them from the tall cedars and Douglas firs as they got out of the car, sword ferns lining the path on either side. There weren't a lot of flowers out yet, but here and there the dogwoods showed out delicate pink blooms, dappled beneath the taller trees. The Queen Anne's lace, shooting stars, and a few wild lilies were more than enough for Starla, and she breathed in the fresh air deeply as they walked. She was such an Oregon girl; apparently, her dad's trailside botany lectures had sunk in, after all. She should probably try to pay that forward.

"Look, Em," she said, "this big white flower that looks like a starburst? That's called—"

"My feet hurt," Emily complained. "Will you carry me, Mom?"

"Nope," Starla said, popping the 'p' with extra attitude like a bit of bubble gum. "You're a big girl. You can walk."

"This is so booorring," Aiden griped.

"Boy, there is just no pleasing you two, is there? You're bored in the library. You're bored in the apartment. You're bored out here in the woods. I bet I could take you to Disneyland, and you'd be bored there, too."

"Wasn't bored at the zoo," Aiden mumbled, and Starla chose to ignore the comment so clearly intended to hurt her.

"Go ahead and you lead, then."

A shadow passed over them, and the three of them looked up. That ominous cloud bank was now directly overhead, and the warm summer air seemed to drop ten degrees around them now that the sun was hidden. Starla paused to look up, glaring, as if to scare it off. *You have no business here. Be gone.*

"I wouldn't worry about that," she said, still staring up at the threatening clouds. "That's nothing. That's just . . . I don't know what. But it's not going to rain. It'll be fine; there was no inclement weather forecast today." But the air smelled damp, and a gust of wind rattled the undergrowth. She could've sworn the flowers were closing up.

Not ten minutes later, she heard it before she felt it, cold on her skin. It wasn't just raining: the sky opened up and tried to drown them. Over the sound of the heavy droplets pelting the dirt, she could barely hear Emily crying and Aiden trying to shout advice; she had the urge to cover her ears to block it all out. Starla's wet hair whipped her in the face as she looked this way and that, feeling frantic. She pushed her hat back a little, trying to look for their footprints that had already washed away. They pounded back down the path, but it forked unhelpfully. Her fogging glasses made it that much harder to see. Which way was the car? Why had she let Aiden lead? Why had she come out here, anyway? She was no outdoorswoman; countless childhood camping trips had proven that. She should've stayed inside where there were books and tea (she still couldn't stomach coffee) and warmth. No, she'd had to try to one-up Charlie. The kids had their shirts up over their heads now, and she pulled them toward the left fork in the trail . . . it looked like it was going to open up to the main road.

She looked up and down the gravel road—there. Smoke. Maybe they could hang out with whoever was in their cabin just until the storm passed. It was probably someone she knew.

"Come on, guys!" she yelled. She charged up the hill, and she heard them scrambling to keep up with her on the loose gravel; she prayed Emily wouldn't fall and turned back to grab her hand. There'd be no consoling her then. The child thought the sky was falling every time she saw her own blood.

Though, to be fair, it was actually falling now. Starla pushed her way through the undergrowth, tripping over ferns and pushing her way past rhododendrons, cutting across the forest instead of sticking to the gravel road. She corralled the kids forward, trying to keep the column of smoke in view. She clung to that bit of hope like the Israelites fleeing Egypt.

"Mom," Aiden howled, "we're going the wrong way!"

"I'm trying to get to that cabin," she said, pointing. "It looks like there's someone home. Maybe they'll let us come in for a while." They stumbled out onto a driveway, and she took both their hands as they broke into a run again. It opened out into a large parking area; there were several ATVs parked near the house, and a green truck with a trailer still attached. A large lodge of log construction stood in the center of the clearing, and she ran up to it. Starla cupped her hands against the windows to see inside. The panes were clean, and inside, it looked reasonably lived in; there was a grocery store bouquet on the kitchen table, and a basket of snacks on the counter. That screamed rental, and for the first time, she hesitated. She looked around the porch as the kids collapsed onto the swing, trying to catch their breath. There was firewood stacked against the building, and someone had swept the porch recently. She knocked tentatively.

"Hello?" she called. Her kids took up the call and yelled it twice as loud. She looked around; the smoke had been coming from this lodge, right? Starla adjusted her pink baseball cap with the BB-8 stitched on it with the words, 'This is how I roll,' trying to keep the rain off her face. She stepped off the porch and backed up until she could see the chimney: it appeared cold and lifeless. *Huh.* Starla looked around, her gaze catching on her kids, who were huddled together on the porch. Water hit her face where it was dripping off the brim, and she wiped her face with an already-wet hand. *There.* There was the smoke she'd seen; it wasn't coming from the lodge. It was coming from over there.

"Wait here," she called to the kids, and then she jogged over to the large, open barn-type structure. It was a garage, upon closer inspection. She pushed the door open with one finger, not wanting to intrude, and found only a gleaming row of motorcycles. "Hello?" she called again, but the Harley-Davidsons, Suzukis, and Hondas didn't answer her. Just as before, the lights were all off. Giving up on the garage, she jogged around the side of the large wooden structure, not bothering to avoid the puddles that were forming in the driveway. There was an herb garden, still at that early spring, not-yet-flourishing height, and she caught sight of dill and basil interspersed with lavender and thyme as she followed a stone path around the back of the garage. Set back from the rest of the buildings was a small, simple log cabin, lit up, smoke lazily rising from the chimney. Some weary father was probably retreating, trying to get some fishing in, or some restless mama trying to write her novel. *Good for them.*

Starla turned and ran back through the rain to where her kids were waiting, and she motioned for them to follow her this time. The three of them splashed around the corner of the garage to the cabin. Aiden knocked on the front door before she could get there.

"Hello?" Emily yelled. "We need help!"

Through the window in the door, she could see someone approaching, and her whole body shook with relief. Maybe it was a little cold. Or maybe she was just stressed. After the week she'd had, it could be all of the above. The door swung open, and the last person she expected to see stood there, barefoot, looking as hot as always in his jeans and a T-shirt, looking as surprised to see them as she was to see him.

# CHAPTER FIVE

SAWYER STOOD THERE, slack-jawed, staring at them. He'd expected maybe Jehovah's Witnesses or Mormon missionaries when he opened the door. Not his cousin Ainsley's childhood friend, the object of his secret affections, wet and shivering, standing on his porch with her two children, also shivering. *What on earth . . . ?*

"C-c-c-an we c-c-come in?" Aiden chattered, and the boy's need propelled him into action.

"Of course, of course. What are y'all doing up here?"

"We were *hiking*. We got *caught* in the *storm*!" Emily wailed, clearly at the emotional limit of her six years. She was such a little drama llama, unlike her mama.

"Oh, my," he said, herding them into the house, ignoring how much water they were dripping all over his wood floors. "Let me get you some towels . . ." Starla still hadn't said anything as he handed her a big, fluffy white towel.

"Thank you," she murmured. "I'm sorry to barge in on you like this . . ."

"It's no trouble," he mumbled back. "Can't have you standing out there in the rain." It was still coming down hard. She helped the kids dry their hair and faces, and he just stood there, watching them, hooking his thumbs into his jeans, then jamming them into his back pockets, then crossing them over his chest. He scrambled to think of some way to be helpful without being overly familiar. *They're cold, right?*

"Y'all want something to warm up?"

"Oh no, don't go to any—"

Her polite refusal was drowned out by her two children squealing and chattering about cocoa.

"Let's see what we've got here," he muttered, striding into the kitchen, opening cupboards and peering into them like it wasn't his house. "I've got tea?"

"It's really okay, Sawyer," she said. *Sawyer.* She didn't usually use his name . . . but then again, she'd never been to his house before, either. They didn't usually see each other outside the library, even though his cousin was her best friend. He wasn't much for events happening in town.

"Oh, it's really okay?" he parroted, rubbing his smooth chin. "You don't think these kids deserve cocoa? It looks to me like they do. Good kids, good sports, going on a hike that was probably Mom's idea to get them out of the house." He raised an eyebrow at her, and her mouth fell open, her cheeks pinking at the insinuation. Sawyer put his hands on his knees, making his body a right angle to see them better. "Did y'all complain?"

The kids shook their heads ardently, at which Starla snorted. "What was that 'this is boring' and 'Mama, carry me,' business, hmm?"

"Sounds like the jury's still out on that one, guys. Did y'all obey your mama this morning?"

Both nodded their heads, and when he glanced up at her, she was still skeptical, but she didn't disagree.

"See, Mama? Good as gold, these two." They beamed up at him, and Sawyer knew the cocoa was definitely happening. He liked the Miller kids; he tried to always say hi at the library, if only to give them something to do while they waited for Starla. Aiden was always quick to show him something in the games he was playing on his tablet while Em mostly ignored him, preferring to stick to her own imagination. About a month ago, though, he'd made the mistake of offering to read her a book she was looking at, and now he had to do it every week. And they were always about magic ponies. Always.

"Okay, okay," Starla assented. "Do you have any, though? Now that you've convinced them that they deserve it?"

Sawyer turned back toward the cupboards, hoping like heck, shuffling things around, muttering, pulling things out to look behind them, but finally turned back to them with a slightly defeated expression.

"I'm afraid not."

"Do you have cocoa powder?"

He pawed through a baking cupboard. "Yep."

"What about sugar? Vanilla? Milk? Salt?"

"I've got all but the sugar. I've got honey, though."

"We can just make it from scratch then," she said softly, and the kids cheered, dancing around the kitchen, their still-drying hair flicking water over the two adults. With a quiet smile, Starla poked around in his cupboards, pulled out the ingredients and found a medium-sized saucepan to get it going. He stared at her for a moment, still unsure he could believe what he was seeing: *Starla. is. in. my. house.* The kids had remembered that they had packed their bathing suits for the hot springs and were currently stripping off their wet clothes, paying his presence no heed. Maybe Starla would like to change, too? He slipped into his bedroom to give the kids some unasked-for privacy and went to his dresser. He could at least give her one of his smaller T-shirts and a pair of shorts. His gaze fell to his favorite sweatshirt, and he grabbed that, too.

She was still facing the stove, stirring with a whisk, but she turned toward him a moment later when he cleared his throat behind her.

He held out a pair of cotton basketball shorts, a white T-shirt, and a navy blue sweatshirt with 'EMORY' printed in white block letters. "For you. I know you're wetter than they are, and I don't have anything for them, but these might fit you."

"Oh . . ." She looked like she wanted to say more, but her attention was on the cocoa and the kids behind him climbing on his furniture like monkeys. "Thank you."

"Sure." He turned back toward the kids. "You guys ever heard of Boggle?"

They shook their heads, gravitating toward him as he went to a low cupboard and opened the glass doors, pulling out the board game. "It's pretty easy. Here, let's pull it out. Aiden, get the paper and pencils; they're in the drawer under the microwave in the kitchen. Em, you can pull more chairs around the table." There was only one right now; he didn't have many guests. When his mama or his sister made the trek up the mountain, they usually just ate on the couches.

"And me?" Starla teased. "Don't I get a job?"

"Of course you do," he replied, deadpan. "You're doin' it right now: Chief Cocoa Maker." He paused as he moved the low vase of wildflowers he'd gathered this morning from the table. "You made enough for me, too, didn't you?"

"Of course. I'm not the worst guest in the universe, just because I crashed whatever you were doing and took over your kitchen."

He shook his head, holding back a smile. Of course she'd think that way. How she could see herself as a burden was beyond him. She was the best part of his week, every week.

"Well, then you just focus on that, and if you wanted to pop some popcorn, I wouldn't object." This was now officially the longest conversation he'd ever had with Starla. Words didn't always come easily to him; the banter that he wanted came out as quips and grunts.

"I will after I change," she said, and she sounded tired. She bent to pick up the kids' wet clothes off the floor, and her eyes went a little unfocused and hazy. She put a hand out, as if to steady herself, and he took two paces forward before he stopped himself. She shook her head a little as she righted herself, like she was trying to clear it, and suddenly, he was at her elbow, frowning, carried forward by concern, apart from his thinking brain, apparently. *Something's wrong.*

"You all right?"

"Of course," she smiled. "Just got dizzy for a second there." She gestured to the clothes in her hands. "Be right back."

He wanted to stop her, put a hand on her shoulder, stare deep into her eyes to see the truth or the lie of what she'd just said. *You can't ignore that stuff,* he wanted to say. *It could be more. It could be something really bad. Like mine was.* But what if they weren't that kind of friends? He couldn't have her stomping off, back out into the rain.

"Holler if you need anything," he called after her, and she turned to smile at him over her shoulder. The kids were setting up the game, shaking the letter cubes at an ear-splitting volume, and he sat down at the table to help them. They turned the timer, and he was supposed to be looking for words—big, get, tab, bat—but his mind was back in Guatemala. He'd been exhausted since he'd arrived there on his first Doctors Without Borders assignment. But it hadn't been fatigue. His diagnosis two years ago had hit his life like a hurricane, destroying his carefully-arranged plans. And he hadn't stood in front of an operating table since.

The kids were comparing words they had found. Under Sawyer's instruction, Aiden crossed out the duplicates. Where was Starla? What if she'd passed out in there? The bathroom door opened, and his concerns dispelled as Emily ran over to her mom, giving her an ardent hug, pulling her to the table. He couldn't help but notice the longing look she threw at her damp purple backpack still sitting by the front door.

"You can be on my team," Emily said to Starla.

"You're in first grade now, kiddo. I think you can be on your own team," she said, but she put the girl on her lap and picked up a pencil nonetheless.

"They crossed out my words, though!" she protested indignantly.

"That's how you play the game, dummy," Aiden sniped.

"No name-calling," Starla corrected without irritation, and Sawyer slid a red mug of cocoa toward her. He must have been asking questions with his gaze, because she pressed her lips into a flat smile to try to reassure him she was fine. She sipped it, and he couldn't stop watching her. Things must have been hard for her these last few months, going through a public break-up in a small town. He hated it when people talked about him; his guess was that she'd feel the same. He could see the strain in the way she held herself: a little defeated, a lot tired. He wished there was something he could do to help. He could at least back her up with Aiden.

"That's right. Name-callers have to wait out the storm on the front porch. Cabin rules," he said.

"Sorry," Aiden mumbled. "Can I shake it this time?"

"Sure," Sawyer said, pushing the game toward him. Starla glanced outside, so he did, too; it was still raining. She took a sip of the cocoa and a small smile lit her face, which allowed him to relax a little. She and Emily scorched both him and Aiden in the next round—of course they did. He'd forgotten to never play word games with a bookworm—so he and Aiden decided that they should team up, too. For the next twenty minutes, they traded wins back and forth; if she hadn't gotten 'flimsy' on the last round, they would've won. The cocoa was gone by then, and she got up to make the popcorn that he'd hinted he wanted. He watched her carefully, but she didn't seem shaky anymore. *Good.*

"Looks like the weather's clearing," she said, as she set down a bowl in front of each of them. "So we should get out of Sawyer's hair soon."

With an exaggerated frown, he lifted his hands to his head and probed his own hair, and the kids giggled. "Nope, no Millers up there. Stay as long as you like."

"I'm sure you were in the middle of something," she protested as she sat back down, pulling her own bowl toward her.

"Nothing important," he said, popping a few kernels in his mouth. "Truth be told, I've finished my work for the week, so you all broke up a Friday that was on its way to Dullsville. So really, I owe you a thank you." It wasn't true, but they had saved him from a dreary afternoon of invoicing and calling delinquent accounts. He put it off until Friday for a reason.

"You're welcome," Aiden said sincerely with all the arrogance of youth, reaching to reset the Boggle cubes. Sawyer and Starla shared a private smile over his behavior, then her gaze just

. . . lingered. She was staring at him, and he had no idea what she was thinking. He raised an eyebrow at her, and she quickly looked away, reaching down to pick up the popcorn Em had spilled already. *Hmm.*

The roof was still dripping when she got the kids back into their sopping sneakers, much to their dismay. They at least had dry clothes; she'd popped them all in the dryer in the bathroom like the wise woman she was. She'd changed quickly and gave Sawyer back his clothes with a shy thank you. He suddenly felt very strange about the whole thing; not that they'd infringed on his time, but that it *hadn't* really felt like infringing. He genuinely enjoyed all of them, had enjoyed seeing the kids open up a little more, away from the library.

She re-shouldered her backpack, and he gave them directions back to the main road.

"You're sure you don't want a ride? It's no trouble. I know the trail head you're talking about, I use it all the time. They're gonna get blisters in those wet shoes."

She froze when he said that. "You use it all time?"

"Yeah. Is that strange?"

"Oh, no. No, it's not, it's just . . ." Was she blushing? "Your cousin's a real piece of work, did you know that?"

"As a matter of fact, I did. I am well-acquainted with her busybody ways. What's she done now?"

"She recommended this trail. I'm sure it was a coincidence."

He chuckled. *Unlikely*.

"You're sure? No ride?"

"Oh, no. We're fine. You've done more than enough," Starla assured him. "Thank you so much." He waved from the front door as they started back to the main road. That little detail about the trail head, though, stuck in his mind like a thrown axe, still quivering from the force of it. *Ainsley*. She'd been trying to push them together since Christmas, and while there was no way she could've arranged the rain storm, it was obvious she'd intended for them to run into each other. For goodness' sake, didn't she have enough to do, teaching and planning her wedding? He'd told her he wasn't going to ask Starla out. Not yet, anyway. His health had been stable for a while, but that's why they called it relapsing-remitting multiple sclerosis . . . like those Mormon missionaries, it would be back eventually.

# CHAPTER SIX

SAWYER WAS HALFWAY through a plate of eggs and bacon when his phone rang the next morning. He glanced at the screen to see who it was, then he winced as he answered it.

A female voice with a hint of a smoker's rasp didn't wait for him to speak. "You didn't check in yesterday. You know our deal."

"Hello to you, too, Mama," Sawyer replied calmly. "I'm proud of you for not roaring up here to see if I was passed out on the floor. As it happens, I had some unexpected visitors, and it threw my schedule off a bit."

"Was it Mormons or Jehovah's Witnesses? You didn't argue with them again, did you? I'm in a knitting circle with Debbie Jensen, and I'll hear about it if you did."

Sawyer chuckled. "No, as it happens, it wasn't anyone concerned about my wicked soul this time. Starla Moore and her kids were hiking up here and they got caught in the rain." He stared at the chair she'd sat in; he was in no hurry to move it back to the living room. It was easier to imagine her still at the table, laughing with her, her feet bare, her wet, silky hair falling in her face, curled up in his favorite sweatshirt. He'd use something else for his computer desk for a while.

There was a long silence on the other end of the line, and he took another bite of his breakfast.

"Are you pulling my leg?" she asked finally.

"No, ma'am," he laughed. "Would I do that to you?"

"Absolutely. You would absolutely give your poor mother hope like that, then dash it like a teacup against a tile floor."

"Mama," he sighed, trying to be patient. "How exactly does it give you hope?"

"You're socializing with a woman I know you're attracted to. I'll let you put it together."

"Mama, it was basic hospitality." It was also the nicest Friday afternoon he'd had in the longest time.

"Uh-huh. Well, it must've been a good visit if it made you forget our call."

"It was. We had a real nice time, actually. I taught the kids how to play Boggle."

"You didn't!" She cackled, and he scowled good-naturedly.

"What's wrong with Boggle?"

"Gosh, we played that game to death when you were a kid. I can die happy if I never hear that noise again."

"Just because I always bested you . . ."

"Yes, you did," she admitted, then he heard her voice fade, as if she'd moved the phone away from her mouth and spoken quietly to someone else.

"Who're you with?" She stuck her nose in his business often enough. It only seemed fair to return the favor.

"Why don't you come by and see?"

"Nice try. It's not Thursday."

He could hear Rhea's smile in her voice. "Well, it's the only way you're gonna find out."

"You know I don't mind a mystery. I'm sure I can figure it out without coming down there . . ." He tapped his spoon against the side of the bowl as he thought. "Let's see. It's Saturday morning, and I know you're not seeing anybody right now . . ."

"How would you know that?"

"Paige keeps track," he said dismissively.

"Your sister doesn't know everything about my social life."

"I trust her intel. She's very thorough in these matters. Y'all care far too much about romance." He cleared his throat. "As I was *sayin'*, you're not seeing anyone, and it's too quiet in the background for you to be at Riverside, so my guess is Mr. Powell dropped off more yarn."

"Am I that predictable?" She laughed, then he heard the phone change hands.

"Good morning, young Devereaux. How are the woods these days?" Mr. Powell's quiet Scottish brogue rolled through the phone.

"Fine, sir, just fine. How are the sheep?"

"Dumb as a post, as usual."

Sawyer laughed. "Fair enough." The clock on the microwave caught his eye; it was already after nine. "I've gotta get to work . . ." A sudden urge to pee grabbed him, and he tried to hold it back while listening, but it was breaking his concentration.

"Speaking of, I've sent a new customer your way; you should get a call next week from a Bobby Parrot. He's got an Indian he wants rebuilt, and I knew you'd be up to the challenge."

Sawyer rushed toward the bathroom as he replied to the man. "Wow. All right. Well, thank you, sir, that's a compliment I don't take lightly."

"My pleasure, young man. You have a good weekend."

"You too, sir."

The phone changed hands again. "Love you, son. Take care of yourself, please."

"Will do. Love you, Mama." As soon as was humanly possible after she said goodbye, he had his zipper down and let go of what he'd been holding back. *That was close.* He'd been dealing with incontinence for a while now . . . he'd been hoping it would diminish on its own. Instead, he was going to have to either start carrying around a change of pants or talk to his doctor about it. *Great. Stupid, screwed-up body.*

His eggs were cold now, but he didn't care. Eating had largely lost its pleasure for him since his diagnosis. If he couldn't eat the wheat pancakes and maple syrup he wanted on a Saturday, he might as well eat what was good for him. It'd make his family happy, anyway. He washed his plate and went out to the garage, only to find a customer pulling up the driveway.

"Morning, Ken," Sawyer called, waving, as the man rolled down his truck window. He was pulling a trailer with a motorcycle on the back. Not just any motorcycle: a Ducati Hypermotard 950 SP Special, the new model. Liquid cooled, sleek and sporty, it just *looked* fun. But apparently, someone had had too much fun already, because the front suspension was badly bent. His client saw him looking ruefully at the machine.

"Son took it on a joy ride."

"Oh boy."

"Don't worry, he's still alive. For now." Ken was a scary dude, as far as Sawyer was concerned; he taught martial arts in Mill City, and while he seemed like a nice guy, Sawyer wouldn't want to piss him off. He was pretty sure Ken could take him apart in two seconds flat. "He'll be paying for this."

Sawyer nodded. "Do we need to put him on an installment plan?"

Ken nodded. "I'd appreciate that. It'll mean more if he owes you than me."

"That's fine. I appreciate that you're teaching him responsibility."

He snorted. "Not well enough, apparently."

"I went for plenty of joy rides as a teenager. I think we all did. Part of growing up."

Ken put his elbow up on the open window. "How many did you crash, though?"

"Oh, none. I knew my uncle would kill me."

"Exactly." He moved to get out and unload the machine from the trailer.

Sawyer went immediately into triage mode. "Looks like the brake disk is shot, and the wheel rim . . . man. I don't know if I can straighten that out. You may need a new one. I'm headed up to Portland on Monday, and I could pick one up then."

"Thanks, man. I know you'll take good care of her. How much?"

"I'll have to talk to the parts distributer. I'll send you an estimate before I start work, how's that?"

"Works for me." Ken gave him a firm handshake. "See you."

"Yup." He spent the rest of the morning taking it apart and doing what he could to straighten things out. If only his body were that simple.

# CHAPTER SEVEN

IT WAS HER DAY OFF, and Starla was going through her boxes. The newest historical romance from Lisa Kleypas, a present from the book fairy, was calling to her, taunting her from the armchair where she'd left it, but she ignored its siren call. The boxes were taking up too much space in the small bedroom, and she was tired of stubbing her toes in the dark. She didn't even know what was in half these . . . she'd packed in such a hurry, Charlie watching her, pleading with her to stay. It had been the most uncomfortable three hours of her life. She'd finally put on headphones and decided to just ignore him. As a result, the contents were pretty disjointed.

As she pulled a cardboard box open, she sighed and asked herself again why she hadn't gone to pack when she knew Charlie would be at the dealership. She grabbed a small trashcan from the bathroom; she had a feeling she was going to need it. Or maybe the bigger one from the kitchen . . . but she'd start with this one. The first box was full of all sorts of bathroom stuff: soap that was shaped like the Death Star (keep), bright orange temporary hair gel from Halloween (toss), expired daytime cold medicine (goodbye), hot rollers (when had she even bought those?), tampons . . . tampons. She stared down at the blue box, cold awareness creeping over her like frost spreading across a window as night falls. But unlike frost, this was an ugly awareness. That she hadn't needed these in a while. Too long. Not since . . .

Starla dropped the box like it was a snake. "No," she whispered. "No, no. Can't be. That's not possible . . ." She put a hand to her belly, as if she could tell what was going on in there, just by touching her skin. Bile rose in her throat, and her mind was pulled back to her stomach problems lately . . . the ginger tea at Riverside, Paige's comments about her looking unwell. The dizziness at Sawyer's. She'd had that when she was pregnant with Aiden, too . . . she remembered running a hand down the gray lockers, making sure she didn't lose her footing in the crowded high school hallways. Starla sat down hard on the bed to keep from passing out, then put her head between her knees. *Not happening, not happening . . .* The shame was familiar, too, only now the knife of it was shoved deeper, because she wasn't a stupid, lovesick teenager. She was a stupid, weak adult, or so it felt. Why was she always screwing up her life? She thought she'd turned a corner, and now here she was, twice as bad off as before. No money, no partner, no choices. Abortion wasn't an option; as trapped as she felt now, the guilt of that would end her. She'd already considered that with Aiden and never regretted her decision.

She swallowed down the acid in her throat, her mind blank, her hands clammy as she pushed the hair away from her face. Before she could freak out, she needed to know for sure. Now. She slid on a pair of sisal sandals she didn't remember owning, grabbing her purse from the bed where she'd tossed it.

It only took her half an hour to get to the grocery store. Shaking, Starla ran over her list again and checked it against her cart. Food coloring for the Easter eggs. Corn chips for taco night. Menthol rub for that lingering cough of Em's. Frozen pizza for Friday night. Pregnancy test. She had too much stuff for the self-check line; why hadn't she just gotten the test? Starla got in line behind Claire Durand, Ainsley's fiancé's sister-in-law. She seemed like a safe choice; some of the other Timberites had been giving her dirty looks lately. Funny, they didn't do that when she and Charlie were married. *Guess I'm not under the Millers' protection now that I've put their cheating son in his place.* But interacting with Claire would mean she needed to act normal. She put on her best cheerful persona.

"Hey, Claire. Hey, Hannah. Oh my goodness, she's getting so big." She was going to be such a cute flower girl at Kyle and Ainsley's upcoming wedding; her hair was longer, starting to take on a reddish hue like Claire's.

"Say hi, Hannah," Claire prompted, still unloading her cart onto the conveyor belt, and Hannah tried to hide her face in her mother's shirt. "Sorry, she's a bit shy."

"Oh, no big deal. I understand." *I feel you, kid. I'd like to hide away, too.*

"How are you doing, Starla? I haven't seen you in a while . . ." Unsure if she was trying to talk about her divorce or just being polite, Starla fidgeted with her phone.

"Oh, I'm doing fine. How are you?"

"Oh, we're doing fine. Happy to have Ainsley almost in the family. Happy to have someone to who'll feed Kyle. Although it was nice getting Cooper picked up all those months

. . . I should've figured there was some ulterior motive. It didn't make sense that he'd just keep doing it out of the goodness of his heart. Though he does have a sweet spot for his nephew . . ."

"Uh-huh." Starla didn't like talking about other people, but she did like Kyle. He was a good match for her friend, and eminently practical. She appreciated that. And he'd given them some excellent advice about how to improve the library setup for patrons with physical limitations. She didn't want people getting hurt or feeling excluded; everyone should feel welcome at the library.

"Starla?"

"Yes?" She'd been totally in her own head, and Claire stood at the end of the checkout, watching her expectantly. *So much for acting normal.*

"You okay?"

"Yes," she smiled, "of course." *No, not for months. And now I think I know why.* "Just tired."

"Well, it's all yours. Have a great day."

"You too, Claire."

Starla unloaded the rest of her cart onto the conveyor belt, trying to group like things together in order to be considerate. She slid the test under two loaves of whole wheat bread, praying no one would notice. She liked it when her receipt was orderly. It was hard to fit everything on the belt, and this checker was slow. She was a nice older lady who Starla had made friends with before.

"Hey, Cheryl."

"Hey, Mrs. Miller. How are you today?" She didn't correct her; it still said Mrs. Miller on her credit card, and there hadn't been time yet to go down to the courthouse and get her name changed back. Also, she was considering keeping it so she could share a last name with her kids. She was never remarrying anyway, so it couldn't hurt to keep it. Charlie wouldn't care . . . hopefully, it wouldn't give him hope. If she knew where the body kept hope, she'd cut it out with a rusty kitchen knife and crush it at his feet. If only she'd had that mentality in February; she'd underestimated how much it would encourage him to think they were getting back together. And another baby would make things that much worse.

"Just fine, and you?"

"Oh, fine, fine. It looks like your total comes to $206.70 today."

"Okay, great. Let me just . . ." She stuck her credit card into the chip reader. The screen flashed: *card error.*

"What's it saying?" Cheryl asked, and Starla turned it so she could see. "Oh, hmm. Well, that machine's been acting up. Can you try another one?"

"Sure . . ." Starla pulled out her debit card, hoping she could remember the PIN; she hadn't used it in a long time. She pushed it into the slot: *insufficient funds.* Starla sucked in a shocked breath. Had Charlie cut her off? They hadn't really talked about it, but she needed stuff for the kids. Almost all this stuff was for them, and he'd promised to continue to take care of them. Hot shame washed over her, and she glanced nervously at the line stacking up behind her.

"Looks like that one's no good, Mrs. Miller," Cheryl said, obviously trying to keep her voice from being heard by anyone but Starla. "Do you have cash, maybe?"

"I got it." Southern accent, nice forearms, flannel.

*No. Not him.*

She didn't want anyone witnessing this pathetic situation, but especially not Sawyer. She knew what was expected at the library: she was the librarian, the employee, and he, the patron, was the employer, in as much as anyone in town owned the library. Running a library was its own art form, and she really did think of them as patrons; she appreciated them. But after sharing an afternoon board game, popcorn, and cocoa, this patron felt more like a friend. A friend who was going to quickly tire of saving her from embarrassing situations. Shelter from a storm and cocoa, she could swallow. An entire grocery bill she couldn't. There were plenty of other ways to damage her pride. And if he saw the pregnancy test . . .

"Thanks, Sawyer, but I got it." She didn't turn to look at him, still feeling awkward; she pulled out his card and held it out in the general direction he'd come from. His warm, calloused hand closed over hers and pushed it gently back toward the card reader.

"You can pay me back on Thursday."

"I don't need to." She put it down on the counter with a snap. "I'm sure I have

something . . ." She dug through her purse until she found her checkbook. But Cheryl was already shaking her head.

"If your debit card's been declined, I'm not allowed to take a check. I'm sorry."

She sighed. "Can you put this stuff back for me, please?" Starla said, forcing her voice above a whisper. "I'm so sorry about this . . ."

"No," Sawyer rumbled, and she glanced at him just long enough to see him shifting his weight agitatedly. "Please let me help."

She lifted her chin and turned to face him then. "It's just a miscommunication. I'll talk to Charlie and come back later . . ."

"Not with perfectly good cash in my wallet, you won't. What are y'all gonna eat this week? You're not going to let those kids starve for the sake of your pride, are you? Take the money, Starla." He didn't usually use her first name, and it sent a little tingle of excitement through her, which she ruthlessly snuffed out. This was not the time to be getting emotional over Sawyer Devereaux. But he wasn't wrong . . . it wasn't about her. It was about Aiden and Em. They'd been looking forward to pizza night. And that test . . . she needed that test. She needed to know. But she couldn't make herself say the words. Her gaze drifted past him to the other customers, who were starting to lose patience with this stand-off, and she felt herself shrinking with embarrassment. He cleared his throat as if to say, "Well?" His jaw ticked like a metronome as they continued their staring contest.

"She's with me," he said to the cashier without releasing her gaze. "Just ring it all up for me, will you, Cheryl?"

*Stubborn, ridiculous man. Fine, be my white knight. Hope it makes you happy.*

The older woman was clearly torn, bouncing her gaze back and forth between them, but Starla gave her a shy, silent nod, and she continued to scan his groceries along with hers.

"Thank you," Starla murmured, looking down at his groceries, sliding by on the conveyor belt, wishing she could leave.

"It's no trouble."

She drummed her fingers on the little check-writing counter. "It's maybe a little bit of a trouble."

He snorted softly. "Well, it's the right kind of trouble, then."

"Is that like in a historical romance when a duke and the miller's daughter get caught kissing in the library and have to get married for propriety's sake?"

Sawyer's eyebrows danced briefly as he seemed to consider her words. "I couldn't speak to that particular situation, I'm afraid."

She giggled a little, and her shoulders shrugged automatically. "That's all right. If you let me pick your book the next time you come in, I'll help you rectify that."

"I've been getting by picking my own books for years, thank you very much." His words distracted her from the fact that he was leaning past her again to slip his card back into the machine.

"Come on. Everyone else in town lets me recommend them a book from time to time. They're hardly ever disappointed."

He leaned a hip on the conveyor belt and looked at her hard. "You really want to pick a book for me?"

She nodded as she loaded her groceries back into her cart, just to have something to do with her hands. "And it won't be a mystery, I can tell you that much."

Sawyer chuckled. "I don't know if I'm interested, then . . ."

"Well, you think it over, and I'll see you Thursday. And I'll pay you back."

"That'd be fine." He didn't have nearly as much stuff, so he'd already gathered it up. He was obviously waiting for her. She'd planned to put her groceries in the car, then come back in to use the bathroom, but that would probably be suspicious and hard to explain. They walked in silence out to the parking lot, and when she started up the second row, he was right there at her elbow. When she got to her truck, he paused. "Say hi to Aiden and Em for me."

"Sure. Say hi to the tall trees for me."

He cocked an eyebrow at her.

"I mean, are there any other organisms up there on your mountain?"

"Yes. But mostly, it's just me and the trees."

She hummed as she put her bags in the back of her Traverse. "That sounds like the start of a lovely poem."

He laughed again, quietly, like he didn't want anyone to hear. "If you say so."

Starla tucked her hair behind her ears. "See you. Thanks again."

"Yup." Sawyer crossed the row to his big blue truck, and she made a point not to watch in her rearview mirror as he put his groceries into his truck two bags at a time, his back muscles undoubtedly rippling, as she backed out of her spot. Well, she watched out for him, but that was just what she'd normally do. This was normal. Nothing weird happening here. A library patron and dear friend's cousin was allowed to pay for her groceries—*loan her money* for her groceries—once in a while. That was a normal thing. Sure. Why not? Starla spoke into the silent vehicle. "Call Charlie."

"Calling Charlie," the car responded in the creepy AI voice that always made her skin crawl. She wasn't going to pick Sawyer a futuristic book, either. Nothing dystopian. She only had one chance to impress him.

"Hey, babe," Charlie answered. She rolled her eyes.

"I've asked you to stop calling me that," she said evenly, not letting her frustration bleed into her words. "There's a problem with my credit and debit cards."

"Oh, right. My lawyer said to cut them off. Makes it easier to divide up assets if we're both paying for our own stuff right now."

"And you didn't think to mention this to me?"

"Well," he said slowly, "you do have your own money."

"But not my own accounts! You know my money goes into our retirement." *But it won't be after today.* "I thought you were going to help out with expenses because of Aiden and Emily?"

"Of course I will, babe. Just let me know what you need and I'll cut you a check. I can cut you one on Sunday, at my parents' house. You're still coming, right?"

She huffed. Humiliation; it was certainly a feeling she'd experienced before, having crossed the stage of her high school graduation six months pregnant. But the idea of going crawling on her belly to her ex-husband every time she needed grocery money was just appalling. All her income had always gone into their joint account.

"That's really inconvenient, Charlie. What do you want, an itemized list of what I bought?"

"That'd be nice." She could hear him grinning, and it galled her that he was enjoying holding this over her head.

"Fine. I'll just pay for their stuff myself." Her mind shot ahead to what she'd need to do to open her own line of credit to hold her over until this month's paycheck.

"Oh, babe. Don't be like that. I was only teasing you. Come on, where's your sense of humor?" *Must have left it at the house when I left you.*

Yet, she had just been laughing with Sawyer . . .

"But there is an easier way, you know . . ." His voice was low, cajoling. "Come home, Starla. Please. I miss you."

She shook her head. *Unbelievable.*

"I forgive you for leaving, for embarrassing me. Let's forget all this divorce nonsense and just—" Starla was fairly sure if she listened any longer, she'd start breathing fire and melt the windshield.

"Goodbye, Charlie." She stabbed a finger onto the steering wheel to hang up on him. Her mind churned. Without Charlie's money, she couldn't afford to pay half Ainsley's rent and also afford things like health insurance, new shoes, gas . . . not to mention hospital bills for a baby. Maybe she should move back in with her parents. That idea grated; not because they didn't love her, but they'd downsized after retirement, and their new place just wasn't big enough for five people . . . no, six? Not that Ainsley's place was either, but . . . she was just one person. It was different with her parents, somehow. That wasn't an option. And the Millers' sprawling estate, while certainly big enough to accommodate them, would be uncomfortable in an entirely different way. She'd seen them in church on Sunday, and they'd greeted the kids warmly, ignoring her completely except to ask her to bring the children over for dinner sometime soon. Yup, that's what she was now. Grandchild dropper-offer. Money-needer. Space taker-upper.

She couldn't wait until she got home. Starla whipped into the parking lot of the Subway and ducked into the bathroom. It was only ten o'clock, so the place was mostly empty. She'd bought five tests—the expensive, early-result kind—despite being on a spending freeze, because everyone knows you can't trust them enough to take just one. Starla waited and waited and waited for it to tell her what she already knew: she was having Charlie's baby. Again. She was waiting to watch her life crumble a little bit more, when she hadn't really thought that was possible. She managed to hold off her tears until the blue plus sign slowly washed across the little window of the white pee stick.

# CHAPTER EIGHT

STARLA SPENT MORE TIME than usual waiting for Sawyer to show up on Thursday. It wasn't like she was wasting time, exactly, but there was more clock-glancing, more foot-tapping, more pointless shelf reorganization. She felt like the envelope of cash she'd scraped together, including money borrowed from Ainsley, was vibrating in her back pocket. She tried to distract herself by processing the book fairy's donations and some they'd gotten from a college library gone defunct. She was knee-deep in dusty books, piled around her rolling chair, when Ainsley showed up. That meant Sawyer would be here soon. Unless he was avoiding her. He'd pushed her to take the money, but the old proverb may have said it best: *Before borrowing money from a friend, decide which you need more.* What if she'd pushed him away before she could officially claim him as a friend? Did he regret his actions now?

"Sorting books?" Ainsley asked, and Starla nodded, pushing the hair out of her eyes. "Do me a solid?" she asked, leaning over the desk on her elbows.

"Sure." Starla picked up another book: keto cookbook. Good one.

"Tell Sawyer he should go to Kyle's bachelor party."

Starla raised an eyebrow. "And why would I do that?"

"Because your opinion matters to him."

Starla let out a snort loud enough to make Pavel look up from his computer, despite the headphones he had on. She waved a little apology to him.

"It does," Ainsley insisted. "And I want him to make friends with the guys. He spends too much time alone up there."

"It's his life, Ains," she said, chucking a book about the USSR from the seventies into the trash. "Leave him alone."

"I like the way you think," a deep voice rumbled, full of humor, and Starla felt her cheeks heat. He seemed to relax a little around Ainsley, and she liked his sass. *Too bad he wants to be left alone. I'd keep him company.* Starla pushed away the thought.

"Where do you even come from?" Ainsley asked, throwing her arms out. "How do you sneak up on us like that?"

"A Green Beret showed me how once."

"Of course he did," Ainsley said, patting his shoulder. Starla hadn't told her what the loan was for, and even though Ainsley was trustworthy, she didn't want to air her dirty laundry in front of her friend any more than she had to. This grocery debt was already killing her, and it had only been a few days.

"Hi there," she greeted him, sounding too eager to her own ears. *Tone it down, Star.*

He just smiled.

"Here for your holds? I didn't see any for you . . ." When he said nothing, she sat up straighter to see him better. He was staring off into the distance, back toward where Aiden usually sat.

"Oh, their dad picked them up. Em had already picked out a book to read with you this week, she was so distraught that they were leaving early . . ."

He still said nothing, his gaze distant, and she wondered if she'd said something wrong. Discomfort filled her chest, and she glanced at Ainsley, unsure of what was happening.

"Sawyer? Hello?" Ainsley waved a hand in front of his face, but his gaze stayed fixed on the stacks.

"Oh no . . ." Ainsley dropped her books onto the desk and un-shouldered her bag. "He's having a seizure."

She sat rooted to the spot, feeling beyond stupid. "He's having a what?"

Starla scrutinized Sawyer's face; his crooked nose, his light eyes, his long blond lashes, the tiny white scar above his right eyebrow. She didn't often let herself really look at him, and even now, she burned with embarrassment to be noticing how good-looking he was in the middle of a potential medical emergency.

"A seizure. Sawyer, honey, can you hear me?"

Starla reached out to touch his arm; his muscles were stiff as a statue, hard as marble, and she gasped. "What do we do? Ainsley, what do we do?"

"Hang on." She was already dialing her phone. "Kyle? Sawyer's having a seizure, what do we do?" As she listened, Starla shuddered; seeing him stand there, so obviously absent, was freaking her out. Then he started to shake.

"Ainsley!" she cried, and her friend turned just in time to drop the phone and catch his dead weight as he collapsed.

"Help," Ainsley grunted. "He's *heavy*."

Starla sat on the desk and swung her legs over, grabbing him on the other side to help Ainsley lower him gently to the ground. She sat down hard and put his head in her lap to keep his head from hitting the ground; it was concrete under that thin carpet. Ainsley scrambled around, searching, until she found her phone and put it back to her ear. "I'm here, I'm here." She listened for a moment, then tilted the phone away from her mouth. "He says to roll him onto his side, in case he vomits." She put Kyle on speaker phone, and together, they grabbed Sawyer by his flannel sleeve and pulled.

"Lord, you weren't kidding; he *is* heavy."

"I know, right?"

The tender feelings toward Sawyer that she usually denied took complete control, and Starla stroked his hair.

"It's okay, I'm here. It'll be okay." She didn't know if he could hear her, and it made her bolder to say what was in her trembling heart. "I'll protect you. You're safe with me. I've got you. I've got you, Sawyer." There was a tangy scent in the air; she knew that scent. It was urine. He must have lost control of his bladder; a glance toward his lower half confirmed it. *How humiliating; poor Sawyer.* The longer this went on, the more she began to fight a hot panic rising in her chest. She turned to Ainsley. "Should we call 911? How much longer?"

"I don't know, we were supposed to start a timer, I think."

"I started one." Kyle's calm voice startled her, coming through Ainsley's phone. "It's just about three minutes since you called. You're in the clonic phase now, he should be almost done. Any second now."

As if on cue, Sawyer's shaking began to slow, his body going limp and heavy against the brown library carpet.

"I think it's done," Ainsley said, picking up her phone again and putting it to her ear. "Hey. Yeah. Okay. Love you. Bye." She leaned over, grabbing her bag, and she pulled a granola bar out of the front pocket. Starla thought obtusely that Ainsley carried a lot of snacks for someone who wasn't a parent yet. Then again, she did work with a lot of children.

Sawyer's eyes blinked open, and he looked around like he wasn't sure where he was. His gaze fell on Ainsley and he tried to push himself up to sitting, but he fell hard back into Starla's lap.

"Easy there, bud. Just give yourself a minute to come back to us."

He strained to sit up again, but this time, Starla gently held him to the floor. He craned his neck to see her better, like he hadn't realized she was there, and his mouth fell open a little when he recognized her. Shock and sadness saturated his expression. "I'm sorry," he murmured.

"No need to apologize," she told him quickly, giving his shoulders a little squeeze that she hoped was reassuring. He was looking around, and she didn't know what he was doing until Ainsley spoke up.

"No, you didn't throw up, which we both appreciate. I know she hates getting out the carpet cleaner, and I get enough of that at school during flu season."

Sawyer snorted softly and shook his head. "How long?"

"Kyle would know, he was timing. We were more focused on making sure your forehead didn't violently meet the edge of the reference desk."

Starla nodded, and Sawyer looked up at her again, still clearly embarrassed. "Home," he mumbled, rubbing at his eyes. "I want to go home." As he pushed himself to sitting, Starla stood, ready to offer her hand. It took both women to get him off the ground, and Starla and Ainsley both immediately tucked themselves under his arms to support him.

"I'm taking you to your mom's," Ainsley informed him, but he glared at her.

"No. *Home. My* home."

Ainsley stopped suddenly, and Starla and Sawyer stumbled forward, Starla trying to support him alone, the full weight him of landing on her shoulders. She planted her feet, bracing her ab muscles and hurting under the strain, determined not to let him fall until she physically couldn't hold him anymore.

"You can't go up to the cabin, Sawyer; you can't be alone up there. Kyle said you need rest."

"Kyle isn't my doctor. I can go home, and I will."

"No, you need rest."

"I can take care of myself. I'll sleep better in my own bed."

"Agreed, and you'll get to in a few days, so stop arguing," Ainsley returned, stepping forward to put his arm over her shoulder again. "I'm supposed to give Kyle an update on you in an hour. He wants to make sure you're doing okay, as well as confirmation that you can still fulfill your duties as a groomsman, or he'll have to start calling his backups. So just chill. I don't want my wedding ruined." Starla didn't think Ainsley's attempt at humor was very appropriate, but Sawyer gave her half a smile, which was more than she could manage just then.

"I can talk to Dr. Rose and get it sorted with him."

Ainsley didn't answer, and Starla leaned forward to see her friend's face better. The firm set of jaw told her that there was no way Ainsley was driving him up the mountain today. But Sawyer didn't seem to interpret her silence the same way.

"Good. It's decided. You can just take me home."

"Sawyer Devereaux, I almost have to admire you. I have never known anyone who could be so wiped out and still put up such a fight; you put the 'can' in 'cantankerous,'" Ainsley quipped. "And you love me, so knock off the surly teenager routine; you're twenty years too late." They shifted as Ainsley tried to get the passenger side door of her truck open. Starla stepped back to let Ainsley get him settled into the front seat, but she was watching him like a hawk; were his eyes glazing over again? She couldn't keep herself from wringing her hands, just a little.

"Do you need me to come with you?"

"No, we're okay. My aunt Rhea is used to him, she won't let him get into trouble." She glanced at her phone. "I don't know if she's home yet, though."

"You can leave him here, if you want. Give her a call," Starla urged. "I don't think you can get him inside without help." Ainsley nodded, moving off to call her aunt.

"He can hear you," Sawyer called, his slumped posture in the seat at odds with his snarky tone, his head tipped back against the head-rest. "What about my truck?"

"It should be safe here in the parking lot overnight. It's well-lit and everything," Starla said. "When I've been here at night, the place is deserted."

"Why were you here at night?" he asked, letting his head flop to the side to see her better.

"I was trying to catch the book fairy."

"Not this again. Why can't you just let people do nice things for you?"

"It's not for me, it's for the library. And I just want them to be properly thanked."

"If they wanted your thanks, they'd drop them off in the daytime. They obviously don't want them."

Starla narrowed her gaze at him. They discussed the book fairy often, and he was often vocal about his opinions, but they were usually more vague than that. This felt different; more pointed? She opened her mouth to ask him more, but Ainsley came back.

"Okay, my mom's going to come hang out with him if Rhea can't get off."

Sawyer groaned, swiping a hand down his face. "No, y'all, don't drag Aunt Nancy into this."

"Aunt Nancy happens to love you and wants to take care of you. She says she can finish her work day from home," she replied. "So just cool it." She closed his door and turned to Starla. "You okay?"

She started to nod, then shook her head. "That was scary. Has that happened before?"

"I don't know. I only recognized it because I had Tanner Wilson in my class last year, and he had several throughout the year." Ainsley looked toward the truck at the man now leaning against the window. "He doesn't like us asking questions about his health."

"Not that that'll stop *you*."

Ainsley smirked in response and gave Starla a one-armed hug. "See you at home."

# CHAPTER NINE

SAWYER FELT LIKE HE'D just run a marathon. Well, what he imagined that would be like; he hadn't exercised like that even before his diagnosis, and after, it became impossible. He'd been sticking to leisurely hiking and swimming since then. But he imagined that running a marathon felt like every cell in your body had been exposed to some kind of extreme radiation. Increased gravity, maybe? He felt pressed into the front seat of his cousin's truck in an almost supernatural way. As if it would take something not-of-this-world to make him feel so weak, so human, so purely exhausted from head to toe.

"I don't know why you feel the need to be so difficult all the time," Ainsley griped as she got into the driver's seat and closed her door. A door which now closed correctly, thanks to her fiancé. He liked Kyle all right; after all, he'd succeeded where Sawyer had failed. He'd been bugging her about that door for months.

"Can't argue with you right now," he mumbled, letting his eyes slide closed. He'd hoped that it would convince his body that he intended to rest, but it did nothing for his fatigue.

"Here." Something hit his lap, and he groped around for it. Smooth. Crinkly. Rectangular. He opened one eye. A chocolate peanut butter granola bar. He knew he should eat it, but he didn't feel like it. It wasn't as if withholding what it needed would make his body cooperate, but he didn't feel like being sensible right now. He'd apparently voided his bladder while he was seizing, and appropriately, he felt angry. And what's worse, he was too tired to do anything about his feelings or his pants.

He hadn't wanted Starla to see him like that. Ever. He didn't want anyone to see him like that, but her most of all. He didn't want her to worry about him; she had worries enough. Seeing her gaze down at him, that little wrinkle between her eyebrows, her fingers stroking his hair, tears dancing in her eyes. He'd been barely conscious, but he'd heard her whispered assurances; that she was there, that it would be okay. He even heard the catch in her voice when she asked Ainsley how much longer. That was the one that slayed him; he'd terrified her.

The problem was that his mom had been threatening to insist that he move in with her for months now. He hadn't had a flare for a few months, and it seemed like his multiple sclerosis was under control. He was working, he could care for himself, mostly, though he didn't mind when she came and filled up his fridge with premade keto meals. But seizures; that was new. This might be the thing that pushed her over the edge. Most people seemed to view Rhea Devereaux as a calm, docile, middle-aged woman, but she certainly was a force to be reckoned with when crossed by her children. She'd been accepting his choices for the last few years tolerably well, but she didn't hesitate to let him know that he was on thin ice. He was afraid he'd just plunged himself right through the ice and into the freezing water.

"Eat," Ainsley prompted, and she turned onto her parents' street. He sighed. Poor Aunt Nancy. He really did hate dragging her into this; no one should have to suffer for his sake. She wasn't due to leave work for another hour. At least Mr. Carpenter didn't seem to mind when she left, since she worked plenty even in her off hours. Harrison Carpenter demanded that kind of commitment.

"Can't," he responded, tossing it back to her.

"Eat," Ainsley insisted, her voice almost a growl. "Kyle said you have to. He said you should eat and rest and hydrate. We're starting with eating."

"Kyle's not the boss of me."

"What are you, five?"

Sawyer rolled his eyes. "Fine. Kyle isn't my neurologist, is that better?"

"Oh, so you're going to call Dr. Rose?"

"Yeah."

"Why don't I believe you?" she asked, and he let his silence speak for itself. He didn't owe her an explanation. She cared too much. She was a good family member. It was damn annoying.

"I will." They'd just had their monthly check-in this morning, so he couldn't go another month without discussing it with him . . .

"Good." She was glancing over at him frequently. She didn't seem half as worried as Starla had, though. Starla . . . oh no. He wasn't going to be able to drive on Wednesday. He wasn't going to be able to . . .

Ainsley pulled into the driveway and killed the engine.

"I need to make a call," he said. "I'll be in after a minute. You go on inside."

She scowled. "What kind of call?"

"The private kind."

Ainsley rolled her eyes, but she grabbed her bag and closed the driver's side door on her way into the house. He pulled out his phone, just staring at it. The real question was who to call. Lord knows his mother and his aunt would not approve, and Ainsley would probably just cry and call Starla immediately to spill the beans. He'd met Ainsley's fiancé, Kyle, a couple of times, and he seemed nice enough, but perhaps not predisposed toward shenanigans.

His brother, however . . . Daniel was Ainsley's best friend, had been for years. The real question was whether he could keep his mouth shut about his secret. He didn't know him well enough to say, and it wasn't like he could call around and find someone to vouch for him. He needed help; he needed someone dependable, but discreet. Daniel Durand didn't exactly scream discretion . . . but maybe he'd enjoy putting one over on Ainsley. With a sigh, he dialed, hoping he wasn't making a huge mistake.

"Hello?" Sawyer didn't hear the constant noise of the hospital behind Daniel.

"Hey. It's Sawyer Devereaux, how are ya?" He let his accent bleed through more than usual; it seemed to put people at ease, mostly.

"Oh, hey! I'm good, how are you?"

"Well, not so good, actually. I had a seizure this afternoon."

Daniel cursed softly. "Geez, I'm sorry. Are you okay?"

"Yes, thanks to Ainsley and Starla, I'm just fine. They reacted quickly. Your brother provided phone support as well, and I'm mighty grateful for that."

"Kyle's the best at stuff like that. I'm glad they didn't call me, I'm useless in emergencies."

"Oh, see, I'm hopin' that's not true. I need a favor. Kind of a big one."

"What kind of favor?"

"The top-secret kind. I'm not real social around town, so I don't have many people I can turn to, but there's a large pepperoni pizza from Annie's in it for you if you can pull it off without getting caught."

"Getting caught?" His voice went higher with piqued interest. "Really? Interesting . . . nothing illegal, right?"

"No, nothing illegal, I swear. I'm willing to bet you won't mind at all." There was a long silence on the other end of the phone, and now it was Sawyer's desperation that was piqued. "Help me, Dr. Durand, you're my only hope," Sawyer drawled, and the other man laughed.

"If you're okay with being Leia, I can commit to this scenario. What's the droid?"

"Well, it's a package, actually. I'll need it picked up from my house on Wednesday and dropped off elsewhere. I'll text you the details."

"Okay if it's kind of late? I don't get off until midnight."

Sawyer grinned. "That's even better." Relief suffused his heart, but with his personal crisis averted, the exhaustion returned. He should really hang up and go inside, while he still could.

"Can I ask what's in the package?"

"You'll know when you see it. Don't forget to get rid of the packaging; I can't be identified by the recipient."

"Well, I'm certainly intrigued. All right. Send me the info."

"Thank you. Seriously, man. I appreciate this."

"Something tells me it's for a good cause. I think I might even know which one."

Sawyer just chuckled. "I'll be in touch."

A sharp knock on his window startled him, and Sawyer turned to see his mom, giving him her patented firm look through the window. He motioned for her to back up, then opened his door and climbed out carefully, making sure to hold onto something; he was that tired. Sawyer mustered up a grin. "Hi, Mama."

"That's all you have to say? 'Hi, Mama'?"

"You didn't need to leave work. Bossypants could've looked after me."

She stared at him, ire in her gaze, her face hard. He decided to try a different tack.

"You look beautiful today. Is that a new perfume?"

Her lower lip trembled. "You promised me. You said you had a handle on your health. You said you could live up there safely by yourself."

He put his hands on her shoulders under the auspices of soothing her, but the additional support didn't hurt. "My doctor and I will be discussing this new development."

"I want you to move down to Timber Falls." He lifted an eyebrow at her, as if to remind her that he wasn't a teenager. "Please," she added quickly. "I'm getting more gray hair by the day, and that was before you collapsed at the library. You don't want to see me in an early grave, do you?"

"Before me? Unlikely."

"Stop. MS isn't a death sentence, and you know it."

He nodded, thinking privately that it must seem that way to someone who didn't have it. Multiple sclerosis had stolen his life, his real life; what he was doing now wasn't living. Just hanging around. So the fact that it hadn't also killed him yet felt a little unfair, if he was being honest. "Mama, I'm not moving into Timber Falls. I like my little cabin. I don't have my tools down here."

"Who's going to drive you up and down the mountain until you get your meds figured out?"

His interaction with Starla at the grocery store flashed into his mind, and he slipped an arm around his mom's shoulders as he led them up onto the porch. "I've got an idea."

# CHAPTER TEN

STARLA LAY IN BED THAT night between Aiden and Em, staring at the ceiling. Usually, their warmth and quiet breathing paired with the forced stillness of trying not to wake them lulled her into quick sleep. But tonight, every time she closed her eyes, she saw Sawyer's vacant eyes and seizing body thrashing on the floor in front of her desk. Ainsley had said he didn't like to talk about his health—which probably meant there was something to talk about—and he didn't seem confused about what had happened—which probably meant it had happened before. But how many times? Why? Was it going to happen again? What if Ainsley wasn't around to help, what if he was driving a car? Taking a shower? That prompted images in her mind of Sawyer and steam and not a stitch on, and she quickly shut it down. Both kids rolled toward her at the same time, as if sensing that she wanted to get up and read for a while, and she kissed the tops of their heads. Starla forced her eyes closed, and sleep finally came.

The next morning was rough. A lack of coffee (thanks, surprise baby) did not help. Her children whining definitely did not help. And once again, there was a line outside the library. Mavis Johnson was supposed to be opening today, but she'd texted this morning that she was sick. That troubled Starla, too, because she'd been doing so well since her breast cancer treatment. She hoped it was nothing serious; Mavis wasn't as young as she used to be. Starla gently edged her way to the front of the group, some of whom were grumbling about punctuality. But the person who was closest to the door said nothing. Sawyer stood there in the same clothes he'd worn yesterday (though they appeared freshly laundered), hands in his pockets, a mischievous sparkle in his gaze. Starla stared at him, feet rooted to the spot a few feet from the door. Sawyer never came to the library on Friday. Never.

"What are you doing here?" She loved that look on him, and she stared at him a little too long.

"Can we go inside? I'm going to be late for my online class," Pavel Kovalenko griped.

"And I need to get to work," Mr. Kirschbaum added. *Mr. K, I cannot wait until you retire.* It wouldn't get rid of his grumpy butt, but at least he wouldn't be in such a hurry all the time. There was no getting rid of anyone around here; they were born here, they lived here, they died here. Even ones like the Horowitzes, who'd moved away, eventually came back. *But what if* you *didn't?* A small voice inside her whispered. *You could put this town in your rear view mirror and never come back. You could wipe this divorce off your boots and move on, really move on.* It was a disturbing thought, mostly because in that moment, it appealed to her. But there was no time to dwell on it.

"Sorry, everyone. Give me just a minute here." She dug around in her purse until she found her keys. The moment the door was open, Pavel shot forward to get to the computers, Mr. Kirschbaum strode inside after him, and the rest of the patrons filed in at a more leisurely pace. Starla went to her desk and stowed her purse, then helped Mr. K., reset the internet for Pavel, found Sir Poops-a-Lot's evening delivery, and wandered through the picture book section with Mrs. Fisher gathering a stack of books her soon-to-be-visiting grandchildren would enjoy. She'd finally sat down to check her email when a voice startled her.

"Wow." Sawyer was sitting on the edge of her desk. He wasn't disturbing any of her stacks or writing utensils, but she wanted to poke his backside with a ruler until he moved anyway.

"What?"

"I thought librarians sat around all day and shushed people."

Starla straightened her glasses. "An unfortunate stereotype, I'm afraid. What can I do for you?"

"I bet y'all are tight as sardines over at Ainsley's . . ." His eyes held a question he hadn't asked yet.

She smiled at the analogy. "I guess you could say that."

"You lookin' for somewhere else? What's the plan once Ainsley moves to Kyle's?"

"I guess I don't have one yet." She rubbed her throbbing temples. "I'm kind of taking it one day at a time. Crisis mode." She'd had time, but she was infuriated with her own naiveté, looking back. She hadn't realized how far her planning would need to go: there were too many factors she hadn't thought through, and now here she was, stuck trying to cobble a life together with nothing but her wits and her meager income.

"I've got a proposition for you . . ."

There was nothing sexy or suggestive about the way he said it, but it still made her stomach clench a little.

"And what's that?"

"Why don't you come stay in the lodge, the three of you? And since I know from our grocery store moment that you're prideful to a fault, in payment, you can drive me to town until it seems like my health issues have stabilized, just until I get my meds figured out. It'll make my mama happy to know that someone's keeping an eye on me Friday through Wednesday."

Lord. That was tempting. She gave him the side-eye as she fussed with a stack of unruly papers on her desk, just to give her hands something to do while she thought it through. She needed to be smarter this time, not just jump at the first opportunity.

"Don't you need the income from your rental property?"

He shrugged one shoulder. "Not as much as I need to be able to live in my own place. I've been living in town less than 24 hours, and I'm already stir-crazy."

"As evidenced by you showing up here at 8 a.m. on a Friday . . ."

"Exactly," he grinned. That smile could charm the pants off a bear. If bears wore pants. She'd been reading a lot of picture books lately; possible too many, if that was the best analogy she could come up with.

Was it safe for him to be walking around by himself? What if he'd seized on the way here? Worry swamped her thoughts, and she tried to push it away, even as she scanned his body for signs of illness. He seemed okay, but how could she really know?

"It's kind of a long drive back and forth," she said.

"It's only twenty-five minutes."

She blinked. "Really?"

"Yeah."

"I don't know," she hedged. "I have enough trouble getting here on time even from Ainsley's place."

"That's a function of time management, not distance," he teased, and she had a strange urge to stick her tongue out at him. "And you'll sleep better if you have your own bed."

That was assuredly true, especially since her belly was about to grow. If she needed to hide, she could think of worse places to do it.

"If it's so close, why do you only come down once a week?"

He crossed his arms. "I don't people well."

"What does that mean?"

He grunted, looking out the window. "It means the town doesn't like me too much."

"I don't think that's true," she scowled.

"Let's put it this way," he said, leaning closer, lowering his volume. "If the library delivered, I might never come down at all."

*Then I'll never suggest it to the oversight committee.*

"We have e-books, you know."

"I like to read at night. Screens and I don't mix too well at that time of day."

"Because of your epilepsy?"

He smiled like she'd said something funny. "I don't have epilepsy."

"You don't? The internet said . . ."

"First of all, you shouldn't google other people's health problems. Dr. Internet doesn't know everything."

"Sorry," she said, tucking her hair behind her ears . . . wait, *she* hadn't done anything wrong. Why was she capitulating like this? Starla straightened and stared him down. "Sorry," she repeated, "but when a library patron—and more importantly, a *friend*—collapses in front of my desk, I don't think it's odd that I wanted to know more about what happened to him."

He tapped her desk. "Quit sticking your nose where it doesn't belong. I'm fine."

"You didn't seem fine when your head was in my lap."

"Touché." He looked down at his boots, his blond locks falling forward into his face, even as his cheeks went rosy. "I appreciate your concern, but it's baseless. You've got worries enough of your own." Wow. He did not know the half of it, and he was still right. He gestured toward the window with his thumb, and she saw that Charlie was coming up the walk. That was strange; he was usually opening the dealership and going over Jason's plan for the day around this time. She didn't want anyone to get the wrong impression; she should get rid of Sawyer before Charlie showed up.

"Let's discuss this later. Do you have my number?"

Sawyer shook his head, and she quickly dashed it off on an index card and passed it over to him. He took it just as Charlie stepped up to the desk.

"What's happening here? Is my wife flirting?"

"I'm not your wife anymore," she reminded him. "Talk to you later, Sawyer."

He gave her a nod, and as he turned toward the door, he smiled at her over his shoulder behind Charlie's back. Still trying to process her previous conversation, she turned back to Charlie; his expression was blank. "Aiden's in the car."

Alarm seized her. "Why?"

Her ex-husband smirked a little. "He got in a fight before school on the playground. Gave Timothy Carver a black eye."

Starla groaned. "This isn't funny, Charlie. Aiden's out of control lately."

He leaned forward with his hands flat against her desk, his yellow silk tie swinging. "And we know what's to blame. So why don't you come home, baby?"

"That is not the answer," she said through gritted teeth. "Aiden is responsible for his own decisions, just like the rest of us. And if he's going to choose to fight, then he can deal with the consequences. Better to teach him now than let him think someone else is always to blame for his own bad behavior." She gave Charlie a pointed look over the top of her glasses, but he just laughed.

"Can he stay with you? They sent him home, and the principal's going to call us in for a meeting later today."

"Fine."

"Thank you, Star," he crooned, and when he leaned down to kiss her cheek, she jerked away.

"Don't."

Charlie just laughed. "I'll send him in. He's in a *mood*, FYI."

Starla sighed. "Did you decide on any punishments?"

"No, I wanted to talk to you first, since you're the one who has to enforce it."

She blinked at him. "Oh. Thank you."

"You're welcome, beautiful." He winked at her. Well, that ruined it; it felt so different being on the receiving end of his flirting when she'd told him she didn't want it. The urge to throw a nearby copy of *War and Peace*—hardback—at him was strong. Instead, Starla turned back to her email and attempted to prioritize what needed her attention most before her sulking son came in, then groaned. She'd forgotten to pay Sawyer back. Again.

# CHAPTER ELEVEN

SAWYER STARED AT STARLA'S number, rubbing his thumb over the corner of the index card she'd scribbled it on. He should just call her. That's what he'd said he'd do, and he was serious about his offer to trade her labor for housing. Trouble was, persuasion wasn't his strong suit, and he had a feeling that Starla had some strong reservations about this. Did she doubt his intentions were . . . pure? They were. She could have absolute confidence in that; being up in the mountains, away from prying eyes, he wasn't going to treat her any differently than he did every Thursday at the library. He had a deep respect for her, and he'd never push a woman into something she didn't want; he'd been raised better than that. Maybe he should've been more clear about that from the start.

Being six years older, he hadn't known her well when they were kids. The Devereauxs had bounced back and forth between Georgia and Oregon . . . when Mom and Dad were getting along, they lived in the South. But when they were on the outs, they'd come back to Timber Falls. Maybe that's why it'd never exactly been his favorite place. He remembered Starla's pregnancy scandal; he'd heard about it in medical school from his mama, his first year at Emory. Felt bad for her, but it wasn't like he could do anything.

Hearing footsteps approach, he shoved the index card back into the pocket of his jeans.

"Do you need anything before I go?" his mom asked, kissing the top of his head.

"Yes. I need to go home. Would you please drive me?"

"Sorry, no time," she chirped. She was still pleased as punch that he was stuck here with her until his doctor's appointment on Monday. Her cheerfulness wasn't meant to hurt him, but it felt downright cruel at the moment.

"Then I suppose not."

"All right, sweet pea. I'll call and check on you later."

"That's not necessary. I'll just be sitting here on your sofa, contemplating my own demise."

"Not funny, Sawyer Abbott." Her hurt gaze said she meant it.

"Sorry," he muttered, and she softened a little.

"I know these past two years haven't been easy for you," she said, sitting on the edge of the couch, so he was forced to move his legs to make room for her. "But I would like you to start to move past this . . ."

With considerable effort, he kept his voice calm. "Hard to do when it affects every decision all day." The medications, his chosen diet, metering his energy. She didn't understand.

"I'm not saying it's not hard, I'm saying it's *necessary*." Sawyer glanced up at her momentarily, then looked away from her firm gaze. "You're stuck, son. It's time to get moving again."

*How?* He wanted to snap. *How? How do I stop being angry? Is there some med I don't know about? One that takes away the grief of this?* He kept his face carefully blank; his mama didn't need to know about that part of it, and she didn't deserve to be ranted at.

"Why won't you go back to medicine?" she asked, arms crossed.

"Because no one wants surgery from someone whose hands have a mind of their own," he said, digging deeper into the yogurt.

"Don't be flippant with me. There are other things you could do."

"Not the same," he muttered. "Once you specialize, it's not that easy, Mama."

"You don't know. You haven't tried."

"Please don't start . . ."

"You've got a whole long life ahead of you, full of adventure and goodness."

"Like what?" He really did want to know. He picked up the Greek yogurt she'd brought him for breakfast and took a bite.

"Well," she faltered, "you've got your motorcycle business."

"My work is fine, but I wouldn't call it something to live for."

"Okay." Rhea patted his leg. "But you've got me and Paige."

"I do. And you're both important, but you've got your own lives to live, dreams to realize. You'd be fine without me."

"If you really believe that," she said softly, "then you don't know how much I love you." His mom leaned forward and kissed him on the forehead. "Have a good day, sweetheart."

"You, too," he said, scooping another big bite of the tangy yogurt out of the container. When he heard the garage door go up, he pulled the index card out again. She'd written her name on the top of it in cursive; he liked that she didn't print everything like most people did. She was a cut above. He tossed it onto the coffee table with a sigh, then slid down to rest his head on the armrest of the couch and turned on the TV. Why should she say yes to this crazy scheme? There was very little in it for her, really. He'd be considerate, of course, and consolidate his grocery trips with hers and time his trips into town with her schedule. But she had a lot of friends in town; why wouldn't she stay with someone she knew better? There was no reason for her to say yes to him. Well, beyond her stubborn pride. He'd enjoyed sparring with her in the grocery store a little too much; not just the battle of wits, but being able to be genuinely helpful to her in a moment of need. He'd seen her deep reluctance to accept his help, and he respected that. He'd gotten scholarships for both undergrad and medical school, working in the summers, then spreading out his money all year. He knew how it felt to want to take care of yourself. She just needed a little boost. This would be another boost, but she'd never take it unless she thought she was earning it some-how.

A knock at the front door had him glancing toward it. If it was Mormons again, he was definitely going to argue with them; he was bored out of his gourd. Maybe it would give his mom more incentive to let him go home. He swiped at the drip on his stained black shirt, which said, upside down, 'Is my bike okay?' He'd gotten it a bunch of birthdays ago, and he still thought it was pretty funny, but at any rate, no one at the door would care that he'd spilled almond butter on it. Sawyer opened the door, and Starla smiled up at him.

"Hey." She was wearing that tan corduroy skirt he liked with a black blouse and a denim jacket over the top . . . not that he had any right to have favorites when it came to what she wore. Besides, she always looked great.

"Hey."

*Dude. Say more. Say something. Anything. Open your mouth and let words come out.*

"What are you doing here?" he asked.

*Facepalm. Not* those *words. Smooth words.*

She jingled her keys, like she was tempting him. "You want to go for a ride?"

"Yes," he said, letting go of the front door he'd been clinging to like a security blanket so he could close it behind him.

Starla laughed softly. "Don't you even want to know where we're going?"

"Nope. Lead the way, lady." It was a cool April morning, but he didn't need a jacket. Not if they were going in her car.

"I feel like I'm springing you out of the joint," she whispered, glancing around conspiratorially as they went to the car.

"Did you see my mama? You didn't miss her by much."

Starla blushed, and Sawyer couldn't help letting a chuckle escape.

"You avoided her, didn't you?" Sawyer accused. "Ms. Moore, I'm ashamed of you. My mama's a darn sweet lady. She would've loved the chance to give you a hug and thank you for helping me during my episode at the library."

"Well," she said, tucking her hair behind her ears on both sides, "I just didn't want to get you into trouble for going out."

"I'm allowed to go out, I'm just not allowed to drive," he said. "So drive as far as you want. Drive until we hit the Mexican border for all I care. I habla the español."

"Do you really?" she asked, glancing at him as they pulled out of the driveway.

"Really. I spent a year down in Honduras with Doctors Without Borders after I graduated, helping out with a hospital down there. Real rough conditions, but it was good experience."

"I can imagine. That was very generous of you."

"Not really."

The memories themselves of that time were not particularly sweet, since that was where his MS symptoms had first started to make themselves known. He remembered standing in the operating theater, willing his hands to stop shaking, wondering if he was just sick with something like dengue fever or cholera. He should've known better, he felt now. As young as he was, it was easy to explain his symptoms away. The chronic fatigue he'd attributed to jet lag and long hours. The strange urinary symptoms, he'd called a UTI. But the hand shaking, that he couldn't ignore.

"Well, I don't have the gas to get us all the way to Mexico, so I thought maybe we could go up to your property instead . . ."

"Oh?" He tried not to look too eager. "Why?"

She shrugged. "Thought you might like some clean clothes, the chance to grab some things. Water your plants or whatever. Oh, and here." She tossed him an envelope, and based on its thickness, he was guessing it was repayment for his grocery assistance.

He smiled. She'd noticed his plants. That was considerate. The deer who hung out around his place was probably having a heyday in his new garden, without anyone there to run him and his girlfriend off.

"Well, thanks, that's very considerate of you."

"And . . ." She hesitated as she turned off the highway onto the forest service road that led to his house. "And I wanted to see the big house again, just to see. If it would work for us." When his stunned silence lasted too long, she cleared her throat. "If you still need someone to drive you around, that is." Yup, her pride was both stubborn and reliable.

"I do. I definitely do. I'm just surprised you actually said yes, I wasn't sure you'd want to be so far out of town."

"Someone said it was only twenty-five minutes out of town."

"It is," he said. "Less if I drive."

"But you can't drive, that's the point," she said with a smirk. "What kind of driving would you need done?"

"Just the basics. Grocery store. Library. Doctor's appointments. Nothing too substantial. I'll have the motorcycle parts that I need delivered, so I won't need to go up to Portland as much, but occasionally, there may be something that's too big to ship, and I might need help with that."

"That doesn't sound too bad. No late-night clubbing?"

"No, ma'am," he said somberly. "I'm always in bed by ten." That was a lie; it was nine, but he didn't want to seem like a nerd. It wasn't his fault.

"Very responsible," she said approvingly. "No drugs, right?"

"Just the prescription kind."

"Got any guns?" As a man who'd grown up in the South, he couldn't imagine not owning a gun, but around here, not everyone felt the same way.

"Just one, but I keep it locked up. Your kiddos won't get their hands on it, if that's your concern."

"Yes, it was." Starla fell quiet, and he watched her as she drove.

"Do I get to ask you questions?"

"Of course, landlord," she said, gesturing for him to go ahead. "Ask away."

"How long do you think you'd want to stay, if you like it?"

She scratched her nose a little. "I'm not sure yet. Probably just through the summer. It'd be better to be closer to town once school starts up again. I don't think the bus will make it up this hill."

"Most likely not," he agreed. "Would you want to sign a contract?"

"I don't think so," she said, but she didn't sound sure. "Surely the word of a friend is good enough. You don't seem like the type to take me to court."

"I'm not the litigious sort, no."

Starla smiled at him again, and he felt better than he had in days. "You're really considering this?"

"Sure," she said, shrugging again. "I do need a place to live. Ainsley's been very kind to let us crash with her, but it's time to find something a little less . . ."

"Cramped?"

"That's the word," she agreed. "Not to mention expensive."

"It's right here," he said, pointing for her to turn where the plywood "Devereaux Motors" sign was tacked to the tree with a nail. She turned into his long driveway and parked in front of the garage. He had to grab the keys from the cabin, then he walked her through the big house, pointing out its features without sounding too much like he was trying to sell it. Even though, in his head, he was 100% trying to sell it.

"Big windows, a bedroom for each of you, and a fully-equipped kitchen," he said, waltzing into the living room as she opened cupboards and peeked inside closets. "If you have things you need to store, there's room in the loft of the garage or up in the attic of this house." He'd dropped by Ainsley's to return a book a few weeks ago and noticed the large stack of boxes cluttering up the second bedroom.

Starla wandered around with her phone out, making notes. Then she lifted her head. "You're sure about this? We're not taking away your rental income?"

He shook his head. "I'd lose it anyway if I'm not here. Can't leave people unsupervised up here or they tend to get into all sorts of trouble."

She nodded slowly, turning around in the living room. "I do have one more question."

"Shoot," he said.

"It isn't housing-related, I've just always wondered . . ."

Now that piqued his curiosity. "Yes?"

"Why won't you let me pick a book for you?" Those big brown eyes were so sincere behind her glasses; he scanned her face. She wasn't mad, but maybe a little hurt.

*Because I didn't want another reason to like you. Because I like getting you all riled up.*

"I'm just real particular when it comes to books . . ."

"Oh, I know," she said, shaking her hands excitedly. "But there's this Swedish author named Henning Mankell, and he writes this character named Kurt Wallander . . ."

The name rang a bell. "I think I've seen the TV show . . ."

She huffed impatiently. "But the books are so much better!"

*That* was a surprise. "You've read them?"

Starla blushed. Actually blushed, the full tomato impression. "I knew they were popular, and I don't like to recommend things I haven't at least tried . . ."

Sawyer was pretty sure that was partly a lie. She'd read them because she thought he might like them, based on the way she was avoiding his gaze, squeezing her hands together anxiously . . .

"All right. I'll give them a try."

He didn't know where the words had come from, because he'd made such a point of it all this time. But if he was going to see her, get rides from her, bump into her in the morning all the time, well . . . he was sure he was going to find more things to like about her anyway. What would it hurt? He couldn't let her stand there disappointed like that.

"You will not regret this," she said, sounding more like a used car salesman than a librarian.

"But you have to let me pick one for you. Fair's fair." The irony was not lost on him; he'd been picking books for her for months, leaving them behind the library. But she could never know about that.

"Fine," she said, shrugging, grinning, looking pleased. "And we'll take the lodge."

"Great." He couldn't keep the grin off his face. Not only had he just gotten some of his independence back, he'd gained a lovely next-door neighbor. "Welcome to the neighborhood."

"Gee, thanks," she grinned, rolling her eyes. "You ready to go grab your stuff?"

"Yep." He started toward the door, but out of the corner of his eye, he noticed her put a hand to her head, her steps stuttering. He turned, alarmed. "You okay?"

"Yes, I just get lightheaded sometimes."

He frowned. That wasn't good. "Didn't this happen when you were here before?"

Starla rolled her eyes again. "Put away your prescription pad, doctor. No diagnosis necessary, I'm sure I'm fine."

Maybe she was allergic to mold? Did his rental have mold? Maybe he'd have it checked before she moved in . . .

"If you say so." He held the door open for her, mostly so that he could keep an eye on her. He had a sixth sense about things sometimes, and something told him there was more to this situation than met the eye, but he wasn't going to say so. Nope. He was going to take this gift horse and lead it right into the stable. Starla Moore was now officially his unofficial renter . . . as soon as he canceled the renters he'd already lined up.

# CHAPTER TWELVE

ABOUT A WEEK LATER, Sawyer got up early. He watched the coffee drip into the pot, bleary-eyed, then took his mug out to the front porch.

"Morning, Lucky," he called, his voice a little rusty with early morning grime. The young buck lifted his head, then went back to his snack at the edge of the woods. "Yeah, I wouldn't pay any attention to me, either," Sawyer said, sipping his coffee. He was a frequent connoisseur of mornings, and this one was starting to feel like a true spring day. His breath didn't crystalize in the air, and dew didn't cling to the ground. The deer grabbed his attention again. Looked like Lucky had brought his girlfriend again today. She was pretty pregnant, and Sawyer didn't bother hiding his happiness at seeing them together. At least he'd finally built a tall enough mesh wall around the garden to keep Lucky and his lady out of *there* . . . he hoped. So far, the sprouts were doing their thing. It was hard to tell with plants.

"Good morning, Lucky's Lady," he added. "Didn't see you there." The buck stared harder at him this time, almost as if he was warning him off his girl, and the deep scar on his right cheek made him look all the more tough. "Hey, man, she's all yours. Not my type."

As if the deer didn't believe him, they moved off together, the buck herding the doe, turning to glare at Sawyer again, and he chuckled. "Sorry I crashed your date. See you tomorrow." It was just as well; he wasn't crazy about having an audience when he exercised. Sawyer balanced his metal, speckled coffee cup on the railing of his cabin and stepped out into the yard. He took a deep breath, parting his feet, then lifted his hands and let his body start to go through the motions. He'd never been able to sit still long enough to meditate, but for some reason, if he was moving, he could clear his head, let go of the things holding him down. Tai chi allowed him that relief. Today promised to be busy, which was all the more reason to make time for it. He loved his cousin dearly, but Ainsley provoked him to meditation.

She had already been texting this morning, confirming that he'd be at the wedding rehearsal six weeks from now (he would), that he would pick up his own tux (he would, with Starla's help), and that he really didn't want to go to the bachelor party (he really didn't).

"They won't be drinking," she cajoled via voicemail. "Kyle doesn't like how he feels when he's intoxicated. So you should go. You don't have to stay late. Just go and play video games and do the food part, and then you can go." She said that, and he had no doubt that she believed it, but the problem was that social obligations never worked that way. Once they had you, they didn't want to let you go. His firm nine o'clock bedtime didn't mesh well with the social activities of most young people, and he had no interest in enduring weird looks or needling about it.

His phone buzzed, and without looking at the screen, he took it out of his pocket and turned it off. His mama would blow her stack if she knew he was doing that. When Starla brought him home, he'd just decided to stay, much to both women's dismay. But he was still wearing the stupid Life Alert bracelet she'd gotten him, so that assuaged his conscience a little bit. It looked more like a Fitbit than a goofy red button hanging around his neck, but it was just one more reason to wear long sleeves. Ainsley could tease him all she wanted about his trademark flannel.

He pushed the thoughts away gently, even as he pushed his hands out in front of him on a long exhale. He let his shoulders sink, his elbows drop. He didn't take it too slowly . . . he'd tried to join a group of old people in a park once, but the pace put him to sleep. It was like a dance, and the imagery of it worked for him. Grasp sparrow's tail, hold a bouquet of flowers, white crane spreads its wings, play the pipa. Whatever that was. He assumed it was some kind of musical instrument. He was not musical; he was more analytical than creative, and that seemed to serve him just fine.

He stepped forward smoothly, rhythmically. Stepped to the side, letting his knees sink slowly, letting his thoughts settle with his body. Normally, this was his best chance at relaxation . . . but Starla was moving in today. He felt like a kid waking up the first morning of summer vacation; all sorts of wonderful possibilities lay before him. He couldn't ever ask her out, but he'd get to see her a lot, maybe even every day. Sawyer tried to force his thoughts back to his exercise, toward listening to how his body felt, toward internal rest, even as the outside of him moved through his routine. But today, he was stuck in his imagination: having casual conversations with her, playing with her kids together, maybe even eating together occasionally. It seemed too good to be true. Grumbling at his own brain, eventually, he gave up and turned his phone back on, just in case she tried to call.

In order to play it cool, he changed the oil in both the bikes that were in the garage. They probably didn't need it, but it would allow him to pause what he was doing without losing track so he could help her unload. He did not anticipate how much help she would bring with her. As her van pulled up, he was surprised to see Ainsley's truck and Kyle's minivan caravaning along behind her. Could three people, two of them children, really have enough stuff to necessitate that? Daniel and Winnie hopped out of Kyle's van with Aiden and Emily.

"That was a *long* drive," Emily announced loudly, and he smiled. Despite her good behavior in the library, he wasn't surprised that this was her preferred volume.

"It wasn't that long," Aiden said, and Sawyer watched the boy's face light up as he looked around at the tall trees, the garage, the garden. Wiping his hands on a rag, he stepped out of the darkened garage, and Aiden's face lit up when he saw him step out of the shadows. "Mr. Devereaux! We're here."

"So I see," he said, giving the kid a grin. "Did you get everything packed up?"

"Yeah. My stuff didn't take very long. Mom and Em took longer. Waaayyy longer," he said, rolling his eyes.

"I'd say that sounds like a common situation for people who care about how they look. More clothes, more cosmetics, you know. Let's go help carry things inside," he said, moving to the truck, and Aiden hurried to catch up with him.

"Were you working on your motorcycles?"

"They're not mine," he clarified, picking up a box and starting toward the house. "But yes, I was working on them."

"Cool," he said, doing the same, and Sawyer recognized the devious gleam in his eye. "Maybe you could give me a ride on one later?"

"No, no," Starla said, coming out of the house, just as they were going in. "No motorcycle rides. We talked about this, Aiden. Your dad said no."

"Maybe I could just show you how to check the tire pressure," Sawyer suggested. If the kid was anything like Sawyer had been at his age, he probably loved anything with wheels. Since his uncle and his dad had worked on motorcycles, it was a logical hobby through his growing up years. The first time Sawyer had gotten the wind in his hair, he'd been hooked on the feeling. After working in the OR, he'd traded that feeling for a helmet. But the need for the freedom of the road with the sun shining on his shoulders was something that still tugged at him. He wouldn't be indulging in such things for a while . . . at least not until his new meds were given a chance to work.

"Not really the same," Aiden sulked, marching into the house and up the stairs.

"Aiden, you're the room next to mine, not the bathroom," Starla called after him. She stopped next to Sawyer, trying to stay out of the flow of helpers in and out of the house. "Hi," she smiled, and he couldn't help but smile back. He wondered how long he'd had this reflex.

"Hi. Where do you want this?" Sawyer was carrying what appeared to be a collection of very specialized kitchen appliances—a quesadilla maker, a toaster oven, an air fryer, a panini press—that had been unceremoniously dumped into the bottom of a peach box.

"Um," she rubbed her own shoulder with one hand, "I don't know. The kitchen, I guess? Are the cabinets full?"

"Shouldn't be."

"But I don't want it to get mixed up . . .. Sorry. I'm thinking."

"No need to apologize," he said, shifting it to his hip. "I didn't do any weight training this morning, so . . ."

Starla snickered. "I really am trying to stop apologizing. I think I do it too much." She put a hand on his arm. "You can remind me, since you'll be around." It was a casual touch; friendly. It shouldn't have been enough throw his thoughts into turmoil and tie his stomach into knots.

"Yeah, okay," he muttered. "So, the box?"

"Kitchen," she said decisively. "Definitely kitchen."

"I haven't been asking," Ainsley announced, "so that you'll have to call me a lot to find out where things are."

Starla punched her friend lightly on the arm. "You know that's not necessary. I'm going to call you anyway."

"So you say," Ainsley sniffed, "but this whole move was very sudden, and I'm having trouble processing it all."

"I told you," Starla said, taking the suitcase from her, "it's not sudden. You're leaving your apartment soon, and I can't afford to rent it by myself."

"And I told *you*," Ainsley replied, "that I'm sure the rental company would've worked with you to keep it rented without having to find someone else, but suit yourself." She glanced at Saywer, and behind her innocent facade, he knew the mischief she'd be capable of. "I guess this is a bit more comfortable." Sawyer glared at her to get her to back off; nothing was going to happen between him and Starla. She was recovering from a divorce, and his health situation was . . . complicated. He wasn't going to ask anyone to insert themselves into that. Well, he sort of already had, but there was mutual benefit there.

"Much more," Starla confirmed, oblivious to Ainsley's insinuations, and Sawyer turned and went back out to the truck so he didn't have to listen to her try to subtly push them together. Daniel was at the truck already.

"Thanks for your help on Wednesday with the package," Sawyer said, offering him his hand for a firm shake.

"No problem," he said with a grin. "Winnie almost caught me, though. I'll have to be more careful next time." Kyle approached them, so they quickly dropped the conversation.

"Hey. Thanks for helping out," Sawyer said.

"I don't mind," Kyle said. "All my wedding tasks are done for the moment, so I had some free time." He lowered his voice. "And if we move them out, I can be alone with Ainsley in her apartment again. That's a win." Without waiting for a response, he continued into the house, and Sawyer blinked after him, not sure how to take his blatant honesty.

"Are your wedding tasks all done?" Sawyer teased Ainsley, who just shook her head ruefully.

"Soooo far from done . . . and I was counting on my roommate to help me out."

"I can still help you out," Starla said, pushing her glasses up her nose. "I'll just drive down."

"And we can hang out with Mr. Devereaux!" Emily piped up, grabbing his hand.

Sawyer smiled down at her, giving her small hand a gentle squeeze, pleased as punch that she'd put the idea forth, until he looked up: Ainsley was smiling wickedly, Starla looked embarrassed, Kyle looked confused, and Daniel and Winnie were ignoring all of them and actually doing the job they'd come to do.

"Em, you can't just assume that other people want to watch you," Starla chided. "Mr. Devereaux has his own life, his own work to do. He's just kindly letting us stay here for a few months. Now go inside and start unpacking, please." Her daughter scampered inside, and Starla turned to him.

"Sorry about that."

"Stop apologizing." He turned and went back to the truck, and he heard her trailing after him.

"What?"

"You said you were going to stop apologizing. She didn't do anything wrong, anyway. I like her, too. It's not like I'm doing anything. I bet she can even dial 911 for me if I seize again."

"That's not going to happen, is it?" Her face had gone very pale, and he wanted to reach out and steady her, just in case she passed out. Her concern was very sweet; most women would be running for the hills rather than get involved with someone with a chronic illness. *Not that we're involved.*

"Unknown," he said, carrying a box of stuffed animals up the porch steps. "Don't worry about it."

She tried to take the box from him, but he held onto it. "I can't help it. Let me take this. You shouldn't be carrying that."

He narrowed his eyes at her, letting a little of his irritation come through. "How do you know? Are *you* a doctor?"

Starla tugged on the box insistently. "No, but . . ."

He had the advantage of a few inches, and he leveraged it to pull it away from her. "Then let me manage my health. I've got this." Sawyer turned and continued through the living room, glancing over his shoulder toward the front door when he hit the steps. She was still staring after him, her arms now crossed defiantly over her belly, and he smirked at her. Shaking her head, she went back out the front door. *No, that'll never do.* He wanted to be clear about this right up front. He grunted, dropping the box where he stood at the bottom of the stairs and pacing after her. Catching her shirt sleeve, he tugged her away from the trucks, over closer to his garage.

"Why do you think I proposed this?" he asked, turning to face her.

Starla shrugged, but he shook his head.

"I didn't hire a nurse, you'll notice."

She stayed silent, arms crossed so tight, her shoulders were almost up by her ears.

"What you told Ainsley in the library is exactly right: it's my life. This is how I want to live it. And I don't like to be coddled or fussed over. You and me, we're alike. Fiercely independent. We respect each other. So even though you're here to help me out, trust me to tell you if I need something." Her body language was still tight, and he could see that there were a lot of things she wanted to say. She leaned forward onto the motorcycle between them.

"And you're not going to be proud and pretend everything's fine when it's not?"

He made an X over his chest, then held up his hand in a mock pledge. "Scout's honor."

Her mouth twisted to one side. "Were you a Boy Scout?"

"Nope." He grinned and mimicked her posture, putting his palms on the bike. "But I think I can tell the truth anyway."

A smile played at the corner of her mouth. "Fine. We agree to stay out of each other's business, then?"

"Agreed."

She straightened up, smiling now, and she looked him up and down in a slow, appraising way that made the hair on the back of his neck stand up. "You won't last a month."

"I can outlast *you*. That much I know."

"Oh, you think so?" She laughed, then put out her hand, and he shook it firmly. "I don't believe it. You've got Buchanan blood in you. It's in your nature to meddle."

"Not mine . . ."

She turned to go back to work, then stopped. "Why aren't you doing anything?"

"Pardon?"

"Earlier, when Em asked if you could watch them, you said you weren't doing anything. Why aren't you doing anything? Why aren't you out there, tomcatting around or something? Shouldn't you be fixing your bikes? Wait, aren't you a doctor?"

"I used to be."

"You're pretty young for 'used to be,'" she mused, and he smiled at his shoes. Thirty-three felt old, faced with this fresh-faced twenty-seven year old, even if she did have two kids.

"Yeah, I guess that's right."

"Why aren't you a doctor anymore?"

"That's not a short conversation," he said, indicating toward her friends, who were waiting around to say goodbye. *And it's one I don't want to have, anyway.* "And that sounds an awful lot like poking around in my business."

With a grin, she turned and went back over to her friends, but his attention was ripped away by a truck he didn't recognize coming up the driveway. Sawyer shaded his eyes to try to see who was in the shiny silver Tahoe . . . oh. It was Charlie. He should've figured he'd show up here eventually, but he'd thought they might get more of a reprieve than this.

"Hey guys," he called, whipping off sunglasses that looked like they'd been designed in the 80s. "Am I too late to help?"

Sawyer was glad he wasn't standing over there so he could mumble, "Yes. Shocker."

He watched out of the corner of his eye as Charlie talked to Starla and his kids, play boxing with Aiden and swinging Emily around. He noticed with amusement that Ainsley was clearly not buying Charlie's act, and she and Kyle moved to leave. He should probably go over and thank them.

"Bye, cousin," he said, giving her a side hug and a kiss on the temple.

"Bye," she said. "Be good. Make sure you're being *neighborly* to your new chauffeur." She waggled her eyebrows meaningfully, and he shook his head.

"It's not like that."

"Whatever you say. It's just nice seeing you and Starla together, getting along so well."

"We're not *together*, cousin. We just need each other."

"You can hear yourself, right?" She looked between him and her fiancé. "Kyle, back me up here."

"Yes. She's right. When even I'm picking up the sexy vibes between two people, you know it's obvious."

He rolled his eyes. "I don't mean *need each other* like that. We're friends. Friends help each other."

"Help of *all kinds*," Ainsley teased, and Sawyer rolled his eyes. Kyle looked at Ainsley, and the humor that danced in her eyes made him at once happy for his cousin and very aware that the same humor often danced in Starla's gaze when she looked at him. The fact got under his skin and made it prickle uncomfortably.

"Go make googly eyes at your fiancé somewhere else and mind your own business."

She folded her arms over her belly. "You are my business, Sawyer."

"You don't fuss over Travis like this. Or Tara."

"Because they don't need it. You do."

"Lord, woman. I *have* a mother. Go find someone else to fix." He looked away before he could see the hurt in her eyes. It was necessary. She had a tendency to pick a project, and he didn't want her focus on Starla to extend to him as well. They were not a unit. Just two people who needed—scratch that. Two people who were in need and happened to be able to help each other. That's all. He didn't need Starla Moore. He couldn't. He wouldn't even let himself admire her lovely dark hair, currently escaping its rubber band again, as she walked up to the group. Wanting her was one thing; needing was something else entirely.

"Okay, well, I guess we'll see you Thursday," Ainsley called after him. "And of course, the bachelor party in a few weeks."

"Oh," Kyle said, frowning. "Are you coming? I thought you RSVP'd that you were unavailable."

"And sadly, that's still the case," Sawyer confirmed, glaring at Ainsley. "Hope y'all have a great time, though." He glanced at Kyle. "Nothing personal, man."

Kyle nodded. "I too prefer to avoid social obligations when I can."

Ainsley nudged Starla with her elbow, and Starla nudged her back. When Ainsley nudged her a second time, Starla rolled her eyes and said robotically, "I would be happy to drive you, if you want to go. Which I know you don't."

"The kids will be in bed by then," Sawyer said, smirking. "That's reason enough to stay home." At that moment, Charlie came back to the group, out of breath from chasing the kids around, and Sawyer felt his smile disappear. Charlie slung an arm around Starla's shoulders, who grimaced and stepped away from him, letting it fall. Ainsley immediately turned away and got into her truck, and the rest of the helpers followed suit.

"What's with the attitude, babe?" he called after Starla, as she went into the house.

"Go home, Charlie," she replied, not turning around, and relief coursed through Sawyer that she was telling him to shove off.

"Charles," Sawyer said in greeting, trying to be polite.

"It's Charlie, actually," the dark-haired man grinned. "You've spent enough time at my dealership that you should know that. You and my brother, thick as thieves back there, elbow-deep in grease." He looked so confident in his own superiority. He shouldn't be. Charlie started toward the house, and for a moment, Sawyer was stunned speechless. Hadn't she *just* told him to leave?

"Hey!"

Charlie ignored him, and Sawyer put on some speed to get in front of him before he got to the porch steps, hoping like heck his balance would cooperate. Sawyer put a hand on his chest, blocking his way into the house.

"Charles," Sawyer continued, "just so we're clear, this is private property. I'd hate to have to call the sheriff and explain that someone's trespassing on my property. Or worse yet, go down and file a restraining order against you."

The man crossed his arms. "Are you threatening me?"

"Threats are idle. This is a promise." Sawyer stepped closer, and he knew by the flash of fear in the man's eyes that he was coming off as serious as he intended to. "She wants you here? Fine. She doesn't want you here? You stay away. She's the boss. You'll finally give her the respect she deserves, as long as she's staying on my property."

Charlie hesitated for a moment, then sneered. "You won't do anything to me. You're all talk. You think that because you're out here in the woods, outside of town, you two can just play house and no one will notice . . ." That sparked his temper, but he kept his voice low.

"I ain't playing. That's what you did. And you lost. Thinking it was a game was probably your first mistake, but not your last. But me? I don't play with people's hearts. And I ain't scared of you, either. You think you can win her back, you go right ahead. But I'm not *playing* when I tell you that it'll be on her terms or you'll be getting a visit from the sheriff." He grinned, and he made sure it was the menacing kind. "Just a bit of advice from me to you, Charles."

"If you touch my wife, you redneck piece of . . ." Charlie started, jabbing a finger in Sawyer's face. He didn't even have time to get angry about it before Starla's yell made them both turn their heads toward the front door.

"Hey!" She was hurrying toward them, while the kids stood watched them through the front windows with big eyes. Sawyer stepped back a little; he didn't want to scare them. Just Charlie.

"Hey, guys," she said, coming between them. "Let's not do this, huh?"

"Just having a friendly conversation," Sawyer said, turning back to smile at Charlie. It wasn't lost on him that she'd turned toward Charlie when she inserted herself in their 'conversation' . . . did she not want to turn her back to Charlie? *Did he hit her?* He'd never noticed bruises on her, but they could've been hidden, and the very thought made him want to vomit. *Is that why she always wears sweaters? If he laid one finger on her, I'll . . .*

"Thank you for stopping by, Charlie, but as you can see, the work is all done," Starla said, her voice quiet.

Uncharacteristically violent thoughts were still running through Sawyer's head, which frightened him a little. He wasn't that guy, that alpha male, pushy, aggressive. But just the thought of Starla being harmed by someone she couldn't get away from him made him want to punch the nearest douchebag. The only thing that was keeping him in check now was that she wasn't stuck with Charlie anymore.

"Starla, all I want is to—"

"You heard her. Sounds like it's time to go." Sawyer kept his voice calm, but held his ground, his chest against Starla's back.

Charlie's demeanor changed instantly from pompous to pleading. "Can't I just have lunch with the kids? I kind of promised them I would . . ." *What a weasel.* If he thought he could leverage his way into that house using the kids as an excuse, he had another think coming.

"Don't make me throw you off this property in front of your kids, man." He'd do it, too. He'd enjoy every second of it. Watching this wonderful woman get more and more broken by Charlie every week had cost him more sleep and heartache than he could tabulate. Sawyer was startled by the depth of his own agitation toward this man. Apparently, he'd been banking it up, all this time. If Charlie was going to keep coming around, it was going to take a lot of tai chi to keep it in check.

"You'll see them all day tomorrow," Starla said, turning Charlie by his shoulders and giving him a little push toward his Tahoe. "Say goodbye, Charlie." Sawyer took a step to follow him, but she put out her arm and shook her head. He stayed. He'd probably overstepped already.

Head hung low, Charlie called to the kids. "No lunch today, guys. But I'll see you tomorrow." He got into his car as Aiden clenched his fists and turned, running into the house. Emily just gave him a sad little wave as she watched him drive away.

"You know what I was thinking of for lunch? Tacos!" Starla said brightly, heading into the house with Em. At the door, she turned back to him and mouthed, "Thank you."

He gave her a single nod, his hands stuffed deep in his pockets, then he went back to his cabin and plopped down on the couch with a sigh before he remembered that he had two motorcycles drained of oil waiting for him in the garage. So much for maintaining the illusion that he wasn't emotionally involved . . .

# CHAPTER THIRTEEN

SUNDAY WAS QUIET; SAWYER opted to go for a hike instead of doing tai chi, because he wasn't sure what time Starla would be leaving to go to church. Soon, it would be too hot for him to go at all, and he'd be stuck swimming. When he got back, her car was gone. She returned about half an hour later, and a few minutes later, there was a quiet knock on his cabin door.

"Come in," he called from the couch, where he had invoices and purchase order paperwork spread out in piles.

Starla stuck her head in the door. "Sorry, I just . . ."

He gave her a lopsided smile. "No apologizing."

She smiled back. "Let me start over." She cleared her throat. "Good morning! I hope I'm not bothering you, I just wanted to say that I can take you wherever today; I just have to pick up the kids at seven o'clock."

He scratched his unshaven chin. "I usually go grocery shopping on Thursdays, but I'm guessing that might not work so well for you."

She nodded in agreement. "Today would be better, if you can. I work all day on Thursday. I could go Tuesday, if you want? I only work a half day."

"No, today's fine. Thank you."

She narrowed her eyes at him. "If I don't get to say sorry, I think you shouldn't get to say thank you. You don't owe me; if anything, I owe you."

"Let's just call it even," he said, looking at his papers. "Five o'clock?"

"Sure. Sounds good." She closed the door gently, and he watched her go back to her house. Strangely, it felt much quieter in his cabin than usual; he could see her, occasionally, moving past the windows of the bigger house, and it made him feel less alone. But that quiet persisted until he went outside to meet her at 4:58. She wasn't there. He chuckled, then bounced up the steps to knock on the door. He had a weird amount of energy today.

"Coming!" she called from inside the house. "I'm coming, I'm coming." He saw her hopping around on one foot, trying to get her shoe on. He stepped back as she opened the door and came rushing out, purse over one shoulder, hair flying.

"Okay! Let's go," she said, rushing to the car, and he strolled after her. It felt intimate, sitting in her passenger seat. He hadn't noticed it last time, this strange closeness. The car was clean enough, but it just felt odd going from his motorcycle, where it was just him and the weather and his bike to this enclosed capsule, contained with another person. She pulled out a tiny bottle of lotion and squirted a bit into her hands, rubbing them together quickly before she backed out, the scent of pineapple filling the vehicle. Some kind of kid music started playing—a cover of *Havana* with the bad words changed—and she shut it off, muttering to herself, and adjusted the small statue of Lando Calrissian on her dashboard.

"Star Wars, right?" he asked, and she gave him a big smile. "I noticed you had that BB-8 hat when you showed up on my porch."

"Yes, Star Wars. Always Star Wars. Feel free to pick something else," she said, gesturing toward the buttons, so he tuned it to the modern country station. "Mmm, good choice," she hummed, tapping the steering wheel and bobbing her head. He sat back with a smile, trying not to stare at her.

"Even Episode One?"

"We don't talk about Episode One."

"It was bad."

"I said *we don't talk about Episode One*." Goading her was his new favorite sport, and he'd clearly hit a hot spot.

He put his feet up on the dash. "Jar Jar ruined the whole thing; apart from that, it was still pretty—"

"Okay," Starla said, shaking her head, "you brought this on yourself. First of all, there is credible evidence that Jar Jar was actually a Sith lord . . ."

Sawyer made a face, but she pressed on. "Think about it. What's better camouflage than someone who seems to be a bumbling idiot, but actually helps the Empire with everything he does? Didn't Yoda play the fool with Luke when he first arrived on Dagobah?"

"I guess so . . . still. It seems like a stretch."

"I'll send you a link," she said, and she touched the microphone icon on her phone. "Remind me to send my landlord Jar Jar Sith lord conspiracy theory articles."

Sawyer laughed, shaking his head. His phone vibrated in his back pocket, and he pulled it out.

**Daniel:** Hey man. I just got my schedule this week, and I'm on an overnight rotation on Wednesday. :sad face: Did you already send it?

Books tended to be slow, so he'd ordered them on Friday; the box was supposed to arrive tomorrow at Daniel and Winnie's house. His heart sank. If he couldn't make this happen, Starla was going to figure it out.

**Sawyer:** Yeah

**Daniel:** Okay, I have a solution: my sister Maggie. She's always up to make a quick buck, no questions asked.

**Daniel:** Do you want me to talk to her?

**Sawyer:** Sure, that'd be great. Thanks, man.

**Daniel:** Okay, she's game. She'll pick them up from my front porch. Just let me know when they've been delivered.

**Sawyer:** Perfect. Thank you so much.

**Daniel:** She says you can Venmo her the cash.

**Sawyer:** Okay.

He sent her email address, and Sawyer stared at it. *Venmo?* What was that? Some kind of Paypal thing? He switched messages to text his sister.

**Sawyer:** What's Venmo?
**Paige:** Some kind of Paypal thing. Young people use it, which rules you out.
**Sawyer:** Ha. Ha. Ha.
**Paige:** Seriously, though, I've got one set up.
**Paige:** Just tell me how much and to who and you can pay me back.
**Sawyer:** Okay. I'll call you tomorrow.

"Awful lot of text activity for a forest hermit," Starla commented. "Who're you talking to?"

"A friend." It was true; he'd certainly put Daniel in that category from now on. He was going above and beyond on this, and Sawyer wasn't going to forget it. He owed him more than a pizza.

"Fine," she pouted, "don't tell me. But it's not like I would spread it around. You're allowed to have friends, you know. A girlfriend?"

Was that simple curiosity or subtle jealousy on her face? It was difficult to tell. He tried so hard to keep a straight face and nearly succeeded; the tiniest slip of a smile escaped, but he got it back before she noticed. The irony of the situation was too funny; here he was, arranging a courier for the secret book delivery he'd been doing every week for almost two years now, sitting right next to the woman he'd been doing it for as she queried him. He felt bad ignoring Starla; now that his problem was solved, he could put the phone away.

"No, not a girlfriend," he murmured, as she pulled into the grocery store parking lot.

"We're here," she announced, throwing it in park. *Of course we are. As soon as I put the phone away.* They went inside and each claimed a cart in silence.

"So how do you want to do this?" she asked, curving toward the produce section. "Go together or meet up at the end?"

"Might as well go together so no one's left standing around." *Also, I ignored you in the car and I feel bad.*

"Well, I have money this time, so you don't have to worry about that," she said, focusing hard on the cantaloupe she was probing for ripeness.

"I wasn't worried," he said, grabbing a bag of gala apples. It was hard not to peek into her cart. Some of it was normal: cucumbers, salsa, salad mix . . . but some of it . . .

"You really like tortillas, huh?" There must have been ten packs of the burrito size in her cart.

"Not me," she said, rolling her eyes. "Em. It's practically all she'll eat. She's always been picky, but if you wrap almost anything in a tortilla, she'll eat it. Don't ask me why."

"Why?" Sawyer asked immediately, and Starla gave him a glare that said she wasn't really annoyed, and they both snickered. "Well, let me know if you want to learn how to make them. No pressure."

"You can make tortillas?"

He nodded. "It's not too hard. Here, let's get a rolling pin, too. I don't know if the lodge has one." They wandered over to the kitchen implement section and he put one in his cart, then he showed her where the masa was. It was sort of cheating, but it worked. Not as good as the ones in Honduras, but it'd do in a pinch.

"How'd you find your place, anyway?"

"It's kind of a weird story, actually," he said, grabbing a block of Tillamook pepper jack cheese. "My mama, she'd been trying to get me to move back after I . . ." He trailed off, not sure how to explain this. "Well, when I was in Honduras, I ended up having to come home early."

"Because you were sick?" She wasn't announcing it, just confirming what she already knew.

"Right. Anyway, it'd been for sale a long time. It was in pretty bad shape. But Hattie knew a guy who—"

"How did I know?" she crowed. "How did I know that Hattie would somehow factor into this story?" She leaned closer conspiratorially. "I should lower my voice. She has spies everywhere."

Sawyer chuckled. "You're interrupting my story, lady."

"So sorry. Do go on," she said, getting a rotisserie chicken. "Hattie orchestrated something because she's everywhere?"

"That's right. Contractor owed her a favor. He turned the barn into a garage for me for a song, added electricity and some insulation. Mama, Paige, and I put elbow grease into the two houses, replaced a few broken windows and we split the rental income."

"Wait," she said, putting a hand on his arm. "I'm taking from your mom and your sister, too?" *Uh-oh.* She was actually wringing her hands, a little crease between her eyebrows, and his heart perked up.

"Don't fret over it. I know they're happy to know someone's watching over me right now." His mama's consternation at finding him gone when she'd come home to check on him at lunchtime had melted away when he'd told her his scheme. "She mentioned she'd like to have y'all over for dinner to thank you."

"Oh, that's not necessary. And my children aren't great on company manners, so . . ."

"You're braver than I thought," he tisked, getting in line to check out.

"How so?"

"I haven't known many people who thought they could out-stubborn my mama."

She nudged him with her elbow. "I bet you give her a run for her money."

"As often as I can, s-s-s"—dang, he'd almost called her 'sweet-heart'—"Starla."

She gave him a funny look, then pointed toward the register. "I think she's ready for you."

He looked down at his cart as he unloaded it. He hadn't gotten half the stuff on his list; he hadn't even *looked* at his list, he'd been so distracted by chatting with her. Now she was just going to have to bring him back here in a few days. *Oh gee, what a shame,* his brain purred, *you'll be locked in her car again, getting her undivided attention. Maybe you won't ignore her this time.* He pushed the voice away, chiding himself for wasting her time like that. He paid for his stuff; it was the same cashier as last time, when he'd paid for Starla's stuff, and she was glancing between them with amusement in her gaze. Clearly, she thought there was something going on here that wasn't; not that he cared. People were going to talk no matter what you did. Might as well live the way you wanted to. *No eggs, Devereaux? Really?* Eggs were Keto Staple #1. He paid and moved off to the side to wait for her. His phone buzzed again.

**Unknown number:** Hey. This is Maggie Durand. My brother said you had a package for me to pick up.

**Unknown number:** Just let me know what you want me to do with it. $20.

**Sawyer:** Okay, great. I'll figure out that Venmo thing.

He programmed her number into his phone.

**Maggie:** I also accept cash. No checks.

**Sawyer:** Cool. No questions for me?

**Maggie:** Daniel said it's not illegal.

**Sawyer:** No, nothing illegal. I swear.

**Maggie:** Then I'm sure it's fine.

**Sawyer:** Just rip the address off the flap, take out the invoice and deliver it to the service entrance of the library on Wednesday night without getting caught.

**Maggie:** . . .

**Maggie:** You're the book fairy??

**Sawyer:** Confidentiality is part of the job.

**Maggie:** That's badass. Does Starla know?

**Sawyer:** No, and she can't find out.

**Maggie:** Got it.

**Maggie:** I love Starla. She introduced me to Terry Pratchett.

**Maggie:** This is a good cause. I'll waive my fee. Just send me the details.

Sawyer scowled. He didn't know this girl; she was still in high school. Was she going to be reliable if she wasn't getting paid? Daniel said they could trust her . . . but how much did he trust Daniel? He seemed a little immature sometimes . . . he chuckled when he remembered that Daniel was the same age as Starla. She seemed leagues more mature than he was.

**Sawyer:** There'll be a new Pratchett in the next box for you. I don't think the library has them all.

**Maggie:** They don't. Thanks.

"You coming?" Starla asked, watching him quizzically again. He gave her a smile and shoved his phone in his pocket, hurrying after her, hoping that Maggie would keep her end of the bargain, including keeping her mouth shut.

# CHAPTER
# FOURTEEN

MONDAY MORNING, STARLA stared at herself in the full-length mirror in the corner of her bedroom, trying to smooth the bump down somehow. It had just . . . popped overnight; Starla's belly seemed to have caught on to its resident and decided to make room for it.

"Mom?" Aiden's voice came through the door.

"Yeah?"

"Aren't we supposed to be going?" She looked at her phone; it was seven forty-five already. Starla cursed, lunging for her open suitcase.

"Yes," she yelled down. "Go get in the car. I'll be right there." She found a big chunky tan sweater; it was still April, right? A sweater wasn't inconceivable. Maybe no one would notice. She hurried down the stairs in her red suede heels, gathering her purse from the post at the bottom of the stairs.

"Let's go, let's go, let's go," she chanted, herding them toward the car.

"What about lunches?" Emily asked, and Starla groaned.

"I'll give you money. Let's just go." *I shouldn't do that*, she chided herself; just last night, she'd been trying to decide if she should sell her car to buy something cheaper . . . but Charlie was on the title, and he wouldn't agree. She couldn't exactly donate plasma if she was pregnant. Her cell phone plan was already bare bones, and she needed reliable coverage in case something happened. If she canceled Netflix, her kids would build barricades and sing revolution songs in French. There just wasn't that much fat to cut . . .

She'd just found her keys to press the unlock button when her breakfast suddenly decided to give her an encore. Starla tried to slap a hand over her mouth, but she wasn't quick enough. She bent over, putting one hand on her car, leaning as far forward as she could to make sure it didn't land on her shoes: these were her most comfortable fancy shoes. She really didn't want vomit on them.

"Whoa." Aiden and Emily were staring at her, disgusted, while laid-back Sawyer Devereaux was running—*stumbling*—across the clearing toward her, a socket wrench still in his hand.

"What happened? Are you all—" He must have caught a whiff of her erstwhile food. "Oh."

"Sorry about that," she said, and she felt the apology was completely appropriate this time. "I'll clean it up when I get back."

He put a hand on her back. "Why don't you call Ainsley or Charlie to come get the kids for school? If you're sick, you should stay home . . ."

"I'm fine. Really." It has a hard case to make with puke all over one hand. She used her clean hand to get a pack of wipes from her purse, and she wiped her face and hands as Sawyer watched her, his head cocked, his eyes assessing. *You don't see anything*, she thought. *Nothing to worry about here. Move along.* She wasn't a Jedi, but maybe through the power of suggestion, she could get him to go back to the garage.

"You just threw up in my driveway, and you expect me to just go on with my day like nothing happened?"

*Damn it.* What she wouldn't give to have the Force at her disposal right now; she'd wipe that information right from his brain. She'd have to go back to their original agreement.

Starla wiped her mouth on the back of her cuff. "That's right," she said coolly. "Problem, landlord?"

Grimacing, he pulled out his phone.

"What are you doing?"

"I'm calling my cousin."

"No, you're not." Her voice was low, then turning her head, she called to her kids. "Get in the car, please." Wide-eyed, they hustled to the van and climbed into the back, bickering over who got to get in first. There appeared to be nothing they couldn't fight about. She stared up at him, vacillating in her mind between begging and commanding him.

"Don't call Ainsley. Please. I am not ready to have this conversation with her yet." There, that was a nice mix of the two.

His blue-grey eyes narrowed. "What conversation is that, exactly?"

"I'm pregnant," she whispered, and she made herself watch as his eyes widened and his mouth fell open in shock. She rubbed her belly protectively, as if she could somehow protect them from the chaos this was going to bring into their lives.

"What's your due date?"

"I'm not sure." She pushed her hair out of her face, but it slid right back. "I conceived on February 14th." His face hardened with momentary anger, but then it was gone. And she really wanted to know what he was thinking, but she lacked the guts to ask him. Most of her guts were already on the driveway.

"How romantic," he quipped, and she detected a note of bitterness that she resented. "When did you miss your period?"

"I don't track my menstrual cycles, Dr. Devereaux. And just so you know, I'm not completely irresponsible. The condom didn't work, because that's the kind of luck I have."

"It's mister now." He took her by the shoulders. "I'm sorry, I'm not judging you. That ain't my style. Just . . ." He sighed. "I still think you should tell somebody."

"I just did," she smiled ruefully. "I told you." Starla shook him off and stepped carefully around her mess as she went to the driver's seat.

"And see a medical professional!" he called after her, his breath clouding in front of him.

"Again, I just did."

He stomped after her. "You gonna let me examine you, then?"

She had the good sense to pale. "What?"

He held the driver's side door closed. "I said, when do I get to examine you?"

*Oh, not going to happen, dude.* If Sawyer Devereaux ever saw her naked, it was going to be under very different circumstances.

"You can't do that," she sputtered, reddening.

"Then go see a real doctor. Or Winnie Durand, if you don't want anyone in town to know. But if I noticed, others will, too." She pulled the cream sweater tighter around herself. "And soon, you won't be able to hide it. You should think about what Charlie and the rest of the Miller family will say."

"Oh, I know what they'll say. The usual guilt about me 'coming home,' but here's the thing: that's not my home anymore."

He seemed to soften a little at that. "You can stay here as long as you need to, all right? Forget what we said before." He ran a hand through his hair, ruffling it adorably. "I'm here for you. For whatever."

She nodded, giving him a little smile as she got into the car. "Thanks. I appreciate that." Her kids were fighting about something they were building together in Minecraft, but she tuned them out. It was one thing to say that, but people were going to talk. About him. About her. About whose baby it was, and whether she was a slut or a whore or just unfortunate. She'd been largely sheltered from that last time, when she married Charlie right away. Their indiscretion had been waved off as a teenage mistake. But not this time. Everyone knew they'd separated in November; now everyone would know what a giant mistake she'd made.

*We could just take off,* a little voice prompted. *Start over somewhere warm.* It was something she'd been thinking about more and more. She couldn't do anything until school was over in June, and she'd need Charlie's approval because of their plan to have shared custody, but . . . but she'd keep thinking about it. Somewhere else, she wouldn't be the town joke. She'd just be Starla Moore.

# CHAPTER FIFTEEN

"WHY ARE WE DOING THIS again?" Aiden skulked into the kitchen and washed his hands with all the enthusiasm of a man about to be electrocuted. Starla had asked days ago if Sawyer could watch them after school today; she had an evening meeting for the Harry Potter night the library was planning and wouldn't be home until dinnertime.

"Your mama had a hard week, being sick and all, and chocolate generally cheers people up." He wasn't sure what she'd told them about her pregnancy, and he sure wasn't going to be the one to try to explain it to them. He was still reeling from the news himself. His gut had burned at the unexpected revelation, wondering who the hell she'd been sleeping with when she'd just left her husband. He should've figured she'd cave to Charlie . . . they seemed to be each other's weakness. A little voice asked him if he really wanted to insert himself in such a screwed-up relationship . . . but it was irrelevant anyway, right? They were just friends. That was a good place to be. And if living up here could help her maintain her privacy a little longer, he couldn't be sorry about that.

"I like chocolate. And I like helping," Emily chirped.

"Kiss-up," the boy muttered under his breath.

"Hey! Mr. Devereaux, Aiden called me a kiss-up."

"My ears work fine, so I heard him. Also, lower your volume a bit. Aiden, don't call names, it's rude." Sawyer had known the little one would be an easy sell. But he had a strategy for the big one. "Now. We're making a specialty from my childhood called Texas cake."

Aiden perked up. The kid loved the Dallas Cowboys, so Sawyer had been betting that anything Texas-themed would be a hit. He'd work on helping him have good taste in football teams later.

"Why's it called Texas cake?"

"Because it's the biggest cake you'll ever make."

The siblings shared a gleeful glance, and Sawyer remembered what it was like having that with Paige. Remembered with regret; he should call her. He hadn't been a very good big brother lately. They used to hang out all the time.

"Aiden, what's the first thing we need?"

The boy's eyes widened. "Me?"

"Yes, you. You're in charge. What's the first thing we need to do?" He tapped the recipe he'd printed out. Sawyer reached over and helped Em roll up her sleeves as Aiden read.

"Preheat the oven to 350 degrees. Grease an 18x13 pan."

"I did that already, keep going."

His dark eyes scanned the page. "We need water, eggs, butter, cocoa powder . . ."

"Wait a second, we gotta get it all out.

Aiden went on. "Sour cream, vanilla, baking soda, salt . . ."

"Wait." Sawyer scowled. "Sour cream? Really?"

The boy nodded. "Right here." He pointed to the page, and Sawyer craned his neck to see.

"Well, I'll be d— uh, darned." He put his hands on the counter. "I guess we're outta luck, then."

"Why?" Emily asked, wide-eyed.

"Because I don't have any. I'm not much of a condiment guy."

"Could we use something else?" Before he could answer, Emily had hopped off the stool and opened his fridge. He held back a smirk as she dug through it, muttering to herself.

"What do you think, Aiden?" The boy liked to be in charge; he'd keep throwing it back at him.

He was still scowling at the recipe. "I don't know. Could we maybe substitute milk? Or something else that's thick? What about coconut milk?"

"Hmm. Haven't got that, either. What about—"

"Ah-HA!" Emily held a white and blue carton triumphantly above her head. "Yogurt!"

"I like that," said Aiden. "Yogurt would taste kind of like sour cream, right?"

"Here's the thing, though, chickpea," Sawyer said, taking the carton from her and cracking the lid. "I don't remember buyin' this."

All three of them gathered around the container. Sawyer could feel their trepidation . . . and secretly, he loved that they'd bought into his idea so hard. That they were now stressed they wouldn't be able to make this happen for Starla. He gave it a sniff. Sour, but not too bad. There was some kind of yellowish liquid floating on top, but they could probably pour that off. There was a little mold on the side, but it wasn't touching the actual yogurt. He took the lid all the way off and let them look. "What do you think, kids?"

Aiden piped up first. "I say we use it. We have to try to follow the recipe exactly or it won't turn out right."

"We could find a different recipe," Emily pointed out. "Maybe there's one that uses milk." Sawyer felt a strange sense of satisfaction, watching them. He felt that they were right in the thick of learning, so distracted by the issue at hand that they didn't even notice. It gave him a sense of glee he hadn't felt since . . . *since the last time I operated.*

"All right. Aiden, I put you in charge. What do you want to do?" He thought Emily might go storming off, but to his surprise, she just waited for his decision.

"Let's use it."

Sawyer held up his palm for a high-five, and Aiden gave him one with a grin. Emily did, too, but her pragmatic side immediately took over. "Now we all have to wash our hands again!" After some water flicking, soap squirting, and towel snapping, they got down to business. Forty minutes later, they were pouring the frosting over the hot cake as Starla pulled up outside. The kids didn't hear her tires on the gravel over the music blasting in the kitchen . . . should they be listening to The Killers? Based on the way Emily was singing along, she'd either heard it before or had a high aptitude for music.

"Mr. Devereaux, this was really fun," she said, licking the wooden spoon, chocolate on the end of her nose, and Sawyer couldn't help but smile.

"Yeah," grunted Aiden. "Thanks." He didn't have time to reply before the front door opened and Starla walked in.

"Ooh, what's happening here?" She put down her keys and her book bags to lean over the cake, hair held back, and take a long, deep sniff.

"It's TEXAS CAKE," Aiden taunted, and Starla groaned.

"I don't know if I can eat this, then. Couldn't you have made Seattle sundaes? Or Washington cupcakes?"

Emily giggled and squeezed her middle, and he saw Starla pale a little, probably hoping she wouldn't feel anything different. Now that he saw her from this angle, he could see a little bump happening there after all, and it made his heart go a little melty. She was already too adorable; seeing her pregnant was going to be even worse.

"Surprise!"

"Yes, I'm so surprised! Thank you both," she said. Then glancing at Sawyer, she cleared her throat. "Thank you all."

Sawyer cleared his throat uncomfortably. "It's still too warm to eat."

"That's not a thing," Starla grinned. She began to reach for the knife block, but he put a hand over hers. Her skin was a little dry, and he wondered if she was drinking enough water.

"No, really. The frosting hasn't set yet. You gotta wait. Just a few minutes. Here, we'll stick it in the fridge."

She crossed her arms over her stomach. "Who's this for, anyway?"

"It's for you," he soothed, "but I want you to have the whole experience. Sit down and rest your feet for a bit, and I'll make supper."

He watched her expression move from relief to guilt without a moment in between for him to enjoy the first emotion.

"You don't have to. Really. I'm fine."

"Oh." He rubbed his chin like he was thinking it over. "I don't have to?"

Her lips twitched like she was fighting a smile. "No, you don't have to."

"If I want to, though, I could?" He stepped behind her and put his hands gently on her shoulders, steering her toward the couch.

"I suppose so," she mumbled, and the fatigue in her voice was obvious. He turned her so she was in front of her favorite spot, the big recliner, and guided her into it. Sawyer handed her a book—he didn't look at which one—and popped the foot rest.

"I think I want to."

"You think?"

"I'm thinkin' I do, yes. Tell you what; if I change my mind partway through, I'll let you know."

Starla pulled her knees up to her chest. "What are we having?"

"Spaghetti with meatballs." His noodles were the vegetable, steam-in-the-bag kind. Somewhat unpalatable, but they worked.

"Sounds delicious."

"Does it?" He was really asking. If her in-utero kiddo wasn't down with spaghetti, he could make something else. She seemed to understand, and she nodded.

"Really. Sounds amazing."

"And you'll have chocolate cake for dessert," Emily piped up, crashing into Starla's legs, squeezing her and giving her knee a kiss. "When it's ready."

"Of course," Starla agreed with a smile.

"*Texas* cake," Aiden taunted from the corner, where he was bent over some kind of school workbook. "Like the Dallas Cowboys, not your dumb Sea-chickens."

"It's *Seahawks*, and that hurts me, son." Starla mimed pulling a knife out of her chest, and Sawyer turned so they wouldn't see him grinning on his way back into the kitchen. Since the meatballs were frozen and already made, it was easy enough work to pull it all together, but at least she didn't have to be on her feet. He kept stealing glances at her; he couldn't help it. She was pregnant. No wonder she'd fled Timber Falls; he couldn't imagine having an unplanned pregnancy twice in a small town where gossip was an Olympic sport. The fact that he'd kept his own situation private prompted plenty of speculation, and he didn't care for that, even on a much lower level. This warm feeling in his chest, watching her snuggle with Emily and correct Aiden's math homework . . . that was just a normal, secret crush sort of feeling, he was sure. Not love. They were in the same boat; birds of a feather and all that. Never mind that he'd wanted her in his flock since he started looking forward to seeing her on his weekly library visits. That he'd already made her a part of his flock without notifying her, exactly. It didn't matter; he couldn't get married. He drained the pasta and called into the living room.

"Let's eat, y'all." The kids went to wash hands without being asked, and he sidled up next to Starla. "Did you make that appointment we talked about?"

"Not yet."

"Are you taking your prenatals?"

"Yes, doctor," she said, sliding into her chair. The kids came to the table, and he chafed at not getting to discuss it further with her. So he took two fingers and pointed at his eyes, then pointed them at her in an 'I'm watching you' gesture, and she snickered. Dinner passed quickly, and before he knew it, she was getting up to do the dishes.

"No, no. Guests don't do dishes."

She continued to stack plates, gathering the utensils into her water glass. "Technically, *you're* the guest."

"Then you're a terrible host. Why change things up now?" He gently pulled the plates from her grasp and Starla put a hand on her hip.

"The person who cooks does not clean up. Everyone knows that."

"Everyone?" He rubbed his chin as if in thought. "Em, did you know that?" Sawyer winked at her, to let her in on the right response.

"No, I didn't know that," she said, grinning. She was such a good sport. He grinned back at her.

"What about you, Aiden?"

"As long as I don't have to do them, I don't care," he said, snatching his backpack off the couch on his way upstairs.

"Oh good, more cake for the rest of us," Sawyer called after him, but to his surprise, Aiden didn't stop.

"Oh, I forgot about cake," Starla said, rubbing her belly. "I should've saved more room. Your sauce was so good; I need that recipe."

"Recipe?" He set the dishes in the sink and turned on the water to get it hot. "Well, that'll be tricky. I don't know that the manufacturer will want to share that proprietary information with you." When she stopped laughing (a sound that lit up his soul like a Van de Graaff generator), he suggested she and Emily read a book. This, of course, resulted in Emily reading to Starla and Starla falling asleep.

"Mom?" she whispered, poking at Starla's shoulder.

"No, chickpea, don't wake her. You just go on and take your shower and get into your PJ's, and your mama'll be up to tuck you into bed in a bit, all right?"

"Okay, Mr. Devereaux." She scampered up the log steps, and he turned back to Starla.

"What are we going to do with you, pregnant lady? You're wearing yourself out." He itched to slot in behind her in the big chair, hold her while she slept. Listen to the rise and fall of her breathing from close up, let their heart rates sync.

She turned over, pressing her face into the back of the chair, as if trying to block out his voice. Shaking his head at both of them, Sawyer went back to her dishes, carefully scrubbing each one until he got to the sauce pan. He'd scorched the bottom a little, and it was going to take some elbow grease to put it right again. He heard Starla put down the foot rest on the chair, and he peeked around the corner. As she stretched, looking around a bit dazedly, he cut her a piece of cake and put it on a plate. She wandered into the kitchen yawning, and she startled at the sight of him.

"You're still here?"

"Had to finish your dishes, terrible host that you are." He handed her the plate, and she took it, digging into the dessert immediately.

"I don't know how I could be hungry again already," she groaned, stuffing her mouth full of cake, and his whole body tensed at the sound of her pleasure. "This is good," she said through a huge bite

"Tell your kids. They did most of it."

"Really?" She wiped the corner of her mouth with the back of her hand. "I kind of thought you were just being generous."

"I'm not the generous sort, occupant."

"I beg to differ, landlord," she said, stabbing the cake again. "Thank you for coming over. It's really not necessary."

"It feels awful necessary when you're throwing up on my driveway. Are you keeping food down, mostly?"

Starla shrugged, getting a bit of just frosting on the back of her fork and licking it off. He tried not to think about the other things he'd like her to lick. He failed. *Get it together, Devereaux. She's not for you.*

"Not in the mornings."

"Try eating some crackers before you get out of bed. That might help."

"I don't need you to take care of me." She glared at him without pausing her assault on the cake. He liked a lady who could multitask.

"I'm not saying you do. Just a little friendly advice from a guy who used to be a doctor. Are you having any spotting? Cramping?"

"We're not having this conversation, Sawyer." She pushed the empty plate into his hands and started toward the stairs. He caught her arm gently, and she stopped.

"I just want to see you cared for. That's all. If I'm making you uncomfortable, I'll stop, but please make an appointment with Winnie. Or ask Kyle or Dr. Baker to recommend you to an OB/GYN in Salem."

"It won't matter; the minute I tell one person, everyone will know."

He swallowed hard. "Right. I get that, but . . ."

"No, you don't." She spun to face him, and there was a forceful desperation in her eyes. "You don't get it."

"Hey, I get talked about, too. People make up all kinds of stupid crap: I flunked out of medical school, I killed somebody, I slept with a patient and lost my license. I know that town thinks I'm a loser."

*And what's worse, your gossip is temporary. Mine's forever.* It was one of the things holding him back from rejoining town life, and he knew he should work on it, but he didn't.

"So why don't you tell them the truth?" she asked, pacing closer to him.

*Because I'd rather have them spread lies about me than the truth.* It wasn't his fault, he knew that. But it still felt like failure. It still felt personal. It made him an object of pity, and that he could not abide.

"Why don't you?" he returned.

"Because it's none of their business."

"Exactly."

"And what if they think the baby's yours?" Her eyes were wide, earnest, and Sawyer felt his heart stumble backwards.

"What're you saying? You're protecting *me*?"

She shrugged again, and he was starting to realize that it was the gesture she used when she disliked the truth. "What if I am? It was kind of you to let us stay here. I don't want to bring more trouble into your life."

"Trouble? Oh, no, sugar, that's no trouble. You'd be doing me a favor, in fact; I derive no small pleasure in giving the hens of Timber Falls something to cluck about, much to my sweet mother's dismay. She may set them straight, but if you want to let them believe this child is mine, I'm just fine with that. Pleased as punch, actually. At least they can't say I never do anything."

Despite his sly smile, she scowled. "You do plenty. I'd never let them think that, if anyone asked."

"I'm surprised they haven't pumped you for information yet."

"They tried," she sniffed, folding her arms over her stomach. "Like you said, none of their business."

He couldn't pretend that didn't delight him, too. Starla was nothing if not loyal . . . she'd help him preserve his reputation as a mysterious forest hermit, maybe even enhance it. A forest hermit who takes in divorcees, then woos and impregnates them. What a fantastic scandal, even if it wasn't true.

"All right. I won't say anything to anyone. But don't you worry about my reputation, Star. I can hold my own. Worst case is I get a tattoo that says, 'The baby ain't mine,' and then I can shock them twice. Thrice, if they're grammar savvy."

"You're wicked." Her eyes were twinkling, and he liked that he'd put it there. Heck, he liked all of this. Feeding her, hearing her heart, talking things over, taking care of her . . . that was probably why it was dangerous. He leaned closer to her nonetheless.

"And don't you forget it."

Starla grinned up at him, and all the warm, tender feelings he already felt for her just went supernova. He could smell her tropical body lotion, see distinctly the way the light couldn't penetrate the deep brown of her eyes. *Kiss her,* his body prompted urgently, and his tongue slipped out to wet his lips, just thinking about it. *Red alert! Back away!* his brain countered, and he was forced to agree with his central nervous system; acting on that impulse would be a bad idea. Very bad. He had a feeling her lips would be his own personal addiction.

"I gotta go. I've got stuff to do at home." He shuffled back, and she blinked, her face falling.

"Oh, right. Sorry to keep you, I—"

"Thought you weren't saying sorry anymore," he reminded her, as he swiped his phone from the kitchen counter.

"Right. I'm not." She cleared her throat, tossing her hair in a way that might seem arrogant if you didn't know her. And he did know her now, better than he ever thought he would. "Thank you for staying."

"You're welcome. See you."

"Yup." She gave him a little wave as he closed her front door.

*That was a close one.* Maybe he'd let her make her own dinner tomorrow . . . but maybe he'd make pizza with the kids on Saturday, so she could take a nap. Sawyer shook his head at himself and was startled to see Lucky watching him, chewing a mouthful of arugula.

"Get out of here," he yelled, clapping his hands, and Lucky bounded back just inside the tree line. Sawyer couldn't blame him. Some things were just too tempting.

# CHAPTER SIXTEEN

THE LIBRARY WAS SURPRISINGLY quiet for a Thursday. It had been three days since she threw up in Sawyer's driveway, and since Ainsley hadn't stormed into the library demanding to know everything, she was assuming he hadn't said anything to her.

Maybe it was just strange to not see Sawyer there . . . she saw him every day now, spent time running him around. It was absolutely silly to still miss him on Thursday afternoons around 3:30, and she told herself so all afternoon. She was just getting around to processing the book fairy's delivery when her kids showed up. Ainsley just waved through the window after she dropped them off; she and Starla had plans later. They were doing gift bags tonight and helping her with her seating chart for the reception; it was the first girls night they'd had since she moved out. Word had somehow passed to Charlie that she'd be out for the night, and he'd offered to let the kids sleep over at his house. The wedding was still more than a month out, but she knew her best friend; if Ainsley didn't chip away at the list of tasks with ruthless efficiency, she'd fall behind and never catch up. She was already overcommitted. Why she'd scheduled her wedding for the day after school let out was still a mystery to Starla . . . she was guessing it had something to do with Kyle's moratorium on sex until they said, "I do."

The phone at the front desk rang, and her coworker Mavis answered it. She loved Mavis. She'd been at the library for over thirty years, but she wasn't stuck in her ways; half the time, she was coming to Starla with a new technology or offering she thought they should consider. She noticed Daniel and Winnie come in the front doors. They both gave her a wave, then each went their separate ways: Daniel straight to the audiobooks, Winnie straight to the computers with the medical journals. After a moment, the landline on Starla's desk rang, and she stared at it. No one ever called her extension; it wasn't listed on the website. She looked across the atrium at Mavis, who just shrugged.

"They asked for you," she said, then pantomimed picking it up and putting it to her ear. The school wouldn't call that number; they had her cell. And besides that, her kids were *here*. Charlie, Sawyer, her parents, Charlie's parents . . . they'd all use her cell.

"Rachel Rutherford Memorial Library, Starla Moore speaking."

"Well, hi there, this is Rhea Devereaux. How are you, sweetheart?" Sawyer's mother had a very light southern accent, despite being from Oregon. They'd spent a lot of time bouncing back and forth between Georgia and Oregon, and it must have rubbed off on her.

"Oh, hello, Mrs. Devereaux. I'm fine, how are you?" A thought seized her heart, and she rushed on. "Did something happen to Sawyer? Did he have another seizure?" *Oh, Lord. What if he collapsed up the mountain? How am I going to get him in the car by myself?* She reached under the desk. "I can go to the hospital or go get him right now if you need me to—"

"Oh, no, you've got the wrong end of the stick. No, honey, Sawyer's just fine as far as I know. I just wanted to invite y'all to dinner as a thank you for all the running around you've been doing for him. And he often used to come to dinner on Sunday nights . . . but I'm guessing he hasn't mentioned that to you." Starla could hear the woman smiling, and she smiled, too.

"No, ma'am, he neglected to mention that, for some strange reason. Must have slipped his mind. I'll be sure to add it to my list of weekly events from now on. My kids go to their dad's on Sunday, so that'd be perfect . . . we can pick them up on our way home."

"Sounds wonderful. I wouldn't mind meeting your little ones, too, though. There's nothing sacred in our house, so you don't need to worry about them running wild. I remember those days all too well."

She giggled. "Well, that's good to know. Thank you, Mrs. Devereaux. We'll see you Sunday."

"And if my son says he's busy?"

"I assume I'd still be invited, so I guess we'll have some good girl talk without him."

"Good answer. You're a quick one," Rhea laughed. She made sure she knew their address and that Ainsley's parents would be there, too, and Starla gave Rhea her cell phone number as she suppressed a pang of guilt. She was surprised Rhea wasn't mad at her for springing Sawyer from her coop after his last incident, but she was glad for it. They said goodbye, and Starla sat back in her rolling chair. She wanted to break the news to Sawyer ASAP, just to be polite.

**Starla:** I'm having dinner with your mom on Sunday, FYI.

**Sawyer:** Am I invited?

**Starla:** I guess. But I really think I'd have more fun without you, since she'll be telling me all sorts of stories about you, I'm sure . . .

**Sawyer:** Putting it on my calendar now . . .

**Starla:** LOL. Worried?

**Sawyer:** Are you familiar with a fish story?

**Starla:** Where the fish gets bigger every time it's told?

**Sawyer:** That's the one. Sawyer stories are almost as bad. I get naughtier every year.

**Starla:** You did warn me you were wicked.

While he was typing a response, another message came in.

**Peg:** Congratulations! Your divorce is final. You should be getting a certificate and final decree in the mail in a few days. And my bill, of course. Just kidding.

She knew it was soon, but she hadn't remembered what day (#babybrain). She stared at the words, feeling a tiny stir of hope in her soul. She'd done it. She'd gotten away from Charlie. Then she looked up and saw him coming up the walk to pick up the kids . . . and it hit her hard that he was always going to be right there as long as she was in Timber Falls. It wasn't going to be easy to really move on when she could barely move at all without running into him or his friends or relatives.

**Starla:** Thanks, Peg. Really appreciate all your help. Do send the bill; I'll pay it off eventually.

**Peg:** Hey, we're family. What's a little jurisprudence between cousins?

**Starla:** Well, I owe you. Big. Let me know if you need anything!

**Starla:** Is your mom still in Phoenix?

**Peg:** Yeah. She loves it down there.

**Starla:** I was thinking of visiting. Think she'd mind host-
ing us?

**Peg:** No, I think she'd be thrilled. I'll text you her number.

**Starla:** Thanks, Peg.

She wasn't committing to anything by contacting Aunt Rosie.
It didn't hurt to get some information. Maybe she really would just
take a visit, then come back home. These were the lies she was telling
herself.

Starla went back to her messages: Sawyer had responded.

**Sawyer:** That's right, sugar. I'm a good one to stay away
from.
**Sawyer:** Hey, I didn't mean you couldn't write me back.
**Sawyer:** You okay?

She smiled as she texted him back.

**Starla:** Sorry, my lawyer texted. Divorce is final.

He sent a touchdown emoji, and she sent back a smile.
"Good news?" Charlie asked, both kids in tow; he'd found them
on his own, apparently.
She tried to keep her face neutral; there was no reason to rub it
in. "Yes, actually. We're divorced."
Charlie laughed. "Oh, is that today?" Shaking his head, he
turned to Aiden. "I think we know what that means, don't we?"
Aiden looked puzzled, and Emily's gaze was bouncing between
the adults.
"You've proven your point, Star. I'm humbled. I'm reformed. Are
you ready to come home now?"

Starla stared up at him, completely baffled. "I . . . wasn't making a point, Charlie."

He smirked. "Yeah, okay. If you say so. Come on, kids, I'm ready for Annie's pizza. What are we getting? Pickles and onions?"

Emily giggled. "No, Daddy! Pepperoni!"

"Hard-boiled eggs and bacon?"

"Pepperoni!" Aiden chimed in. "No olives, either. I hate olives."

Starla was staring after her retreating family, trying to figure what had just happened, when she saw Winnie and Daniel standing by the front doors, getting their things together to go. She'd promised Sawyer that she'd start getting care for the baby . . . and here was an opportunity without having to go to Santiam.

"Hey, Winnie?" She jogged across the open space.

"Yes?" They both turned back, and Starla debated about what to say. Thankfully, she didn't have to decide.

Winnie turned to Daniel and gave him a soft smile as she put a hand on his arm. "Will you give us a second?"

"Sure." He dropped a kiss on her lips, then looked at Starla with unadulterated curiosity before going outside.

Winnie turned back to her. "What's wrong?"

Starla adjusted her glasses. "What makes you think something's wrong?"

"I am unfortunately quite often the target of uncomfortable conversations. Your tone of voice, the fear in your eyes, and the nervous way you're fiddling with the edge of your shirt gave you away." Starla hastily dropped the fabric she was rolling between her fingers.

"Oh, that?" Starla huffed out a laugh, and it diffused some of the tension. Winnie waited for her to go on. She cleared her throat. "I need to make an appointment with you."

Winnie got out her phone. "Okay. You need a well woman exam?"

"No."

She looked up from the screen. "A pap smear?"

"No."

That look of broken comprehension on her face. It was the one Starla had been avoiding all this time, pity and heartbreak and pain and sympathy, all rolled together.

"Please don't look at me like that. This little person will be loved. And I will be fine."

Winnie looked at her for a long moment, and to her credit, she wiped much of the sympathy off, but left the compassion. "I apologize. Will a partner be accompanying you?"

"No. Not this time."

She gave her a hard look that reminded Starla of Dr. Baker, and Starla wondered fleetingly whether this little person would take after her as strongly as Winnie took after her mother. "Are we concealing this from anyone?"

"No. Not intentionally, I just . . ." She sighed. "I'm not ready for him to know yet."

The midwife relaxed fractionally. "Okay. I can do Thursday night at six o'clock."

"That'd be great." Starla mentally patted herself on the back. This was a good thing. A very responsible thing. A good idea. "I'll see you then."

"Do you need someone to watch your kids? I bet Daniel would take them on a walk by the river to skip rocks if you want to do your appointment at our house instead of the hospital."

"Oh, would he? Will you ask him?" A tear slipped out. She just wasn't ready to be seen walking into the hospital just yet. Because as soon as the town knew, Charlie would know. And as soon as Charlie knew, she'd never get any peace from him. *Unlike now?* Well, that was a good point. Maybe it wouldn't be so different, but she just wanted to know for sure before she spoke to him. She was still turning over their strange interaction in her head . . . was he just completely ostriching?

Winnie smiled. "Daniel loves kids. Especially yours. I'm sure he won't mind. I can't guarantee they'll come back as clean as they left, but . . ."

"That's not an issue. Sawyer's doing a good job of messing them up, too. I've got stock in Oxyclean."

Her friend laughed. "Thursday. Six o'clock."

"Thank you, Winnie."

"My pleasure. And I'll see you tonight."

Starla felt herself quiver with fear a little. "My news isn't . . . that is, Ainsley doesn't know . . ."

"My lips are sealed," Winnie assured her, patting her shoulder. *There. One hard thing down. A million more to go.*

# CHAPTER SEVENTEEN

"YOU WANT ANOTHER BEER, Star?" Ainsley was in the kitchen, pulling a piece of pepperoni off the leftover pizza and popping it into her mouth.

"No, I'm good," she mumbled. "I'm gonna drive home tonight, so . . ." She'd taken the first one to the bathroom, dumped it out into the toilet and flushed it, then refilled the bottle with water. She even ran the fan to try to dissipate the smell of it. She wasn't sure if anyone was fooled, but they hadn't seemed to notice.

Winnie, Martina, and Lizzie were all sitting on the couch, laughing. A few of Ainsley's teacher friends were gathered by the front windows, putting on their coats, getting ready to go. Gift bag making had been quick work with an assembly line going, and the evening had now devolved into a string of embarrassing confessions that Starla was enjoying. But not as much as Martina.

"Okay, who's next? Ainsley? Winnie? Winnie, we haven't gotten any good ones out of you yet."

"Well," she said, hesitating. "One time, at the hospital, I was so tired, I went into the wrong bathroom . . . and Dr. Pearson was changing." They all groaned; the poor guy had to be pushing eighty. "He didn't see me, so I just ducked out quickly, and I never said a word."

"Until now," Martina cackled, clinking beer bottles with Lizzie. "What about you, girl? Spill it. You've gotta have some great cop stories . . ."

Lizzie shrugged coolly. "Not really."

"Oh, come on," Martina needled. "I know this town. They do all sorts of crazy stuff every day of the week."

Lizzie blushed a bright shade of red, and Starla chuckled; it must be tough being a redhead. "Well," she said, glancing around, "I did get a call last week from Vanessa Rutherford

. . . she'd gotten a call from a neighbor that there were lights on at their family cabin on the lake. When we went to investigate, we didn't see any vehicles . . . so we knocked. And when no one answered, we tried the door . . ."

"Let me guess," said Martina. "It was her teenage son?"

"No," she said blushing harder. "It was her dad. Apparently, he'd parked in the garage. They were getting busy on the couch when we walked in."

"With who?" Winnie asked, leaning forward.

"I can't tell you that," Lizzie chided, then she grinned slyly. "But you'd be shocked if you knew."

"Tell us, tell us!" chanted Martina.

"Forget it. The embarrassing part was me walking in on them, shining my flashlight on them like they were teenagers in the back of a car." She giggled, hiding her face. They all knew Lizzie was a virgin, so she was even more scandalized than they would've been. Laughing, shoulder to shoulder with her friends, Starla felt determination rise inside her. She could hide her news a little longer, but really, she had them all here, and that didn't happen often without her kids or other people around. It made her bold, even if it was going to bring the mood down. She should go home soon anyway.

"I have a confession to make," Starla said, putting down her drink.

"It's not your turn," Martina chided, and the rest of them laughed.

"I'm pregnant."

Everything stopped. It was like someone had dipped the entire room in wax and then hardened them that way. You could've heard a bottle cap drop.

"By whom?" Ainsley demanded, and when Starla dropped her head, she heard the collective gasp. "Oh, Star. I'm sorry. I shouldn't have asked that, it's none of my business."

"No, it's okay. You meant well." The tears started, and she felt herself being surrounded by friends slowly, as if they were afraid of making it worse.

"How far along are you?"

"I don't know yet. Winnie's going to check me out next week." The blonde gave her a kind smile.

"I'm just . . . I just . . ." Ainsley sat back. "Wow."

"Yeah," Starla sniffled. "Wow is right. It sure wasn't on my bullet journal goals page, let's put it that way." She shrugged. "But another kid isn't such a bad thing."

"That's right," Martina said. "You just let Tia Tini rock that little one. I'll be over every day. I bet Willow would love to hold her, too." She was getting married in August . . . it was one of those years, some sort of romance confluence in the town. She'd yearned for couples to socialize with when she and Charlie were first married, but everyone was still dating around, not wanting to settle down. All the young people were finally catching up to her . . . ironic.

"Are you guys going to start trying for kids right away?" She didn't mind picking a tangential topic . . . not one bit.

Martina pouted. "Carter doesn't think we're ready yet. I need someone with babies to come over and help me convince him. And girl, you're now at the top of my list of people to have over."

Ainsley wedged her way onto the couch next to Starla, and Winnie got off the other end so they could all scoot down.

Her best friend laid her head on Starla's shoulder and gave her hand a squeeze. "We're here for you. We'll help you. You'll figure it out."

Starla released a shaky sigh. "That's the thing. I think maybe . . ." She paused too long, afraid to say what she was thinking.

Ainsley lifted her head. "You think what?" Martina passed her a tissue, and she wiped her nose.

"I think I might leave Timber Falls."

"What?" Her friend stared at her, slack-jawed.

"It's just something I've been thinking about."

Now Ainsley was the one crying. "Why?"

"I'm tired of being talked about, Ains."

"But your whole family is here. Your parents and your grandparents and Charlie's

folks . . ."

"And Charlie."

"Screw Charlie!" Ainsley cried, and Starla felt her face heat as everyone stared at them with sympathy.

"Yeah, that's the problem. I *did*. And now everyone's going to know. I know I shouldn't have, I was just lonely and sad and it was Valentine's Day . . ." She wiped her nose. "It was a stupid thing to do."

"Look. Don't let Charlie ruin your life this way. Don't move away from everyone who cares about you." Ainsley put a hand over hers. "You're my best friend."

"You're mine, too." Yes, Ainsley could be annoying, but she cared. Sometimes she was too motherly, but she always supported her. How many friends would let their divorcee friend and her kids crash in her apartment for months? "I'd miss you a lot."

"Then don't go. Please. I hate the thought of you trying to do this on your own. Just wait until the baby's born, then see how you feel."

"That's the thing, though. If I wait until the baby's born, it'll be that much harder to leave. I don't know if I want the baby to be around Charlie, to be fought over their whole life."

Ainsley stared down at the couch, and Starla felt guilty for bringing the party mood down. But they deserved to know.

"Where would you go?" she asked softly, and Starla shrugged.

"I thought about Arizona. I like the heat. My aunt Rosie lives near Phoenix."

"That's super far away, Star."

"I know." *The farther, the better.* It wasn't fair. She knew that. But if she had to stay in this town, she was going to lose her mind. She needed to leave like she needed books; escape. She heard it whispered in every beat of her heart. Especially since it was starting to beat for interactions with a certain woodsy motorcycle man. Better to leave before she fell too hard.

Ainsley sighed. "We're going to have to try on your matron of honor dress again ASAP."

# CHAPTER EIGHTEEN

ON SUNDAY, STARLA WENT to church with the kids, still sitting in the same pew as Charlie and his family. She tried to listen to the sermon, but it was about the woman at the well, a notoriously loose woman, and she couldn't shake the feeling that people were sending her meaningful glances. *Just a few more weeks, people. Then you'll really have something to stare at.* She saw her parents out front, chatting with Charlie's parents, and she ducked out the side so she wouldn't have to pass by, but her dad spotted her.

"Star! Come here, please."

*Head held high, girl.* Shoulders thrown back, she marched over to them. "Yes?"

"Peg tells us that your divorce is now final." All four were frowning at her.

"And?"

"Don't you think this has gone on long enough? Did you two ever look into those counseling resources I sent you? I'm not paying for another ceremony . . ."

"We're concerned," her mother interjected, and Charlie's parents nodded in agreement. "You two need to work this out, before it's too late."

"Too . . . late?"

"For Charlie to take you back," his mom said softly. Was she really being that unclear? What part of this was so confusing? The front of the Timber Falls Baptist Church was not the place to be having this discussion, but they'd started it, so . . .

"I do not want him back. I don't know what gave you that impression."

His mom laughed. "But you two have been thick as thieves ever since that first prom date! Whatever happened, you two can work it out." Her gaze shot to where he was strolling toward the church. Thick, hot anger bubbled up inside her, like a volcano about to blow, complete with tremors.

"Serial adulterers do not just 'work it out,'" Starla snapped, giving air quotes around her former mother-in-law's words. "Charlie needs professional help, but it isn't going to repair our marriage. Our marriage is *over*. In fact, let me just clarify for everyone . . ."

She looked around. There was a large rock with a plaque for Samuel Foster, one of the town fathers, and slipping off her shoes, she climbed up on it. "Excuse me," she called. "Can I have your attention, please, everyone?" The people coming and going and just standing around all turned to stare at her. "As of today, I am now single. I know what people are saying, but contrary to popular belief, I did not quit my marriage. I survived it, as one survives a sinking ship. I bailed water for as long as I could, people. I bailed until everything hurt, and then I got myself into a lifeboat." Charlie appeared next to her, and she felt his hand on her wrist, tugging at her.

"Get down, Star. You're embarrassing yourself." He made no attempt to keep his voice low, and it just fueled her fire.

She ignored him. "Charlie and I are no longer together. That will not be changing. You may call me Ms. Moore; I will no longer be responding to Mrs. Miller. If anyone has any questions, they may direct them to me. Thank you for your attention."

She used his help to balance on her way down and slip her shoes back on, refusing to acknowledge the increased buzzing from the groups scattered in front of the church and, to her surprise, a light smattering of applause.

"What is wrong with you?" Charlie growled, crowding her personal space, following her toward the parking lot.

"Me? Nothing. What's wrong with you? What's wrong with them?" she asked, throwing her hand toward their stunned parents, still standing on the sidewalk. "Why do they seem to think our divorce was some sort of stunt, Charlie? Is that what you've been telling them? Because they're sure as hell not getting that impression from *me*."

He glared daggers at her, but said nothing. She shook her head as she unlocked her car. "Don't forget to pick up the kids from Sunday School. I'll see you at seven." She slammed the door behind her. She stewed all the way down 22 to the forest service road turn-off. As she began to climb the hill, her rage persisted . . . they all thought she was weak. Thought she'd come crawling back to Charlie, like *she* was the one who'd done wrong. Well, they had another think coming. This was it. The last straw. If getting a divorce wasn't a strong enough message, she'd find another one. She had mostly reclaimed her cool by the time she got out of the car at Sawyer's . . . and found him on his stomach, taking pictures of a motorcycle.

"What are you doing?"

At the unexpected sound of her voice, he jumped, and she giggled.

"I didn't hear you pull up."

"The artist at work can't be expected to pay attention to his surroundings."

He dusted off the backside of his jeans, jamming his phone in his pocket. "Just trying to take some pictures for my Instagram. The business Instagram, I mean."

"Let me see." She held out her hand, and he slowly drew out the phone and handed it to her. "You're bad at this."

"Gee, thanks," he said, opening the toolbox drawer to find his 3/4 socket wrench. "That's just what a guy likes to hear."

"No, I mean, you're really bad. You should hire someone to help you."

"No money for that. Plus, I don't think my clients are much into Instagram."

"They don't have to be. Their partners are. And if motorcycles are an interest for both of them, the next time a potential client says, 'My Honda's not working right,' their partner will say, "There's this guy in Timber Falls who can fix that for you . . . so you know what I think your Instagram feed needs?" Starla grinned slyly. "A picture of *you*." What had happened in town was now forgotten, dissipated by the thinner air up here on the mountain.

His gaze narrowed. "Why?"

"Because you're hot," she said, drawing out the last word meaningfully. "That light beard and blue eyes and 'I don't care' haircut plus the leather? Hot." Sawyer snorted and shook his head. "What, you don't believe me? You don't hear all the ladies whispering about you when you come into town? I do. It's a library. The whispers carry better there."

"I ain't got any interest in town girls."

"Can't imagine why not, we're all adorable."

He shook his head, smiling. "Fine. Whatever."

"Put the sunglasses on."

He turned back to the Harley. "I don't work with sunglasses on, Star."

She rolled her neck impatiently. "It's not about your actual work habits, goofball. It's about perception, it's about style. It's about coolness. Like virtually all marketing, it's about sex."

Starla felt like that last word hung in the air between them, heating and stirring it. She cleared her throat as he slowly pulled the sunglasses out of the front of his shirt and slipped them on, waiting to lift his head to look at her until they were on. How did he *do* that? The man just exuded sex all the time, but it was ten times worse now. She couldn't see his eyes, but she knew they were smoldering . . . it was her fault. She'd said the 's' word.

Focusing on taking the picture was a good distraction, and she let her brain tilt toward the artistic side, putting him a little off-center, making sure to get enough of the bike in the picture. She tapped the screen. "Good," she whispered to herself. He had a little smirk on his face, and it was not off-putting. *Not at all.*

"You want me to email it to you?"

"Is email still a thing?"

She tossed her head. "I was trying to speak your language, troglodyte."

"Is that some kind of dinosaur?"

"That would be amazing, but no. Sadly, no." She texted it to him instead.

"Got it. Thanks."

"Any time. We're leaving for dinner in four hours."

"Oh, I forgot about that," he groaned, and he was still complaining when she shut the front door of the big house behind her.

WHEN SAWYER GOT IN the car at 4:30, he was already scowling. He held up his phone and cleared his throat. "Troglodyte: a person who lived in a cave. A hermit. A person who is regarded as being deliberately ignorant or old-fashioned." He let his hand drop. "Really, Star?"

She shrugged, grinning. "You have to admit, you haven't exactly embraced the modern era."

"I have *totally* embraced the modern era," he grumbled. "And if I haven't, why should I? What's so great about it?"

On a whim, she patted his bearded cheek. "Hopeless. Just hopeless." At that little contact, his eyes widened; *oops.* That was too familiar. Her instincts were wrong, again. *No touching. Check.* They chatted all the way down to Timber Falls, which distracted her from being nervous that Rhea wouldn't like her. She didn't know his sister Paige at all, so she focused her questions on her, and before she knew it, they were there.

"Rhea, this is delicious," Starla said, cutting into the roasted chicken and helping herself to another scoop of potato salad.

"I know it's a little early in the year for barbeque food, but I just thought, why not?" she said, passing the watermelon. Starla grinned. This woman was quickly becoming her new heroine; she embodied that IDGAF lifestyle.

"Mama knows her barbeque, that's for sure," Sawyer agreed. He'd been fairly quiet tonight; Starla wanted to ask him if he was okay, but it wasn't her place.

"I made dessert," Paige put in. "So don't let her take credit for that."

"I would never!" Rhea laughed as she sipped her sweet tea. Starla had taken one sip of hers and nearly spit it back out; it was like drinking straight sugar.

"I feel bad you went to all this trouble for me," Starla said, but all the women shook their heads, including Ainsley's mom, Sawyer's aunt Nancy.

"You don't know how much it helps us to know that someone's checking in with him every day," she said, patting her arm. "Someone we know is *responsible*." Starla rolled her lips between her teeth to keep from smiling. How responsible were they going to think she was when they found out about the little surprise she was gestating?

After her outburst at church this morning, maybe she should just tell them . . . but she wasn't ready to lose their love yet.

"Oh, it's been helpful to me, too. It's so nice of him to let us stay in the big house for free." Paige whipped her head in Sawyer's direction, and he immediately held up his hands in innocence.

"All right, I know what you're going to say . . ."

"When my friend Stephanie needed a place to crash," Paige said, leaning forward, "*you* said the big house was only for paying customers!"

"You said you checked with them!" Starla said, aghast.

"Busted," muttered Mr. Buchanan, chuckling, sipping his beer.

"I did!" he protested, blushing. "Well, I checked with Mama, anyway."

"I'm so tickled to have you there, I'd pay *you* to stay," Rhea said, biting her straw with a grin.

"Y'all keep leaving me out of stuff," Paige grumbled. "I put just as much work into the place as you did; you should've asked me, too. Y'all didn't even call me when he collapsed at the library."

"I'm so sorry, Paige," Starla said. "I'll make it up to you. I promise."

"No," said Sawyer, frowning. "I'm the one who did wrong. *I'll* make it up to her."

"Fine. *We'll* make it up to her. Is that better?"

She raised an eyebrow at him, and he raised one right back. It had been a long day, she just wanted Paige to like her, to think well of her before . . . before the baby news came out. Everything kept coming back to that lately. Just dreading it, just waiting for the whispers to start. The universe was playing a giant practical joke on her . . . ending her relationship with Charlie the same way it'd begun. Only she wasn't going to get suckered into staying this time, baby or no baby. Starla held his gaze, feeling like she was in a staring contest she hadn't signed up for. Sawyer didn't seem any less prone to backing down: he glared at her in stony silence.

"Okay," Paige conceded, breaking the tension. "Y'all can start by doing the dishes; it's my night."

"Fine by me," Starla said, standing up, setting her napkin aside.

"No," Sawyer said, taking the dishes out of her hands. "I've got this." He turned toward the kitchen as if the conversation was over. *Oh no, you didn't.* She was marching after him before she knew what she was doing.

"It's not your problem," he said, nudging her away from the sink with his shoulder. "Go back and sit down."

Starla spun in a huff and went back to the dining room—but only to collect more dishes. She set them down with a clank on the butcher block counter tops.

"Do you want to wash or dry?" she asked, using a tone that brokered no discussion. She meant business. It was her fault Paige was losing money when she hadn't even been consulted.

"Both," he said innocently, batting his long eyelashes at her, and she almost laughed.

"You cannot keep me from helping," Starla fumed, snatching a plate and taking it over to the garbage can to scrape the bones into the trash.

"You think so?" he said, sounding like he was musing about a philosophical quandary and not being a stubborn imbecile.

"I know so," she shot back, reaching past him to grab the bottle of eco-friendly dish soap. She was so focused on the soap, she didn't see the sprayer in his hand until it was too late. Sawyer shot the spray directly at her sternum and she gasped as the warm water soaked her T-shirt.

"You did not just do that!" she cried, wiping frantically and uselessly at her chest, while Sawyer doubled over laughing. *Oh, is that how it's going to be?* And since his face was turned away from the sink,

Starla seized her opportunity for retaliation. She grabbed the dangling sprayer and pulled the trigger, aiming directly at his head.

He yelped when the water hit him, lunging for her and taking it full in the face. He pinned her wrist against the side of the refrigerator, his chest heaving.

"Let go." His hair was dripping, but he was grinning from ear to ear like he'd won.

"You let go," she shot back, tilting her chin up to see him better, still trying to wipe the moisture off her shirt. But there was a large man in the way; he'd pinned her waist against the counter now with his hip, nose to nose with her. "I'm going to help."

"You don't have to."

"I want to!"

"You need to stop taking responsibility for every bad thing that happens around you." He shook his head like a dog and sprayed her with water, leaving her sputtering. "That's why you're always apologizing. But I've got this. You're gestating."

"Sawyer Devereaux, you are not going to treat me like I'm porcelain just because I'm pregnant, are you? Because that's downright patronizing."

"You're the one acting like I can't even wash dishes just because of my MS!"

*So that's what it is. MS.* She tried to bend her wrist to spray him again for being so ridiculous, but she couldn't manage it: he was too strong. She raised her voice in irritation.

"It's not about your health at all, you goofball! I just feel responsible!"

"But that's just the point, Star—you're not responsible! I'm responsible! So let me pay my debt on my own!"

"But you wouldn't be in this mess if it weren't for me!"

"Maybe I like being messy with you!" he fired back. "And you're hurting my arm, so let go!"

She dropped the sprayer immediately; the thought that she was hurting him made her cringe . . . she should've been more careful, she shouldn't have played with him so roughly. He caught it and jammed it back in the sink and shut off the water.

"You're so easy," he laughed, bent over again with one hand on the counter. "That's the oldest trick in the chronic illness book."

She stared at him, fighting a smile, putting mock outrage into her voice. "You just used a serious illness to get your own way. You just used my compassion against me."

"And it was soooo easy," he drawled, wiping tears from his eyes. "Starla Moore, I swear, you're the softest touch in all of Linn County."

"And what's wrong with that?" she asked, crossing her arms over her wet chest indignantly.

Sawyer picked up a towel and stepped closer to her. "Nothing, sugar. Nothing at all." Holding her gaze, he carefully wiped the water from her cheeks and neck, and Starla felt all the fight drain right out of her. She hadn't drunk a drop of alcohol, but his bright blue gaze was making her feel warm, wobbly . . . willing. She let her arms fall, and he shuffled a little closer. She wanted to touch his jaw, loop an arm around his neck and pull him closer, feel his lips pressed against hers, feel the heat of his tongue against hers . . . and judging by the look in his eye, he wanted all that and more.

"Y'all haven't even started?" Paige exclaimed from the doorway. Sawyer took a big step back, ruffling his wet hair, looking away as Paige turned and called over her shoulder. "They haven't even started yet!" And the laughter that drifted to them from the other room brought Starla back down to earth. *Foolish.* She must've read him wrong; she was so out of practice with dating. *We're not dating.* He was just being a friend, just messing around. She pivoted to the sink so they couldn't see her face fall.

"Sawyer, will you grab the keto cupcakes? Thanks, Bubba," Paige said, grabbing the cake plate that was already piled high with rich-looking chocolate confections.

"Bubba?" Starla asked softly.

"Bubba Watson, he's a golfer, and he cried a lot when he won the PGA tour a few years back." He rubbed the back of his neck awkwardly. "I'm a bit of an emotional wreck sometimes, and Paige and Mama teased that we were cut from the same cloth. It's meant with love."

She smiled at him, handing him the yellow plate. "Maybe we'll start a club," she said, heading back into the dining room.

# CHAPTER NINETEEN

SHE'D BEEN AVOIDING him all week. Ever since that moment in his mama's kitchen, wiping the water drops off her beautiful skin, getting lost in her trusting, vulnerable gaze, when he'd come as close as he ever could to kissing her. And if he'd done it, maybe she wouldn't feel so awkward around him now. He'd given her a list for the grocery store on Monday instead of going with her, now that she more or less knew what he bought, and he'd just paid her back and padded the payment a little. Just so she'd have more breathing room. *You are so in love with her. You are so screwed.*

So when he knocked on her door Friday afternoon, he wasn't sure how it was going to go down. When Aiden opened the door, he thanked his lucky stars. "How'd you like to learn to make tortillas?"

Aiden tipped his head to the side, considering. "No, thanks. It's screen time." The boy closed the door again, and Sawyer chuckled as he saw Starla sit up straight from the couch and point toward the door, her lips moving and heard her yelling something. Aiden came back to the front door, exuding more bad attitude than an upside-down airplane.

"Come in."

"Try again, Aid," Starla called from across the room.

Aiden pasted a fake cheesy smile on his face and did a sweeping bow. "Welcome, sir, to our temporary home; we are pleased to have you as our guest. What did you wish to show us?"

"Aiden," Starla warned, but Sawyer just ruffled his hair and laughed. *Such a little punk.*

"Tortillas. Your mama said your sister's crazy about them."

"She is," Aiden confirmed, closing the door behind him. Starla had wandered over, clearly curious, but keeping her distance. *And I can't blame her. I'm probably giving her more mixed signals than a drunk air traffic controller.* She sat at the peninsula of the kitchen counter and opened her book again.

Since he knew the kitchen, he got out a mixing bowl and searched her cupboards until he found the masa. "You ever roll out cookie dough?"

"Once," the boy said, "at Christmas time, with my dad."

"Well, it's kind of like that. And I'm letting you in on a secret here: they'll be softer if you put a little olive oil in for some of the water. Pro tip," he said.

"Did your dad teach you how to do this?"

Sawyer's insides clenched a little. "No, my dad wasn't around much. He was a traveling salesman, always on a trip somewhere." *And sometimes, he just didn't bother to come home.*

Out of the corner of his eye, he saw Starla frowning, picking at a bowl of popcorn. *Don't worry about it, soft touch. I'm over it.* Sawyer laid out the tools they'd need at the top of the open space on the counter, then put down a silicone mat.

He and Aiden rolled the balls between their palms; the kid wasn't half bad. Sawyer lined the balls up carefully, not touching each other, then ripped a plastic storage bag apart to use as a barrier. He showed Aiden how to use it to keep the dough from sticking to the rolling pin, while still being able to see through it to see if it was round. He'd never been good at perfectly round, and it still bothered him. An oblong tortilla tasted the same, but it just didn't look as good. The pan was smoking; as he turned it down he noticed Starla was still hanging out near them, just listening.

"You want to try?"

"I'm not great at baking," she said, grabbing more popcorn. "Besides, I kind of like letting two men cook my dinner."

Aiden's chest puffed out, and he remembered how that had felt, taking care of his mom. Being the 'man of the house,' when his dad was gone. Emily snuck into the kitchen, stealing one of the prepared balls off the counter and popping it into her mouth before either of them could stop her.

"Apprehend that thief!" Sawyer bellowed, chasing after her with the rolling pin still in his hand, and he and Aiden both ran after her around the couches until she finally darted upstairs, out of breath from laughter. He only remembered the tortilla that had been in the pan once they caught their breath again, but Starla had quietly snuck into the kitchen and turned it, so it hadn't burned.

"Thank you kindly, ma'am," he said, tipping an imaginary hat to her, and she just smiled, moving to cut up some lettuce and black olives for toppings, her eyes sparkling. Maybe he hadn't screwed things up too badly.

"With kitchen skills like these, you'll make some woman a good partner," she said, moving the olives to a bowl.

"I can't support a wife."

"Like, you can't pick her up, or you can't pay the bills?"

"Both, I guess."

"So what? There's no law that says the man has to be the primary breadwinner."

"Asking her to work so that we can put food on the table doesn't feel right. And what if things progress and I have to use a wheelchair? What then? It just doesn't seem fair, that's all." It was his deepest fear, his waking nightmare, and he'd just blurted out the words at her. For a guy who usually felt like he stumbled his way through conversations, he couldn't seem to shut up around her, even when he should. She'd stopped chopping, and he glanced over at her. He hadn't seen Starla angry, truly angry, too often, but he felt the antarctic fury rolling off her in waves, crashing against his fragile heart.

"Aiden, go play on your tablet." He didn't need to be told twice; he darted from the kitchen in a flash. When she turned back to Sawyer, she enunciated so clearly, he heard every syllable as clear as day.

"That is the biggest pile of ableist shit I've ever heard." She pointed at him with the tip of the knife, and he was actually a little bit afraid. "You take that back right now."

He shook his head. "You don't understand . . ."

"Oh, don't I? Wake up, Sawyer. Life isn't fair. You think it was fair that I got pregnant at eighteen? That I walked for graduation feeling like the Goodyear blimp? That I've been tied to a man who doesn't truly care about me for years? Fair was always a myth. Don't let fair rule your life. Don't let 'fair' decide what makes a good life for you. Because it'll always let you down. Decide what's good for yourself. Decide who and how you want to love." She lifted her chin. "I've got no health problems, but with Charlie, I had little 'quality of life' to speak of. So I fixed it. But fair? It never entered my mind. And it shouldn't enter yours, either."

Sawyer stared down at her, this little spitfire of a woman who didn't know her own strength. He'd never wanted to kiss her more than he did right now. But he wouldn't, because if he did, he knew he'd be handing her his heart permanently. And he rather valued its function as a regulator of his circulatory system; he couldn't go on without it, in fact, and that would mean he couldn't go on without her.

"Fine. I take it back."

She went back to her chopping, but it was far more aggressive than it had been. "I can't believe you said that," she huffed. "Honestly, Sawyer. What a mountain-sized pile of steaming, hot crap."

"If you say so."

"I do, as a matter of fact. You're too smart to believe such stupid, small-minded—"

"Are you finished?"

"No, I'm not finished!" she snapped. "Too *smart* to believe such *stupid, small-minded, media-driven, capitalist, patriarchal—*"

"I meant with the lettuce," he clarified, trying to lighten the mood. "I could tell your rant wasn't finished." Not that he wanted it to be; he was happy to let her yell at him, even if it was poking at some sore spots inside him.

"And it won't be! Not for a long time! You're gonna hear about this for quite a while, buster." She shoved her cutting board toward him, her cheeks pink with barely-controlled rage.

"Okay."

Em came into the kitchen, asking how much longer it would be, and that seemed to put an end to the conversation for the moment. Unsurprisingly, the Miller children knew how to make a mean taco; when Starla called them to wash up, they pulled out two kinds of hot sauce, sour cream, pumpkin seeds, cheddar cheese, green onions, and pinto beans and made a buffet bar for everyone to make their own on the peninsula where Starla had been sitting. Sawyer washed his hands, too, but then made for the door; his work here was done. He'd just needed to look her in the eye, really. He'd needed to see that they were okay. He hadn't expected that she'd try to obliterate his deepest fear: that his health problems made him unlovable.

"You're leaving?" Emily asked, her tone plaintive.

"Can't he stay, Mom?" Aiden added. "Please?"

"I'd like that," Starla said quietly, "but that's up to him."

He looked at their pleading faces; how could he say no to that?

"Well," he said slowly, "I guess since you've already set an extra place, you'll have to wash that plate anyway, huh?" All three of them grinned and nodded, and he moved to grab his plate and get in line. Over dinner, he participated in a lively debate about whether the

Ewoks were necessary or if their role could've been played more effectively by Wookies. He and Em were in agreement: Ewoks were cute and therefore necessary. The other two argued their side ardently, but ultimately lost: you couldn't argue with cute. Then someone pulled out a board game, even though it was a weeknight, and before he knew it, he'd trounced them at Sorry. The kids were yawning hard and it was time for them to go upstairs. He quickly washed up the dishes while Starla was supervising the bathing, the finding of jammies, and the toothbrushing. He slipped out while she was still upstairs; no reason to leave himself open to the temptation of facing her big, brown eyes all alone.

The stars were already out as he wandered back across the yard toward his cabin. He'd meant to get some work done tonight, but it could probably wait. He suddenly remembered he'd never checked his Instagram after Starla posted that picture. He pulled out his phone, its bright glow feeling harsh against the softly falling spring evening.

"Well, I'll be damned." Starla had not been wrong about Instagram; a quick check had his likes and comments at ten times what they usually were. He scrolled through, responding back with gratitude for the comments, until one name made him stop short.

**Dawson Devereaux likes this.** *What?* He hadn't heard from his dad for . . . how many years was it now? Too many. He hadn't known how to invite him to his high school graduation, though the thought had crossed his mind. When he graduated from college, he'd thought about it again. He didn't know why, beyond simple manners. It seemed impolite not to invite the man who'd helped bring him into the world. But then again, that man hadn't decided to stick around to help him navigate said world, so maybe politeness didn't factor. But his mama had never said a harsh word about him, despite his inconsistent visits and inappropriate birthday presents. They were still legally married, as far as he knew.

"Your daddy's going through some things," she'd explained, confiscating the BB gun he'd just unwrapped for his fifth birthday. "He means well. He'll be back around soon, I'm sure." At least his mom had been able to return the gun somehow; she'd bought him some back-to-school clothes with the money. She did let him pick out a dinosaur shirt; he'd worn the heck out of it, told all his new little friends in kindergarten that his dad had gotten it for him. He cried when she threw the threadbare, holey thing away a few years later. Then again, it was well-known in the Devereaux family that Sawyer was the teary one. Paige was the tough one. Mama was the gentle one. And as he remembered it, his dad had been the funny one. Maybe that's why they all stopped laughing for a while every time he left. He couldn't imagine why his father was following him on social media after all this time. Saywer closed the app; he didn't need to think about work now. He shouldn't be looking at screens so close to bedtime, anyway.

# CHAPTER TWENTY

THE NEXT MORNING, SAWYER was out on the porch, drinking his coffee, still waking up, when the quiet of the May morning was broken by a slamming door.

"Are you going to do your karate today? I saw you out the window . . ." Aiden's face popped up over the railing, and Sawyer chuckled.

"It's tai chi, not karate, but they're similar, I guess." He watched the kid for a minute, just thinking. "Yeah, I am. You want to join me?"

"Mom said to tell you no pressure if you didn't want company." Aiden had gotten in trouble again for fighting, and he knew Starla was upset about it. Sawyer had been kind of an angry kid, too, and it didn't help that he teared up when he was upset. It was easier to punch someone who teased you than try to make them understand that it was healthy to be in touch with your emotions. He looked up, and his heart leaped. A sleepy, tousled Starla stood on her porch, holding her mug in front of her mouth with both hands, wearing baby Yoda pajamas. For a brief moment, he imagined waking up next to her like that . . . waking her up with a kiss . . . *nope, no point in thinking that.*

Sawyer gestured to Aiden, and they went out to the open area between the garden boxes and the cabin. For the next twenty minutes, he showed the kid how to do tai chi; he wasn't bad at it, for a beginner. It became their thing: Aiden would quietly show up on the porch in the mornings. They didn't talk, they just moved, watching Lucky and his lady have their breakfast, pointing out brave chipmunks who came up onto the porch to check out Sawyer's coffee cup. Then Aiden would go home, eat his breakfast, and get ready to go to school, and then he'd come back to the garage if he had extra time. Sawyer'd had no shortage of work lately, which was nice.

This had been going on for a couple of weeks when Aiden started opening up, asking him things. Sawyer rarely saw Charlie, but he knew the kids were spending time with him every week. He hadn't been up here since the day they'd moved in, and Sawyer couldn't be sorry about it.

"How's school going?" Sawyer asked as he took the muffler off a Goldwing.

Aiden shrugged, kicking at the metal leg of the stool he was sitting on. "My dad says I need to try harder."

"Mmm. What do you think?"

"I think he wouldn't know how hard I work, because he's never around," he glowered, rubbing one eye, and Sawyer thought he might be covering for tears. Or maybe he was just projecting.

"I know what it's like to have a dad who isn't around as much as you want him to be."

"You do?"

"Mmm-hmm. My dad would take off for long stretches of time, mostly working. I'd miss him a lot. Then he'd come back, and I'd have all these plans for stuff we could do together, and he didn't want to do any of it. And then he'd be gone again."

"I guess I at least get to see my dad every week."

Sawyer bumped him gently on the knee with his fist. "And you have a dad who really cares about you, Aid. I know your dad's made some mistakes, some real whoppers. But you're not one of those. Your mama and daddy love you a whole lot, I can tell. And they're gonna work it out so that you get to see him, no matter where you end up. Your mama said so just the other day."

"She did?" The boy swiped at his face. "I didn't know that," he mumbled.

"That's why *talking* works better than *assuming*, you see. You ask a question, and then you get an answer. It's a strange process, I know, but you'll get used to it."

Aiden punched his arm gently, and Sawyer mouthed "ow," holding his arm protectively, angling his body away from the boy. Aiden laughed.

"You're gonna pick on an invalid? That's cold, Aiden."

"You don't even look sick," Aiden said, going back to his kicking.

"Looks can be deceiving sometimes."

"What does it feel like, when you get sick?" Well, that was only fair. If he was going teach the boy to ask questions, then that opened him up to all sorts of lines of inquiry.

"Well, it doesn't feel good."

Aiden rolled his eyes. "I figured that much."

"I feel real tired. Sometimes, I can't work. Sometimes I have to pee and I can't make it to the toilet. Sometimes my vision gets a little blurry. Sometimes I have pain. Sometimes I have seizures." He shrugged. "It's hard to predict. That's part of what makes it frustrating." *And that's why I haven't asked out your mom; I'm not exactly a catch.*

"Huh." He could see the kid's wheels turning, then Starla called him to come get in the car. "Gotta go, bye." He went running off in a puff of dust that set Sawyer coughing, and Starla called, "Sorry!" across the driveway. He just waved her off. A few minutes later, he heard tires on the gravel again. They were always forgetting something; Starla had been late to work every day this week over forgotten lunches or homework and once, forgotten shoes. How could a kid forget to put on shoes? He shook his head as a shadow fell over the doorway.

"What'd you forget this time?"

"Hey, son."

Sawyer spun toward the door. Dawson Devereaux stood there, hands stuffed deep in his pockets.

Shock rooted him to the spot. His throat felt cast in concrete. "Hey," he choked out. His mind was blank. He couldn't think of a single thing to say. They stared at each other. His dad's hair had gone completely gray; he was wearing it longer, but his beard was neatly trimmed. And glasses. He had glasses now. They were rimless, and they made his eyes look wrinkled, watery. Old. His dad had gotten so *old*. Was his mama old? He couldn't remember now, if he'd ever noticed. Maybe since he saw her every week, he'd gotten used to it as it happened, like his leather coat, cracked and stretched in the right ways. He'd have to look at her again, sometime.

"How did you find me?"

"The photo on Instagram. It was geotagged."

*Yeah, that's not creepy or anything.* He'd have to talk to Starla about her phone security settings.

"Can I come in?"

"Yeah. Sure." He pushed a stool toward him with his boot. It was the least he could do, since he'd come all this way . . . well, Sawyer assumed that he'd come a long way. "Where you living these days?"

"Tacoma." He threw a thumb over his shoulder. "I was just passing through on my way to California and thought I'd stop by and check on you."

"Why?"

"Why?" His father echoed, rubbing his chin, and Sawyer realized with regret that he often did the same thing when he was thinking and didn't know an answer. "Well, I used to do that from time to time, when you were younger." He paused, then looked him in the eye. "Just wanted to make sure you're all right."

"Okay." It was a placating thing to say, which wasn't usually Sawyer's MO. But he was seriously so thrown right now. Strangers didn't just show up on his doorstep; his cabin was too hard to find without good directions. Salesmen didn't bother with him. Even the census takers had ended up stopping him in town. Girl Scouts got him at the grocery store with their tempting treats. And make no mistake, this man was a stranger. As much of a stranger as a salesman.

"You're not having any . . . health problems?"

Sawyer stiffened. "Why would you ask me that?"

Dawson shrugged, hands still in his pockets. "I try to keep up with you, as I can. The internet helps. Followed all your adventures overseas, then it all just . . . stopped. Seemed like you'd found your calling, up until that point."

*I had. I'd found the thing that gave my life meaning, that made the world better. I snatched people out of death's hands. And now I can't.* He didn't know what to tell him. He sure as heck wasn't going to turn his soul over and dump it out onto the concrete floor like a woman's handbag. His soul was not for public consumption.

"I ask again: why would you ask me that?"

Dawson grimaced. "Because I've got MS. And when I first got it, they said it didn't run in families, but now there's new research, and since you're my kid, I wanted to make sure you . . . knew."

"Is that why you left?"

"I don't have any excuse for that. But yeah, I guess so."

They sat in the garage, both of them still, staring at the concrete floor. He didn't know what to say, let alone feel.

"You're fixing motorcycles now?"

"Yup."

"Got any interesting ones for sale? I'm in the market."

Sawyer tipped his head to the side, giving the man what he hoped was an appraising look. He didn't want charity, but if the man wanted to absolve himself of some guilt by buying a bike, who was he to stop him? "Sure, I've got a Goldwing you might like."

"Well, let me see it."

Still unsure of what was happening, Sawyer stood up, moving toward the bike in question. He walked it out into the yard, carefully dodging the others. Dawson walked around it, bending down to see it better. He couldn't stop staring at his dad. Here. At his house. On a random Thursday in late May.

"Can I take it for a test drive?"

"Sure." He must be safe to drive if he'd gotten here on his own. He was driving a blue SUV, older, but he could probably hook a trailer to it if he wanted to take the bike with him. Dawson straddled the bike, revving the engine and setting the ravens in a nearby tree to flight. Sawyer watched him go, then sat down on the porch steps to wait for him to come back. It felt like it took a long time. Waiting for him always had.

# CHAPTER TWENTY-ONE

IT WAS LATE. SAWYER sat in the garage on the concrete floor, a portable work light at his knee, cursing whoever manufactured this ceramic bearing. It should just slide in, but it hadn't seated correctly. He tried gently prying it out with the tip of a screwdriver, but he didn't want to scratch the chrome, and when he tried with his fingers, he couldn't get leverage on it. It wouldn't budge. And his newest client was supposed to pick it up tomorrow morning, first thing. He'd been too distracted earlier, after his dad left, still muttering about needing to think about the Goldwing. Sawyer still didn't know exactly why his dad had come by. He wasn't sure his dad was, either.

"Hey."

He pivoted to see Starla standing in the doorway, shyly, holding one arm in front of her with her other hand. It didn't hide her little baby bump, and her hair was down, loose around her shoulders. He didn't need to turn; he'd known it was her from her voice, he just liked looking at her. It felt nice to admit that, if only to himself. He'd been denying it for so long.

"Hey," he replied, going back to his work. Maybe a magnet would work? He reached for his rolling metal toolbox, opening one of the thin red drawers, finding the place where the tool was seated in the foam.

"Wow," she said, strolling over. "You can take the doctor out of the OR, but not the OR out of the doctor, huh?"

"What?"

"Your tools. They're just very orderly, very organized."

"A lot of people are organized; it's not a doctor trait necessarily."

"So what's with the tray?" she asked, nudging his cookie sheet with the toe of her sandal. Her toenails were painted black with white polka dots, and at first, he thought it was just a random design, until he saw the tie fighter on her big toe. *Star Wars toes. She literally put her fandom on her toes. That's so awesome, it hurts.* She was loyal to a fault. That made it all the more admirable that she'd left Charlie.

"The tray is a matter of efficiency," he explained. "I'm sure lots of people do it. Keeps my nuts and bolts from rolling away."

"But you did the same thing with the tortillas," she said, sitting down on his black rolling stool. "You lined up your ingredients and your rolling pin and your measurement instruments."

"So?"

"So you're a doctor, Sawyer. Maybe there's still a way you could practice medicine."

"I'll take it under consideration," he mumbled, still uselessly digging at the caddywhompus part with his fingernails. "Can you get this out?"

She leaned forward, squinting at it. "This part?"

"Yeah." He scootched back a little, and she rolled forward. Her fingers, which weren't dirty and greasy and were a little bit smaller than his, plucked the part out easily.

"Here you go," she said cheerfully, tossing it to him.

"Unbelievable. Ever thought of giving up books for mechanical work?"

She laughed, pivoting back and forth on the spinning stool. "No, I'm pretty happy where I'm at. Though I'm actually between reads right now. My TBR is as long as Interstate 5, but I can't seem to pick one."

He turned back to the motorcycle. "There's plenty of good books that aren't a mystery. Why don't you try that new Pratchett when Maggie brings it back?"

Starla stopped spinning, and he suddenly realized what he'd said. He scrambled to change the subject.

"I read that 'Jar Jar Binks is a Sith lord' article you sent me, and I still have some serious reservations about—"

"You," she breathed. "You're the book fairy."

*Don't panic. She's just guessing. She doesn't know for sure yet. Bluff.*

"What? That makes no sense, sweetheart," he scoffed, not looking at her, keeping his hands moving. "That baby's stealing your brain cells." If he looked at her, she'd know. He was a terrible liar. Always had been.

"Hey, look at me." He blushed hard, keeping his eyes on the motorcycle. He was glad it was fairly dark in the garage . . . but he was pretty sure she could tell. "You couldn't have known that we had a new Pratchett. I didn't tell you, and you didn't come down this week."

Desperation took over, and he cocked an eyebrow at her. "You must've mentioned it."

"No," she said, shaking her head slowly. "I know I didn't. I noted it, because the fairy's never sent fantasy before, especially not such an old book. Always new releases. But you know who loves Pratchett? Maggie Durand. And she came in and checked out the new one on Friday." Her gaze went thoughtful for a moment. "You couldn't drive, so you asked Maggie to drop them off, didn't you?"

He said nothing. He would plead the Fifth. If he said nothing, maybe she wouldn't know. He kept his gaze on that stupid machine. He felt her gentle fingers on his cheek, turning his face toward her, her eyes searching and hard.

"Sawyer Devereaux, look into my eyes and tell me you're not the book fairy."

His heart was jammed with unknowns, more stuck than that stupid part, trying to calculate all the different ways he could play this, all the different ways she could react. All the different ways he could lose her over something that started as such a simple thing and just spiraled out of control.

"I can't," he muttered.

"Why?" she whispered, and he finally lifted his eyes to give her his gaze. He felt like she was reaching into his chest and squeezing his heart with those big, wild eyes of hers.

"You know why."

"Why would you do this?"

"You know why," he repeated firmly, but she shook her head, a few strands of her dark hair sliding out of her ponytail.

"I really don't. I really can't imagine why—"

"You can't?" he interrupted. "So if you had a friend who was sad and depressed, whose husband treated her badly, you wouldn't do anything—*anything*—to try to make her smile?"

She let her hand fall from his face. "But it didn't make me smile, it just made me *crazy*. I *told you* it was making me crazy!" she cried, gesturing wildly. "We talked about it at length, every week, when you . . . when you . . ." He felt like she'd been undressing him emotionally, and she'd just gotten to his belt buckle. "It gave us something to talk about," she whispered, her eyes still frantic even as comprehension dawned. "You took my mind off my problems. You bought books you knew I'd love, and I did love them. You . . ."

"Star," he said, his voice ragged, pleading her with his eyes to stop. "It wasn't a big deal."

"It was to me." She put her hands on his face, both of them this time, and he shuddered at the tender touch. "It meant *so much* to me. Why didn't you let me thank you? Why didn't you tell me?"

"You were married. I didn't want you to think I was hitting on you."

"But you still came to see me?" Her voice was small.

He nodded. "I did."

"Why?" *I had to. I couldn't stay away.* That first day he'd walked back into the library and seen her sitting there, all grown up, eating her lunch while reading some heady, thick historical fiction novel, he'd just wanted to sit on the corner of her desk forever. He'd asked her where the mysteries were, and she'd politely walked him over to the fiction section, shown him how to look for the question mark symbol on the spine, asked if he'd like his library card renewed, since it had probably expired since he'd last lived in town. On a base level, it was no different from the way he'd seen her treat any of the other patrons, but somehow, it didn't matter. He'd just instantly admired her.

"You had such a hard life, I just . . . I just wanted to make sure you were okay." He paused. "I didn't know how else to . . . to help you. Sometimes I don't people well."

She jerked back, like he'd shocked her with static electricity. "You don't . . ." She burst out laughing. "You don't *people* well?"

Not sure what was happening now, he nodded slowly, warily, not wanting to break their connection. "That's right."

She brought their foreheads together, and he closed his eyes, savoring the closeness, breathing in her pineapple joy. "Oh, you incurably sweet, amazing man. Someday, Sawyer Devereaux," she murmured, "I hope someone does something for you like this, so you can finally understand how *such a big deal* it is." Her slow breaths played over his lips, and he thought she might kiss him. He wanted that; he wanted to kiss her, he wanted it so much, more than his next breath. He was sure once would be enough, since there couldn't ever be more than that. Surely his foolish heart would be satisfied with tasting her just once. But where he was sitting on the floor, he couldn't get any closer to her. She was above him in every way, or so it felt. So he just waited, breathing with her, drinking in her warmth and her touch.

But she drew back suddenly. "I-I-I'm sorry," she stuttered.

"For what?" he asked gruffly, turning back to the bike, trying to pretend like his insides weren't howling with disappointment.

"I don't know," she said, standing up quickly, agitatedly dusting off her skirt like there was a spider on it. "It's late, I should get to bed."

"Sweet dreams," he said, as she spun and hurried out of the garage. He let himself watch her go, listen to her muttering to herself all the way back to the big house until the door slammed behind her. Sawyer flopped backwards onto the floor, completely wrung out by the interaction. It wasn't every day that a two-year secret was revealed to your crush and she almost kissed you before she freaked out for an unknown reason and ran off. He looked up at the ceiling of the converted barn, the way the rafters crisscrossed, the barn swallow nests still clinging to the sides, the darkness trying to engulf them. He'd been afraid of this for so long, that she'd find out. That she'd know how deeply he cared. And now she did. He didn't expect anything back from her; that wasn't why he'd done it. But now he wondered, staring at the stars through the barn door, if she'd want to get anything off her chest, too. Maybe he'd find out tomorrow . . . it was going to be a long night.

# CHAPTER TWENTY-TWO

AS IT TURNED OUT, SAWYER didn't see Starla the next morning. By the time he came out for his morning exercise and coffee, her car was already gone. It was a troubling development to say the least. Would she move out, thinking he was some kind of creep? Maybe he *was* some kind of creep; she'd been married after all. But it's not like he'd asked her out. He'd just sent hundreds of dollars' worth of hand-picked donations to her place of business. He sighed and had just gotten the keys down to unlock the garage before his nine o'clock meeting with Victoria Greene when his phone rang.

"I'm sick!" Ainsley sounded terrible. "You have to go to the town meeting tonight."

"Have you been sniffing the classroom art supplies again?"

"I'm not kidding," she wailed. "I'm at home and I'm sick and I just got the agenda for the town meeting. Starla's on it."

Sawyer frowned. She didn't usually go to the town meeting unless she was supporting something. "She's going into town to speak?"

"No, you're not getting it: they're speaking *about her*. They're upset that she's been late so much, and they want to know what the town council is going to do about it."

That did it. He'd had it up to his eyebrows with this town and their entitled attitude, and he was going to take them to the woodshed and have a come to Jesus meeting. Enough was enough. "I'd need someone to pick me up."

Ainsley's deep sigh came through the phone as static. "Maybe Kyle would. You want me to ask him?"

Sawyer twisted his lips to one side as he considered this. He would not be seen as a charity case, begging all over town for a ride, but this wasn't for him; this was for Star. And for her, he'd sit on a street corner with a tin cup and a fake crutch if that's what it took. That's what you did for a friend, especially a friend who'd fallen on hard times. Or rather, who'd dived into them head first, but only in order to get herself out of a worse situation. He had to admire her for that, and he wasn't going to let the town besmirch her.

"Yes. Please ask him."

Ainsley chuckled. "That was a lot of thinking over a fairly simple question. You didn't have another seizure just now, did you?"

Sawyer lowered his voice and made it as deadpan as he could. "My health is a joke to you?"

"Oh, whatever—I've heard you say way worse. Do you want me to ask him or not?"

"Yeah, ask him. I'll pay him for the gas."

"I doubt he'll let you, but you can offer." She paused, and it was obvious she was hesitating for a reason.

"What?" he growled. He'd had almost no sleep, and he could practically feel a flare coming on. "Just spit it out, Ains."

"When she told me about the baby, she said . . . she said she was thinking of leaving town. For good."

His heart fell in slow-motion, like a video of a wine glass shattering. Only his heart broke into more pieces and would be harder to put back together.

"Did she say when?" His voice was gravely, and he hoped Ainsley didn't notice.

"No. But if she loses her job . . . there'll be nothing to keep her here. Sawyer, we can't let her leave. We have to try to stop her. All alone with her kids, including a baby? I just can't even . . ."

Now he was the one hesitating. "If she wants to go," he said softly, "she should go. She's been living for other people her whole life. It's about time she did something she wants to do. But until she decides, I'll do what I can at the meeting."

WHEN KYLE PULLED UP two hours later, Sawyer tossed twenty dollars next to the minivan's gear shift. The man narrowed his gaze, assessing something on Sawyer's face. "What are you doing?"

"I'm paying you for gas."

"Family doesn't do that. You're basically family now. Please remove your cash from my cup holder."

Sawyer grunted discontentedly and crossed his arms over his chest, pointedly looking out the window.

"Huh. Interesting." Kyle pivoted the car to turn around and began back down the driveway.

"What?"

"Oh, my family often accuses me of being grunty and broody, but I've never been on the other side of it until now. They're right; it is kind of annoying." Kyle picked up the twenty dollars, lowered his window and threw it out onto the driveway, shaking his hand as if it was now sticky or slimy.

"Hey!"

"It'll still be there when you get back. Now, where are we going?"

"Town meeting."

Kyle turned out onto the main road, checking for traffic, then cautiously pulled out. At this rate, they were going to be just in time for next week's meeting rather than the one tonight.

"Oh, good, that's where I'm going anyway." Kyle glanced at him, his curiosity undisguised. "I don't see you there much, though."

"That's because I've never been."

"You're lucky. It's not very interesting, but it's important."

"Tonight's agenda is *interesting* to me, that's for sure." His annoyance was simmering for now, but he had a feeling it wouldn't take much to get it to a full boil.

"How so?"

"Starla's on it. They want to can her. I don't think she should lose her job just because she's pregnant." She was never the most punctual person, but it was nothing like it was now.

"That's a secret."

"Yes," Sawyer said impatiently, "I *know* it's a secret. But I won't see her lose her job over something that's not her fault!"

"It actually is her fault," Kyle said, still driving slow enough to make Sawyer want to tear his hair out. "She slept with her husband."

"But their protection failed!"

Kyle's head whipped to the side. "How do *you* know?"

Sawyer's cheeks heated, but he tried to shrug apathetically. "It's common knowledge."

"It's *definitely* not. I've been wanting to know if she used protection, but Ainsley prohibited me from asking. It was very annoying."

*Crap*. She'd trusted him, and now he'd gone and blown her secret. She hadn't even told Ainsley? That was big. It had him feeling a little disoriented.

"Well," Sawyer said slowly, "if it's not common knowledge, then please keep it to yourself, as a favor to me."

"Can I share it with my fiancée? I'd like to gloat about knowing before she did."

"No. Definitely not with your fiancée. Least of all your fiancée."

Kyle grimaced. "Fine. But if it ever becomes common knowledge, please let me know."

Sawyer coughed out a soft laugh. "Deal. Are you going to get us to the meeting sometime this century, Sunday driver?"

"We should arrive in about fifteen minutes, if my initial trip up the mountain was an accurate indication of how long the trip usually takes."

"I can do it in five. Pull over."

"I don't think so. I don't allow other people to drive my car. Especially not people with seizure disorders, no offense."

Sawyer banged his head lightly against the window, and Kyle snickered.

"When will you get your license back?"

"Another week or two, I hope. Barring any more *events*." 'Events' was what the neurologist called them. 'Pain in the carburetor' was what Sawyer called them.

Kyle nodded. "I'm sure it's inconvenient to depend upon others for transportation. I'm not often available, but when I am, you can depend on me without feeling concerned that you're bothering me. You're very important to Ainsley, and she's very important to me. Therefore, you're important to me as well."

Sawyer rubbed his palms against his jeans; they were sweaty, for some reason. "Thanks, man."

"You're welcome. You did me a favor by agreeing to be in my wedding party; I initially only wanted two groomsmen, and the prospect of picking a third was daunting."

"Let me guess: Ainsley added someone at the last minute."

"No, she gave me plenty of advance warning, but it threw a wrench in my plans nonetheless."

"Women have a way of doing that."

"Preach." His deadpan tone made Sawyer smile.

He glanced at Kyle. "You seem pretty happy with Ainsley, though."

"Of course I am. Ainsley is wonderful." He pulled into the parking lot. "I'll take you home right after the meeting."

"Yeah, I'm not going to want to linger," Sawyer muttered, throwing open the passenger side door. He probably should've changed his shirt before he was going to mingle with all these . . . these . . . *town people*. Sawyer subtly sniffed at his shirt; well, at least it smelled okay. In fact, he kind of smelled like Starla. He'd made an unnecessary trip to the grocery store a few days ago wearing this shirt, he just . . . he just liked talking to her, that was the truth. He'd make any excuse necessary to check on her, to get into her kitchen and clean something. She shouldn't be alone in this. Any of it.

Sawyer slid into a seat in the very back row which was mostly empty, but it didn't keep his aunt from noticing him, even though she was sitting much closer to the front.

"Well, hi there, stranger. You grab a ride from Ainsley?"

"Kyle," he said, gesturing vaguely behind her, but Aunt Nancy didn't take the subtle hint that she should focus on someone else.

"How are you feeling?" He hated the question, but he grudgingly admired her directness.

"Better. Thanks."

"So there's no reason you can't come to Fourth of July with us, then?"

"Oh," he said, rubbing his hand on his jeans, "I don't think I said *that* . . ."

Aunt Nancy grinned. "There will be homemade potato salad, I can guarantee that. And your grumpy uncle."

"Which one?" It was a good joke, because he only had one uncle.

"The handsome one," she said, winking at him. More happily-married people. How nice for them. They were giving him heartburn with all this sweetness. The woman who made him smile would never see him that way, winking about his good looks with her relatives. Starla had bigger and better things ahead of her, he was sure of that.

Starting over would be good for her. Maybe if he was lucky, she'd let him visit her. Aunt Nancy stepped forward and gathered him into a motherly embrace. Softly enough that only he could hear, she whispered, "It would mean a lot to have you there. I really hope you'll decide to join us." He hugged her back. Her intentions were good; at least she'd just asked, instead of laying on the guilt about how it would make his mother happy. But if he had a seizure or if he was feeling poorly and had to leave early, he'd ruin everyone's holiday. It was easier to just stay away . . . but he hated disappointing her.

"I'll think about it."

"Good enough for me," she said, giving him one final squeeze before she let him go. Honestly, these Buchanans. Once they thought you were theirs, they just didn't let go. And now he had Durands doing the same. How much of this town was going to claim him? No matter; they'd all hate him again after tonight. They weren't going to like what he had to say, but he'd made up his mind. No one was going to fire Starla. He'd make sure.

Sawyer bounced his leg anxiously through the first part of the meeting, tuning out through PTA announcements and Fourth of July logistics.

"Now," said Councilman Park, an older Asian man, "the next item on the agenda concerns many of us. The library closures. Mr. Kirschbaum, you proposed the item for the agenda; would you like to address the group?"

The older white man stood up, belatedly removing his hat to reveal a crop of askew white hair, and Sawyer finger combed his own hair in anticipation of speaking next. "I go to work early in the morning, and lately, the library hasn't been open early enough for me to get my books before work. The books are for my wife, and we only have the one car." Sawyer rolled his eyes. This was pitiful; he was clearly playing to the crowd. "Now, I like Mrs. Miller as much as the next man, but she's been derelict in her duties, and it's affecting all of us. We should get somebody in there who can show up on time. That's all I want to say."

*He can't even get her name right*, Sawyer fumed.

"Thank you, George. Anyone else?"

The dark-haired Russian kid who was always hogging the computers raised his hand, and Councilman Park called on him. "Pavel?" Sawyer knew that kid. Half the time, Pavel was diddling around on Twitter when he went in there.

"I have a distance learning class with a discussion component, and it starts at a certain time. If I'm not there, I could lose credit. I don't want to have to retake the class and lose the money I've invested."

"Oh, give me a break," Sawyer muttered, shifting in his seat, and the couple next to him glared at him. Aunt Nancy patted his knee, and he knew she wanted him to calm down, but that wasn't going to happen.

"Did you have something to add, Mr. Devereaux?" He must've said that louder than he meant to.

"Yeah," Sawyer said, standing up before Mr. Park could acknowledge him. "I got something to say. Y'all should be ashamed of yourselves. Every person here knows the hard time Starla's been through these last few months. Is she handling it well? Maybe not. But I bet there's not a person here whose life she hasn't made easier at one time or another. I visit the library every week, and I hear her at the desk, recommending books on grief and medical conditions and helping you with your taxes or checking your email, even though that isn't her job." He was running out of breath; he seldom gave speeches, and his lungs were apparently unused to the exertion. He took a deep breath and plowed on before anyone could interrupt him. "So y'all can just cut her some slack right now while she's getting her feet under her as a single parent. Pavel, you wouldn't even know about those classes if it wasn't for Starla; you'd still be playing video games in your mama's basement all day. And Esther Kirschbaum, I see you out walking for miles with your lady friends. You live less than a mile from the center of town; you're telling me you can't swing by the library on your way home and get your own books?" Pavel avoided his gaze, but Mrs. Kirschbaum nodded sheepishly. "If you've got concerns, don't talk about her behind her back. Work with her to figure it out, or get a high school kid to open it early, and give them some community service credit. It ain't rocket science. But this?" He gestured to the group of riveted spectators. "Y'all are better than this. This is beneath you. And it's certainly not what she deserves." He sat down hard, still glancing around the crowd, silently daring anyone to argue with him.

"Thank you for sharing that, Mr. Devereaux," Councilman Park said, shuffling his papers and adjusting his collar, like he was too warm.

"Dr. Devereaux," Kyle corrected, standing up on the other side. "And I'd like to echo Sawyer's sentiments. Starla is an important member of this community. I believe grace is called for this scenario. My fiancée couldn't be here tonight due to a minor illness, but I believe she might be willing to help keep the library open later one or two nights a week, if that would help. I know she would also express concern at these proceedings occurring without Starla's presence." He sat back down, and Sawyer hid a smile. Having a team was kind of helpful sometimes, apparently.

"Thank you, Dr. Durand. I'll make a note of Ainsley's willingness to help." He jotted something down, and Sawyer doubted it was in any way related to Kyle's comments. "Anyone else?"

Mrs. Foster raised a hand shyly. "I see both sides of the issue; I believe we can find a way to support Mrs. Miller while still acknowledging that her tardiness is a problem for some people. I would be happy to deliver books to those who can't come to the library when it's open. I know the joy I've recently rediscovered in reading, and I'd like to do something to give back."

"Thank you, Alice. I'll note that down as well." He took off his reading glasses. "And I'd just like to clarify that the concern was raised, but no action has been proposed as of yet. This is just a preliminary discussion to gauge how widely this is affecting the community. I believe I speak for the whole council when I say that Mrs. Miller is a valued member of this town, and we will certainly discuss the problem with her before coming to any conclusions about what action ought to be taken." He didn't look at Sawyer, but it was obvious that the man thought he was overreacting. Well, that was just fine. He'd just go back up his mountain and leave them to their pointless meetings. Sawyer got up, grabbing his leather jacket off the back of the chair, and stalked out of the VA hall before anyone could stop him. He'd said what he came to say; it wasn't cold. He'd just wait outside until Kyle was ready to go.

After five minutes, Kyle came out. "Let's go."

"Already?"

"Yes." He certainly wasn't going to complain about that, but he knew the meeting wasn't over yet, so it was a bit perplexing. He felt a bit bad for storming out like that, but it seemed more important to keep his cool. He'd already let his mouth run more than he usually did. The two men got into the minivan, and Kyle pulled out of the parking lot.

"I didn't realize you were in love with Starla," Kyle said, ever matter-of-fact.

"I'm not in love with . . ." He tried to make his lips form the word. It was just a word, just her beautiful name, the name that reminded me him of how she lit up his darkness like a sky full of stars. "Starla," he muttered.

"Are you sure? That doesn't seem right."

"Yes, I'm sure. But thanks for asking." He looked over at his almost cousin-in-law. "You didn't have to leave the meeting."

"I'm sure that was the most interesting thing that was going to happen tonight. Ainsley can get the notes from someone else. I only went because she asked me to pick you up."

The doctor in him was curious. "What's she sick with?" The doctor in him was also nosy as heck, apparently.

"Just a little stomach trouble. Nothing serious. I'd like you to consider joining my teaching staff at the hospital."

"I beg your pardon?" Not only was there zero transition to the subject, but he'd never practiced medicine in Oregon; his license wasn't even valid here. He hadn't bothered transferring it from Georgia when he'd had to leave Honduras.

"You have a lot of knowledge and experience. You can't perform surgery, but you can teach others to do so. And you have integrity, loyalty, compassion . . ." Kyle nodded to himself, as if he felt he was making some very good points. "These are all things I value. I'd have to speak to Dr. Baker about it first, but . . ."

Sawyer cut him off. "There's no need. I can't do that." He wasn't trying to be unkind, but the man was barking up the wrong tree. Unthinkable.

"I understand that you have a condition that's sensitive to stress, but we could start with a part-time position and see how it goes. I'm sure it would pay more than you're making as a grease monkey."

Sawyer closed his eyes. The comment barbed a little, even though he reminded himself that Kyle probably wasn't trying to be insulting. "It's not about the money, man. I can't go back to medicine."

"Why?"

Sawyer turned his whole body toward the man. "You really want to know why?"

Kyle's gaze didn't stray from the road. "Yes. Really."

"Surgery was my first love. My only love, really. I won't say that no other branch of medicine appealed to me, but I'm a surgeon down to my bones. The precision. The challenge. The ability to change someone's life profoundly. I don't know if I can go back and be so close and yet so far from that."

"I believe many of those same draws exist in teaching. I think you'd be a natural. I'd like you to consider it. Please." Sawyer thought back to the fun he'd had teaching Aiden to make tortillas and making the cake with the two of them. It *had* been fun. And teaching adults would be more tolerable than teaching kids, probably. He thought of Starla's teasing about his tool tray . . . maybe . . . something caught Sawyer's eye outside the car as Kyle's headlights swept across the shrubbery by the road, and he shouted.

"Stop the car! Stop!" He had his seatbelt off and the door open before Kyle could even slide to a halt on the gravel road. Lucky lay on the side of the road, eyes wild, breathing ragged, bleeding from his chest and his head; he'd been hit by a car. It must have just clipped him, because there was no smoking heap of a machine. Sawyer fell to his knees next to him, trying to think what he could do for the poor creature. It was so unfair. He heard Kyle get out of the car and come and stand next to him.

"I know this deer," Sawyer tried to explain, but once he heard it out loud, he realized how ridiculous it sounded, so he shut his mouth again. Lucky took one or two more loud breaths, and then stopped. Sawyer stared down at him; he was alive one minute and dead the next. He felt like his heart had been cut out. Lucky was such a beautiful, peaceful part of his life; he'd so looked forward to seeing him. Sorrow settled on his shoulders, bent them low under the weight.

He'd seen it in the operating room before, of course, but somehow, here in the quiet woods, it meant something more to him. Death was part of life, a necessary part. But he felt like the wind was whispering to him he wasn't dead, not yet. And he'd been acting like he was. He'd been acting like his life was over, like an idiot.

So what if the kid she was carrying was someone else's? So what if she was leaving? Any of them could get hit by a car tomorrow. Life was too precious, too unpredictable to let another second go by without grabbing for what he wanted. And what he wanted was Starla.

Sawyer stood up, brushing off his hands. He turned to Kyle. "If Dr. Baker will approve it, I will join your teaching staff on a part-time trial basis."

Kyle beamed. "Awesome." He looked down at the deer and cocked his head. "I'm not sure how this experience convinced you, but I don't really care. I'm glad you said yes."

Sawyer put a hand on Kyle's shoulder in a friendly gesture and gave it a squeeze. "Let's go home. I've got some things I need to do."

# CHAPTER TWENTY-THREE

"THEY DID WHAT?" STARLA found herself staring out the front window, since she couldn't stare in confusion at the person talking to her through the phone.

"They talked about you at the town meeting," Mavis repeated. "That's what Alice Foster said, anyway, when she called me about doing book deliveries. I was as shocked as you are."

The fetal position was sounding really good right about now, but with her growing belly, she could never have managed it. Her slouchy T-shirt slid down her arm as her shoulders slumped forward.

"What did they say?"

"Just that they want you to be on time," she said. "I'm sorry, honey." She'd told Mavis about the baby last week, when she'd caught her unsuccessfully trying to bend over to pick up a fallen copy of the *Dramatist's Sourcebook* in the reference section. "But they said your beau stood up for you."

"Beau?" *Not Charlie.* If he'd made a scene at the town meeting, she was going to hear about it all week . . .

"Yes, your recluse. Mr. Devereaux."

"Thank you for letting me know," Starla murmured. "I'll see you tomorrow." She couldn't lose her job. Not yet, anyway. She'd been looking into positions in Arizona . . . but she hadn't decided yet. Maybe this would make the decision for her. Out the front window, a gray van pulled into the yard, and she squinted. Without her glasses, she couldn't see who it was, but she was guessing Kyle based on the make and model. Sawyer got out of the car, and her annoyance about the town meeting took a sharp right turn. *Where has he been? Why didn't he tell me he needed to go somewhere? I'd have taken him.* She had half a mind to march out there and confront him, but . . . things had been weird between them since she'd unmasked him as the book fairy. Well, more accurately, she'd been avoiding him since then. Ironically, she *was* on time to work this morning, but only because she hadn't wanted to talk to him.

She'd turned back to her spot on the couch and her book when there was a quiet knock on her front door. That could only be one person. She took a deep, steadying breath as she went to the door and opened it.

"Hi, Sawyer. I'm sorry I haven't—"

"I think we're in love." *Well, that's a heck of a greeting.* And based on the way he stood akimbo, eyes blazing, he was ready to fight about it. Well, that worked for her.

"Nope," she said, shaking her head automatically. Starla stepped out onto the porch, pulling the door mostly closed behind her, mindful that her kids were not heavy sleepers. "Can't be. I wasn't going to fall in love again." What was happening to her grammar? She made it sound like it had already happened . . . but it hadn't, had it? Did she just like the way his hair fell into his eyes like that, or did she love it? Did she just like his scruff, his scars, his gentle way, his dry humor, or did she love it? Did she love Sawyer? He didn't give her long enough to really think about it.

"You say that like you had a choice."

"Love is always a choice."

He was coming closer, slowly, almost sheepishly, scraping his boots against the porch.

"Later on, maybe. Not at first."

She snorted derisively. It was the only defense she had left. "You'll forgive me if all your experience as a forest hermit doesn't convince me—"

"Star." He captured her face in his hands, and his rough fingertips against her cheeks made her stomach drop like the time she'd looked over the edge at the Space Needle on their eighth-grade class trip to Seattle. "I'd like to kiss you now. Just to see."

"Is that what it's going to take to convince you?" she muttered, trying to hide how *not flippant* she felt inside. "Fine, get it over with."

Inside, Starla was all nerves. She'd imagined this moment plenty of times. She should probably be stopping him, seeing as she might be leaving. But he was right; what could it hurt to see? She thought he'd come in slow, sultry-like, but with plenty of heat. So when he gave her just a quick taste, his soft lips fluttering against hers for such a brief moment, she felt completely justified in complaining.

"You call that a kiss? Are you punking me, Devereaux?"

He grinned, not releasing her face. "What's wrong with the way I kiss? I was trying to be respectful."

"It just doesn't count like that," she said. "Come here." She pulled him forward by his T-shirt, and his lips met hers much more firmly this time. She felt his hands slide into her hair, holding her gently, like she was breakable. She bit his bottom lip lightly, just so he'd know that she wasn't. Sawyer groaned, and those polite hands lost some of their reticence; one went to the small of her back, pulling her flush against him despite her bump of a belly, and the other went to the back of her neck, twisting his fingers into her hair. He drew a long kiss against her lips, then slid his tongue against the seam of her lips in question. Starla giggled a little as she opened for him, but she lost her humor as soon as his tongue touched hers. That little taste, that tiny bit of intimacy lit her fuse like a firecracker. She was melting in his arms, the smell of leather wafting around them. Sawyer was savoring her like she was better than Texas cake; he seemed determined to try her from every angle, but there was nothing hurried about him. The man was having his way with her, kissing her like he had all night.

And as infuriating as it was to admit it, he was right. She was in love with Sawyer Devereaux. She'd only been in love once before, but it had died a long time ago, and this felt different, anyway. She felt like she was kissing her best friend, but in a good way. Her heart was still racing, but she was thinking about how he was with her kids and how he cooked for her and did her dishes. How he'd helped her laugh her way through the hardest time in her life. She felt like she was trying to pour all the goodness he added to her life into her kiss and failing miserably, but based on his little groans and greedy fingers stroking her, he didn't mind. Politeness had left the porch some time ago, and Sawyer was tugging at the edge of her T-shirt, bending his head to let his lips travel her neck and collarbone, walking her backwards until her backside met the wall next to the front door. Sawyer Devereaux was carefully dismantling her with his lips and his touch, and she felt ready to come apart completely in his arms if he asked her to. She'd always been extra needy during her second trimester.

"Mom?" They both jumped, and Sawyer backed up hastily as they looked down at Emily's sleepy face blinking up at them.

"What, baby?"

"Why are y'all ringing the doorbell?" Starla pivoted her hips and looked behind her; sure enough, the doorbell was right behind her. Based on his shocked expression, Sawyer didn't immediately register the change in her daughter's speech patterns or the doorbell coincidence, but Starla laughed out loud.

"Sorry, kiddo. Mr. Devereaux and I were just . . ."

"Kissing," Emily finished, yawning.

"Yes. Kissing." She leaned down to give her a peck on the forehead, then turned her around and gave her a gentle shove inside.

"Back to bed. I'll be up to tuck you in after a minute." She watched Emily through the open door until she reached the landing of the stairs, then she turned back to Sawyer. She'd never seen him look so dismayed; he rubbed his forehead agitatedly.

"What's wrong?" she asked, resisting the urge to wring her hands.

"Star, that was not what I had in mind, that was . . ." He swallowed hard. "I apologize for getting carried away." The collar of her shirt flopped down her shoulder again, and he choked out an embarrassed note from the back of his throat. Sawyer quickly righted it, patting it once it was back in place, as if to assure himself that no harm was done. Starla grinned in the darkness; he was going to die tomorrow when he saw the hickey she could feel forming on her neck.

She wrapped her arms around his neck, bringing their foreheads together.

"I can't believe you did this to me," she said, shaking her head slowly. She felt his shoulders stiffen, and he tried to pull away.

"Again, I am so sorry, I didn't mean to—"

She put her hand over his mouth. "Not the kissing. The kissing was great. I mean the falling in love part. I really wasn't going to do that again, and now you've screwed it all up. Thanks a lot, Devereaux."

He nodded slowly, letting his shoulders drop, closing his eyes, still holding her close.

"Yeah," she said softly, "all messed up." He sighed contentedly as he smoothed down her shirt, pressing just a few more gentle kisses to her neck.

"I'll pick you up at five o'clock on Sunday."

"For what?"

"Our first date." And with that, he pressed one last kiss to her cheek before he turned and sauntered back toward his cabin, throwing her a wink over his shoulder.

"I take it I'm driving?" she called after him, and his answering laugh had her glowing from head to toe.

# CHAPTER TWENTY-FOUR

THE BAD NEWS WAS THAT Starla spent all day Saturday being a basket of nerves; she hadn't asked nearly enough questions about this date or what his expectations were, and now she was hoping she hadn't given him false hope. The good news was that when she was stressed, she cleaned the living daylights out of her house, so the lodge looked amazing. When she ran out of laundry to fold, she collapsed next to Em, who was watching some kind of Barbie show that probably didn't reflect Starla's feminist values. *Barbie's designing robots now? That feels like a STEM money grab . . .*

Barbie wasn't able to hold her interest, especially after such a frenetic morning, and she didn't wake up until Em shook her shoulder.

"Mom, I'm hungry."

Starla rubbed at her eyes with the heels of her hands. "What time is it?" The living room was darker than she expected, evening light slipping in sideways through the front windows.

"You're always sleeping," Aiden noted from across the room, where he was curled up with his tablet. "Are you sick or something?"

Starla looked at both of them, trying to decide what to say. This seemed as good a time as any to tell them. They might decide to be more helpful or at least feel more included and less blindsided. They were bound to notice sooner or later.

"You know how we talked about where babies come from?"

"Ugh, not this again," Aiden grimaced, getting off the couch.

"Sit down, son," she said firmly, and with an emphatic eye roll, he complied. "I'm not sick. I'm having a baby."

Emily uttered a little cry of ecstasy, like she'd just won Miss Universe and they'd handed her the bouquet of red roses. "I'm going to have a sister?"

"I don't know yet if it's a boy or a girl," she said, rubbing her belly with a smile.

Pushing aside her hand, Emily put her ear to her belly. "I don't hear anything. I think a boy would be making more noise."

Starla laughed and tried to finger comb her daughter's unruly hair. "What about you, Aiden? Are you hoping for a boy or a girl?"

At the silence, she looked up. He was gone. She sighed. When she got to the top of the stairs, he was flopped onto his bed, head under his pillow, tablet on his nightstand. Starla gave a tentative knock on the door. "Can I come in?"

He shrugged, but said nothing. Starla sat on the edge of his bed, reaching under the pillow to scratch at his scalp gently.

"What's up, bud?"

His response was too muffled to make out.

"Sorry, I didn't get that . . ."

He pushed the pillow aside angrily. His eyes were red-rimmed, but he pretended he wasn't crying. "You shouldn't have left Dad. Who's going to take care of us now? Who's going to help you with a *baby*? Who did you make it with?"

*You know why I left, Aiden. You were right there with me.* She didn't want to discuss that day with him again; not now, anyway.

"Your dad and I made the baby before we got divorced, and I think Emily will volunteer to help . . ." she mused, but he didn't smile. Starla sighed. "It'll be okay, honey. Don't worry, okay?"

Aiden gave her a hard look, then pulled the pillow back over his head to hide his tears.

"Buddy?" She rubbed his back in a bid for his attention again, but he didn't move. "Aren't you excited at all? You're getting a new brother or sister. That's pretty cool, huh?" Aiden kicked one foot against the mattress in a subtle "go away, Mom" move. Resigned, she took the hint.

"Dinner's in thirty," Starla said softly, rising from the bed, trying not to let it sting that her son thought she didn't know what she was doing. *Maybe I don't know. I want to learn to trust my own judgment, but I don't know how. It's always led me astray.*

"I'm not hungry," he said, his voice muffled by the pillow. "Shut the door, please."

AIDEN STILL WASN'T speaking to her when she dropped him off at Charlie's the next day after lunch. Emily, on the other hand, hadn't stopped talking about her new baby sister since dinner last night. Starla told her sternly that this was a family secret and not to tell anyone, and she'd promised. Watching them go, she gave it about 50/50. Emily turned around to wave at her, while Aiden just trudged into the house. The drive back up the mountain was too quiet, and she hit play on the audiobook she'd been listening to. She tried to focus on the words, the purple prose about Lord So-and-So and Lady Whatever, but it just wasn't doing it for her. Nothing was going to distract her from the fact that she was going on a date with a man she really liked this afternoon. *No, love. He said love.* That had her feeling all jumbled inside . . . it wasn't that she thought he was wrong. Being her book fairy was the absolute sweetest thing anyone had ever done for her, and the way he'd stood up for her at the town meeting showed that he was willing to step out of his comfort zone for her. But this . . . all this—the divorce, the pregnancy, her kids—how was this not too much for him? It was too much for her, and it was her life, for heaven's sake. Why on earth was he signing up for this? She was afraid to ask him. It wasn't like he'd proposed or anything . . . *he's not going to propose, is he?* That would be way too much, too fast. Sawyer could be kind of an intense guy, but she couldn't see him going that far. And yet, the way he sometimes looked at her, his gaze like a warm blanket around her shoulders . . . he was clearly invested.

Yet, he seemed to think he *couldn't* get married. *I can't support a wife.* She started to get upset again, just thinking about their conversation about his illness . . . she still didn't understand exactly what he had. He'd said something about a wheelchair the other day, but she was unclear on why epilepsy would put him in a wheelchair. Wait, no, he'd said it wasn't epilepsy, just seizures? She didn't know. But she was going to ask. If he was going to come up onto the porch and kiss the daylights out of her, she felt like she had the right to at least put a name to it. Whatever it was, it had been enough to drive him away from medicine. She kept noticing little things about him that made more sense now . . . he was always explaining scientific phenomena to the kids, knocking on their door to show them a tree frog or a garter snake. The kids, of course, needed no excuse to hang out with him . . . she could barely get Aiden to come inside when Sawyer was out in the garage. Unless it was screen time, of course.

She pulled up to the lodge. Sawyer sat on the front steps in his normal jeans and boots and a gray T-shirt with a worn blue Atlanta baseball cap; in other words, he looked as good as usual. Starla muttered to her hormones to simmer down as she got out of the car. He stood up as she approached, giving her a bright smile.

"It occurred to me," he said, stuffing hands into his back pockets, "that your kids would be gone all afternoon, and I don't have to wait until five. Unless you're busy. You're probably busy. Or maybe you were contemplating a nap, seeing as your house will be quiet and it's Sunday."

She smiled. "I think I could make room in my schedule . . . you want to come inside?"

"No," he said quickly. "I kinda . . . planned something. At my place."

"Of course you did," she said. "Because you're the king of secret gifts, apparently."

Sawyer looked away. "You were never supposed to find out about that. Me and my big mouth."

"A nice mouth, though," she said, sauntering nearer. She wanted another kiss, but she wasn't sure what was allowed. It had all happened so quickly the other night; she wanted to know if she'd just imagined the red-hot chemistry between them, or if it was as real as the timber under her feet. Sawyer must've caught on to her implication, because a slow smile spread across his lips.

"Sugar," he said in a low register, "you want something?"

She shrugged with one shoulder, feeling her face heat. She had no reason to be embarrassed; he'd started it. And he'd clearly liked it. But for some reason, saying it out loud was a little scary still.

"Hey." She turned back to face him; she hadn't realized it, but her gaze had wandered. "You want something from me, you just ask, okay? If it's mine to give, you can have it." She wanted to groan. He was always so direct, so earnest. How was it so easy for him?

"I want a kiss," she murmured. "Maybe more than one."

He sighed as if it was an imposition, when she was quite sure it wasn't. "All right, but if you get carried away again, I'll be forced to intervene."

"Me?" she gasped, feigning shock. "That's not how I remember that encounter *at all*."

"Star," he said patiently, wrapping an arm around her waist as he led her toward his cabin, "my mama raised me to be a gentleman. So if anyone tried to swallow anyone's tongue, it was you."

"Oh, silly me," she laughed, enjoying the way he'd seemed to have recovered from the way he'd mauled her on the front porch. It'd been an extremely pleasant mauling. He paused at the door to his cabin, drawing her closer by her elbows.

"I want to clarify something," he said, his thumbs brushing over the backs of her arms. "I know you're leaving. I just want to be together while we've got the chance. I just want to call you mine for a little while. I'm not trying to keep you here."

Dismay filled her. She turned his words over and over, like a rock rolled downriver, pushing along by an inundation of her own thoughts. He didn't want to keep her? Maybe his feelings weren't as strong as he'd initially told her. She was still trying to decide if that was the most gallant thing she'd ever heard or the stupidest when he kept talking.

"Ainsley said something about you wanting to leave town . . ." *Ah. That explains it.* He looked perplexed, like maybe he'd said the wrong thing, and she knew she needed to respond.

"I haven't decided yet. But yes, it's something I'm looking into." She glanced at him nervously. "Do you . . . have you changed your mind?"

He kissed her. "No. God no. I can't imagine what it would take to change my mind about you, sweetheart, but this isn't it. Not even close."

"Well, if you're not put off by the fact that I'm carrying another man's baby, it does seem like you're pretty hard to repel."

"Let's go inside, I can't have you getting eaten by mosquitoes," he muttered, and she smiled. She didn't see any mosquitoes, but she wasn't going to argue. He opened the door for her, and she couldn't help but look around the small cabin. She hadn't been back inside since the day of the big storm. The big windows with open white cotton curtains made the house feel like an extension of the forest. There was a computer against the wall between the windows on a desk stacked with papers, but no television. The brown leather couches were cozy-looking with soft, dark green chenille pillows and a plaid cherry red throw with long fringe. There were photographs of nature on the walls and lantern-like sconces. At the end of the living room, next to the bathroom, there was another door, which she assumed was the bedroom. Paired with the small but functional kitchen, what more did he really need?

"I thought we could make burgoo," he said, ushering her toward his small kitchen, which already smelled delicious.

"It's pronounced 'burgers,'" she said, wrinkling her nose as she leaned over the simmering pot to sniff at its contents. "But this doesn't look like it."

Sawyer chuckled, shaking his head. "You've got a lot to learn about southern cuisine, sweetheart."

"What's in it?"

"If it walked, crawled or flew, it goes into burgoo," he said in a singsong voice. "Here, you can cut up the potatoes for me."

She hesitated, glancing at him as he got more veggies out of the fridge. "So . . . potatoes are keto, then?"

Sawyer slowly put down the peppers and okra he was holding and shifted so that he was caging her in, with one hand on the counter on either side of her, bending down to look her in the eye. "Are you policing my diet?"

"No," she said, wishing she could back away just a little from that intense stare. "I'm just asking." It wasn't threatening, just very pointed, and pointed exclusively in her direction. She adjusted her glasses in an attempt not to look flustered.

"Starla, please let me make my own choices without guilt. I've been good all week. I deserve a treat sometimes, too."

"Okay," she said, nuzzling his cheek with her nose, knowing he wouldn't want an apology. She was getting better at not saying it, but she still felt the need to soothe the annoyance. "I just don't want to be the reason you're sick."

"You're not. You wouldn't be. I don't think you understand what you . . ." He trailed off as he nuzzled her back now, dragging his beard gently over her cheek.

"What I what?" Her good grammar had once again been decimated by his presence.

"You make me feel better, even when I feel lousy. Having you around. Seeing you smile. Touching you . . . I mean, the touching, that's new, but I'm finding it addictive already." He straightened and adjusted his hat. *Addictive, but perhaps not entirely comfortable . . .* he'd reacted the same way after he'd kissed her the first time. Had to make sure everything was okay when he was done. It was pretty stinking cute. Still, she tried to tamp down the disappointment that bloomed in her belly; why hadn't he just kissed her now?

"Potatoes are a weird flex for a treat, you know," she said, turning back to the counter and pulling a knife from the block. "I'm sure I could find you a better keto treat. There are websites. Lots of them."

"Burgoo is not burgoo without potatoes," he said haughtily. "Everyone knows that."

"I didn't know it," she said, bumping him lightly with her hip.

"Hey, knife safety! You're gonna make me slice off my finger. How am I going to teach surgery if I'm missing a finger?"

She brightened at his words. "Teaching surgery? I haven't heard about this." He pursed his lips in thought, and all she could think about was how that beard was really working for her.

"Yeah, it's . . . it's new. Kyle talked me into it. That guy doesn't give up."

"No, he doesn't," Starla agreed, remembering his courtship with Ainsley with amusement. "So what are you teaching?"

"Just some beginning surgery technique for the interns at Santi-am. I have an exercise in mind already, something one of my residents used. It is sadistic and therefore perfect."

She grinned at him. "Full time? When will you need a ride?"

"Nope, just part time. I thought I could go on Tuesday, if you don't mind. Since you work a half-day anyway."

"That sounds perfect," she said, popping a carrot round into her mouth. She was always hungry these days. Pregnancy was the worst. "And your illness, it's not going to be a problem?"

He was focusing hard on those veggies all of a sudden. "We'll see. I mean, my hands shake, so I can't operate on anyone, but as long as I don't overexert myself, it should be okay."

She summoned her courage. She'd promised herself that she would yesterday, overthinking their whole thing. Maybe his librarian wasn't owed any details, but a girlfriend should be.

"I wanted to ask you," she said slowly, suddenly finding it easier to focus on the food herself, "more about your illness."

"Like what?" He slid the okra off the cutting board into the bubbling pot of red stew.

"Like what kind of MS you have, for starters?"

He didn't say anything. *Oops.*

"You don't have to," she rushed on. "I understand if it's too personal or if you—"

"No," he said softly. "It's all right, Star, I just—" He paused, putting down the knife and bracing himself against the counter, like this was going to hurt, going to cost him, just talking about it. "I should've been more upfront with you. You should know the risks."

She went on with her chopping, pulling the celery toward her. "Risks?"

"I know you think I'm being discriminatory toward myself, but I swear, it's not just about other people. If you get involved with me, you might have to take care of me someday, if this thing goes the distance. You should know that going in. It's not a thing to take lightly."

"It's a little tough to know what I'm committing to, when you won't even tell me what you've got," she said, herding the scraps into a little pile on the corner of her cutting board.

"It's relapsing-remitting, so it comes and goes."

"Okay?" She put down the knife and turned to face him, resting her hips against the counter. At least now she'd know what to Google. "And?"

"And it's the degenerative neurological condition that will likely be my cause of death." *And that explains that thing you said to me so long ago, about how some mysteries are best left unsolved.* But he didn't know that; not really. She couldn't help but poke at the assumption.

"Oh, I don't know," she mused, imitating the way he rubbed at his beard when he was thinking on her smooth chin. "You do live out in the woods. You could get eaten by a bear. Or maybe you'll finally tick off your sister bad enough and she'll take you out and claim the rental house for herself." He didn't say anything, and for a tense moment, she thought she'd offended him. But his lips twitched as he fought off a smile.

"This is serious, Star."

"Okay. I'm sorry."

"Has my sister said something about taking me out? That one feels the most plausible."

She gave a mental sigh of relief; joking was good. Joking was better.

"Not within my hearing, hot stuff. I'd have told you."

His eyes widened. "Hot . . . hot stuff? We're doing pet names now? Did you not hear anything I said?"

"I heard it," she shrugged. "I just don't see why I should dread your death any more than anyone else's. I don't see why taking care of you physically should be a bigger deal than caring for me emotionally. You'll be doing plenty of that, I guarantee it."

Sawyer stared at her for a long moment, then he pulled her into a hug that crushed the air from her lungs. Starla hugged him back, feeling emotion well in her, then recede like the tide. In its wake, it left pure affection; she felt a string had been tied between them, a live wire between his heart and hers. They stood there, holding each other, in his tiny kitchen until her back started hurting. She pulled back a little, and he let go. She tucked her hair behind her ears as he straightened his hat again. *Two peas in a pod, aren't we?*

"Where did you get the ingredients for this meal?" she said, trying to gently transition away from the moment. "I don't remember any of this in your cart last time . . ."

He rubbed at his light beard. "I may have paid a helpful Durand to drop it off this morning."

She laughed. "Maggie again? I knew I was right."

"The girl's hard up for cash," he said defensively. "You know how it is in high school. And it's better than calling my mama, who would have way too many questions for me . . ."

"So you didn't tell her about our date?"

"Not yet. I wasn't leaping to label things. Thought we could just take it slow."

"Yes," she drawled, "because nothing says 'slow' like showing up on my porch, professing your love."

Scowling, he threw an okra stem at her, and she went on, undeterred.

"Not to mention the dour lecture I just got about how I might as well stop loving you if I have an aversion to people who aren't ablebodied . . ."

"You're impossible," he grumbled, but he was smiling, and he threw a fluffy, green carrot top at her, too. She threw that one back.

"Don't make me go get the sprayer, Devereaux. I'll do it. You know I will."

"Fine. Do it. See what happens. You don't scare me, woman."

She lunged for the sink on her right, but he was quicker.

"Not as brave as you touted, dude," she taunted as she tried to wrestle the sprayer away from him, but Sawyer just laughed. He danced away when she tried to step on his foot.

"Not fair! I have to be extra careful with you right now." He was trying to get the water on with his elbow, nudging the faucet handle, and her eyes widened. She lowered her shoulder and knocked him back the few inches she needed in order to clamp her left hand down on the faucet.

"Parlay! I call parlay!"

"I look like a pirate to you?" Sawyer deadpanned, still trying to get the water on. "How long you been wearing that prescription?" He'd slid into a deeper accent, and Starla almost wished he would spray her with water, only so she'd stop melting over it.

"I think I see just fine," she said, fluttering her eyelashes a little. She felt on uneven footing with her flirting . . . it'd been a long time since she'd tried it. They were still wrapped up together, octopus-like, locked in their silly battle, but Sawyer had stopped moving. He stared at her lips unabashedly. She tipped her chin up in invitation, and the heat in his gaze had her melting.

"Let go," he breathed, and she realized he meant the sink. He must think it was a trap. A snicker escaped from her lips. She wouldn't use his lust against him like that. Not yet, anyway.

"You first," she parried.

"Never."

"Fine. We'll do it simultaneously. On three."

He gave her a nod. "One."

"Two."

"Three." To her surprise, he did let go, but he reached for her immediately. He cupped her face in both hands as his lips met hers frantically in a storm of kisses; he rained them down upon her, and she felt rocked by them, every one like a drop of rain watering her dry soul. She drank him in, brushing her fingers along the back of his neck, letting her hands wander over him for the first time, learning the way his soft shirt clung to his strong back. He whipped off his hat, and his hair tickled her skin as he dipped his head lower to press soft, sweet kisses to her neck. As intoxicating as he was, her eyes fluttered open again, and the faucet was right in the corner of her peripheral vision. It was tempting. He seemed wholly distracted. Her bounty was right there. Maybe she could just . . .

"Don't even think about it," he said suddenly, lifting his head swiftly to cock an eyebrow at her, spearing her with a stern look, and she grinned back at him so hard, it made her face hurt.

"How did you know?"

"Because that's what I'd be thinking, if I were you." He scooped her up in his arms, and she squeaked out a protest.

"What are you doing?"

"Moving you a safer distance from the sink, that's what. So I can focus on more pleasurable pursuits without having a care for your wicked ways."

"What about the burgoo?"

Sawyer paused halfway between the kitchen and the couch, and the way he glanced back told her he was torn. "It can simmer for a few minutes before we add the rest."

"I'll try not to get carried away," she whispered, laying a hand to his cheek. Sawyer grinned as he settled them on the couch and picked up right where they'd left off.

# CHAPTER TWENTY-FIVE

SAWYER WAS NERVOUS. Sweaty palms, soaked white undershirt under his button down style nervous, and he ran a hand through hair for the thousandth time that morning. Maybe he should've gotten a haircut. He hadn't thought about it.

"Bye kids," Starla said, pulling up to the curb of the school. "Love you guys. Have a great day." On time, for once. It was considerate of her to make sure he wouldn't be late for his first day of work.

*It's just a trial run. Might not work out. Might be a bigger mistake than that whale ODOT tried to blow up on the coast in the seventies.* Either way, he was about to find out, and his hopes were officially up. Starla reached out and squeezed his hand. He looked at her, expecting words, but she just kept driving, holding his hand.

*This is what a partnership would feel like, if she were staying. Just quietly being there for each other. If I were smart, I'd be scared of this, not my first day back in a hospital.* But he wasn't. He let the weight of her hand on his leg stabilize him. Sawyer let his mind drift back to their second date last weekend. Well, he wasn't really sure if it was their second, because she'd been making him come to dinner every night since then. He tried to give her money for his portion of the meal, but she'd just laughed and kissed him. So he'd taken to stuffing it in her purse when she was in the bathroom, which was somewhat frequently. When Aiden caught him, Sawyer hadn't felt comfortable asking the kid to keep a secret from his mom (#creepy), but Aiden must've agreed it was for the best, because Starla didn't come stomping over to the cabin with a fist full of cash. But if it was their second date, it had been a good one, just like their first one. He'd cooked for her again; Dutch pancakes with marionberry syrup. Simple food this time, which left more time for guilt-free kissing, and he'd taken full advantage of that. He loved kissing her; when he wasn't actually kissing her, he'd think about kissing her and replay their highlight reel in his head. It was going to make focusing difficult today. Maybe he could get one for the road to tide him over until tonight after her kids were in bed.

"Sawyer?" He turned to look at her. Starla watched him expectantly. "You good?" They were parked in the drop-off zone of the hospital. He kissed her knuckles, feeling full of gratitude to her just for being her, then gave his neck and shoulders both a roll as he grabbed his backpack off the floor of the van.

"Lunch!" she called after him as he got out, and he poked his head back in to grab his insulated lunch box, too. He walked around the front so she couldn't drive away yet. When he stopped in front of her window, she rolled it down, and he tapped his lips. Starla smiled as she leaned in to meet his kiss.

"You'll be great, hot stuff. Knock 'em dead."

"We usually aim for the opposite in a hospital setting," he reminded her with a grin, as he backed toward the front doors, still not really ready to say goodbye to her. Dogs were probably okay, but was he allowed to bring an emotional support human? Because she'd be perfect.

Sawyer went into the ER, which is where he'd agreed to meet Kyle. Turns out, if he hadn't practiced medicine in the last year, he had to take a qualifying test, so he'd done that last week. He'd mailed off his paperwork, but didn't actually have his license back yet, which is why he'd decided not to wear the white coat today. He didn't want anyone to think he was here to practice medicine just yet. Today was just preliminary stuff: meeting the interns, filling out paperwork.

"Can I help you?" A tall male nurse in green scrubs with short, blond hair greeted him.

"Well, I hope so. I'm looking for Dr. Durand."

"Which one?"

Sawyer chuckled. "Ah, good point. Kyle."

He checked a calendar on the wall. "Rotation schedule says he's supposed to work, but I haven't seen him yet today."

*Great. That figures.* He'd told him he'd be in today, but things sometimes changed on the rotation schedule, he knew.

"Oh. Hmm. Well, all right, then. Thanks, man."

"Are you sure there's nothing I can help you with? I'm Trevor," he said, sticking out his hand.

"Sawyer Devereaux."

"Oh! You're the new guy who's going to help with the surgery instruction, right? Kyle told me about you. Let me see if I can find Dr. Baker." Without waiting for an answer, Trevor took off down the hallway, leaving Sawyer to stare after him. That was better than trying to walk to the library to meet up with Starla, so he'd let the man try at least.

A few minutes later, Trevor came back with Dr. Baker, and he saw the resemblance between her and Ainsley's former roommate Winnie immediately. Her silvery blonde hair was swept back into a bun and her light makeup was flawless.

"Sandra Baker," she said, extending her hand for a firm handshake.

"Nice to meet you, ma'am. I believe I know your daughter and son-in-law."

"Oh, how nice. Dr. Durand is regrettably out sick today. Walk with me."

He did, feeling like a kid who showed up late to the first day of school. The backpack probably wasn't helping.

"Dr. Durand tells me you're a surgeon. Is that correct?"

"Yes, ma'am."

"Where did you study?"

"Oregon State, then Emory for medical school."

"Impressive." She looked like she meant it sincerely. "Why aren't you practicing medicine now?"

He sighed a little. "I joined Doctors Without Borders a few years back. While I was in Honduras, I developed symptoms that were later diagnosed as multiple sclerosis. Surgery was the only branch of medicine I'd ever considered practicing, but my hands were no longer steady enough. It dealt me quite a blow."

"Understandable." She paused and turned to him. "Why don't you shadow me with the interns this morning? You can look at our program, see how you might help. I don't mean to be crass, but we're fairly desperate for help. The program has put more of a strain on my physicians than I anticipated."

*Was that crass?* He made a mental note to keep his 'not in the South' mindset on and not to invite Dr. Baker over for dinner with his family. She'd probably faint.

"That sounds fine. Thanks. I didn't mean to put a wrench in your plans for today."

She waved away his comment. "Let's start with the interns, shall we?"

He met Greg Baker and Tharushi Udawatte; he already knew Daniel Durand, but he made a point to greet him warmly. Even from his cursory observations, they all seemed capable and compassionate. Dr. Baker clearly did not suffer fools, which he appreciated. He just hoped he wasn't one. He watched Dr. Udawatte suture; her patient had injured her finger, using a bread knife to cut apart cardboard, and Sawyer gave her pointers over her shoulder. Even though he wasn't the one doing the surgery, knowing that he was contributing to good care was a rush. Even though he was just following them around, he was amazed at how many questions he could help with, how many little tricks and tips he'd saved up over the years. Maybe Kyle hadn't been as delusional as he'd thought to ask for his help.

The morning went by quickly, and he was surprised to see it was two o'clock already when Starla appeared at his elbow. He hadn't even eaten the lunch he'd so carefully packed. It had him a little disoriented, and not just due to low blood sugar.

"Ready to go?"

"Yeah," he said. "Well, no."

She cocked an eyebrow at him.

"I mean yes, I'm exhausted, and I've still got a Honda to work on this afternoon. But no, because I feel alive again."

"Why?"

"Look around, woman," he said, spreading his arms out. "This is where the action happens."

"An unexpected sentiment from my favorite forest hermit."

Sawyer laughed from his belly, and then it happened. It was too sudden for him to do anything about it. One moment, he was talking, laughing with her; the next moment, he felt his muscles fail as warmth and wetness spread across his dress pants. Sawyer stared down at himself in horror, then quickly moved his hands in front of his pelvis. He'd been so busy all day, he'd neglected to make sure his bladder was emptied often enough. And when he met her gaze, he could tell. He'd covered it too late. She'd seen.

Immediately, she pulled him into a tight hug, covering the spot completely, and he moved his hands to hold her back.

"Hold this," she said, shoving her purse at him, and he took it without arguing. He didn't have a better plan. Unlike at home, there were no extra clothes. He hadn't even brought a jacket; it had been a warm June so far.

"Dr. Devereaux, are you headed out?" Greg Trout was approaching, and even though the spot was covered, Starla stayed in front of him protectively when she turned to face the intern. *Best emotional support human ever.*

He nodded. "Yes. Until I get my driver's license back, I've gotta go when my . . ." He didn't know what to call Starla, and it made an already tense, uncomfortable situation even worse.

*Friend? Make out buddy? Neighbor? Renter?* It was too early for *girlfriend*, he was pretty sure. They'd been on two dates, and she was considering moving out of state. This wasn't anything approaching commitment, no matter how much he wanted it to be. Wishing wouldn't change things . . . but he couldn't help himself.

"Chauffeur," Starla offered, holding out a hand, and Greg shook it.

"Yes, when my chauffeur shows up for me. But I'll talk to Dr. Durand about coming in another day this week."

"Please do, it was really helpful to have you around today. We all thought so."

"Well, I enjoyed working with y'all."

She whipped around so she was still covering him. "The kids are out in the car by themselves, and I don't want them left alone. Would you mind going out to sit with them? I've got to hit the bathroom anyway, so I'll grab your bag."

He nodded slowly. Was it less plausible than him getting his own stuff? Yes. But Dr. Trout didn't seem to notice the discrepancy in the logic; he jumped at the chance to help Starla, leading her down the hall toward the locker room, and he made a dash for the front doors before anyone else stopped to talk to him and realized he was holding a women's purse over his crotch.

He cursed himself all the way to the car. Doctors really did make the worst patients. He could've talked to Dr. Rose about it. But he wasn't ready to manage another symptom; it was easier to pretend it was an isolated event. Easier not to think about another complication, another medication, another round of testing to try to ferret out whether it was nerve damage or just stress incontinence. He cursed inwardly again. He was tired. And something about being around healthy people made him all the more self-conscious. The seizures were bad enough, but this? This made him an object of pity. Anger and helplessness welled inside him, threatening to spill tears. And yet . . . and yet, she'd played it cool. Covering for him. He'd never had that since he'd gotten sick. His mama and Paige had been there for him, but it was in a sad, anxious sort of way. Starla, on the other hand, just seemed to roll with it. She'd rolled with that first seizure, and she'd done the same thing just now.

He opened the passenger side door and got in the front seat. "Hey, you two." He blinked. "Em, isn't that Aiden's tablet?"

"Mine died. He said he wanted to share," she explained and Sawyer pivoted to give him a fist bump. Something had shifted in the kid recently. He couldn't put his finger on it, but he was doing better. He just seemed less angry. Maybe it was the tai chi. Starla came around the front of the car and hopped in.

"Everyone buckled in?"

He lowered his voice as she passed him his backpack. "Did you really have to use the bathroom?"

She snorted. "I'm a pregnant lady, Sawyer. I *always* have to use the bathroom."

He turned toward the window. He appreciated her efforts to protect him, he just . . . wished it wasn't necessary.

"Did you know," she said conversationally, "that ever since Emily projectile vomited on me in church, I keep a spare set of clothes for everyone in my family in the back of my car?"

"How would I know that?" he asked, grumpy.

"It's true. It was mega gross," Aiden added. "I remember." He gave an exaggerated shudder, and Sawyer gave him a small, begrudging smile.

"There's more room in the box, if you're interested," Starla said, then abruptly changed the subject to what they would have for supper. She just seemed to assume he would join them nightly now, and the one time he'd tried to take off right after the meal, she hauled him back over to the front porch and demanded a foot rub in retribution. He had given it to her gladly, of course. She'd played it cool today all right, but he was still shut down inside with embarrassment. It was hard not to want to slink off to his cabin for the night, rather than changing and coming back. *Pity party, table for one? Don't mind if I do.*

She must've sensed it, somehow, his plan to sequester himself. Starla caught him by the shirt sleeve before he'd even made it past the garden boxes.

"You're coming to dinner, right?" she said. Her tone made it clear that it was not actually a suggestion.

"It ain't necessary, Star. I'm fine."

"I didn't say you weren't fine. I said I want you to come to dinner, just like every other night." How she managed a gaze so soft and so hard at the same time, he'd never know. But that was Star all over; tougher than she gave herself credit for, and yet falling apart over little things that made him scratch his head sometimes. Maybe it was the pregnancy hormones.

"Why?" He hated how vulnerable the word came out, how disbelieving, but he couldn't help it. It was as uncontrollable as his bladder, apparently.

"Because you're . . . you're . . ." She seemed to be searching for just the right word, and it made him feel strangely better that he wasn't the only one who couldn't find what he wanted to say sometimes. "Because you belong with us." She stepped closer, close enough that he could see all the shades of variegated brown in her eyes, but he closed his eyes when she kissed his lips. "You belong with us," she repeated more firmly. "On good days. On crap days. All the days." He wasn't sure if he'd want to kiss someone who smelled like urine, but hey, he wasn't going to turn her down. Not when she pulled him forward with such tenacity, such sincerity. Not in a thousand years.

"For what it's worth, it was a crappy day all around." She pulled out her phone and turned it so he could see the screen.

**Charlie:** You're pregnant?

**Charlie:** Don't bother denying it. Em told me.

**Charlie:** It's mine, right? The baby?

**Charlie:** See, the universe is telling us to get back together, baby. It's a sign.

"Ooh. Not good."

"No," she sighed. "He should've heard it from me. I just . . . wasn't ready to tell him yet."

He kissed her again. If she needed distraction tonight, he could provide that.

"Not tacos," he muttered, breaking the kiss. As much as he loved Emily and her Mexican food obsession, he was kind of over it.

"Not tacos," she agreed. "Chicken nuggets and mac and cheese for them, grilled chicken and salad for us. Come back as soon as you've changed, and I'll let you toss the salad. I made a new keto dressing: green goddess!"

"Not tacos?" Emily wailed, and Starla sighed.

"Be back here in twenty or I'm coming after you," she threatened as she went to deal with her daughter, and he had no doubt that she'd make good on it.

# CHAPTER TWENTY-SIX

THE DAY HAD FINALLY arrived: Ainsley and Kyle were getting married today. Starla gave her friend a big hug as she sat in front of the mirror in the fourth grade Sunday school room; all the women were gathered there to get ready, having mostly recovered from the bachelorette party. That is, they were less bloated now from all the chocolate they had eaten and had corrected the bags under their eyes from how late they had stayed up. Starla, of course, had fallen asleep on the couch and had awoken to texts from Sawyer wondering why she hadn't come home. When she texted him back at 1:00 a.m., he answered, making her heart flip around in her chest like a salmon in a rowboat, which was appropriate, because she was completely hooked on him. She had successfully resisted the urge to apologize and had gone back to sleep. As matron of honor, her responsibilities had been blessedly limited until now, but today, she was determined to be there for Ainsley.

"Nervous?" Starla asked. She was. She was about to stand up in front of the whole town, and there were no baggy sweaters to hide behind this time.

"No, just ready to get started," Ainsley said. She could deny it all she wanted, but her hands were shaking as she tried to apply her mascara, and Starla put her palm out for the applicator. Ainsley gave her a tight smile and handed it over gratefully.

"Look up for me," Starla murmured, and she carefully brushed the black makeup onto her friend's lashes. "Is this waterproof?"

"Should it be?"

"You're not going to cry? I always cry at weddings. Mine was no exception."

"I have a handkerchief . . ."

"That's good. Just keep taking deep breaths. Try to enjoy the moment. It goes by fast."

"It already is. How much time do we have left?"

"Plenty. Have you eaten something? I don't think I got a bite of catering at my own wedding." Starla paused to pull a package of almonds out of her purse, but Ainsley put a hand on hers.

"I'm getting married today." She looked a little lost, and Starla chuckled. She set aside everything and wrapped her friend in a warm embrace.

"Yes, you're getting married today. And you're gaining a wonderful life partner, and you're going to be so happy together most of the time. And even when you're not, you'll work through it. I promise."

"I want you to be here to see that," Ainsley whispered back, and Starla heard the catch in her voice. Grief coursed through her, and she hugged Ainsley tighter. She couldn't lie to her, even on her wedding day, a day that was supposed to be perfect in every way.

"Whatever happens, I promise we won't lose touch."

Ainsley nodded, then released her. "I think I'm ready for my dress." Starla adored the dress they'd picked out: a snow white 1950s-style tea dress, knee-length with a full skirt. The satin bodice looked wrapped around her at an angle, and it made Ainsley look a little taller than she actually was. With her bright red lips and her long blonde curls cascading down her back, she looked every bit the bombshell. Her shoes for the ceremony were black with white polka dots, nice and tall, and she had white Chucks for the reception. It was all just so perfectly . . . her. And as a bonus, the dress had pockets.

"Are you still nervous about Kyle's reaction?"

She nodded ardently. "He sent me a bunch of pictures that looked nothing like this. It was all silk and lace, very Victorian. I just don't want him to be disappointed. But I especially don't want him to *tell everyone* he's disappointed." They laughed.

"I'll try to remind him before it starts."

"Thanks, Star," she sighed. "I don't know what I'd do without you."

"You'll be just fine," she said, hoping it was true. Hoping she'd be just fine without Ainsley, too.

"Starla," said Winnie, poking her head into the room. "Kyle's out here, and he needs a moment of your time."

"Be right back," she winked at Ainsley, then slid out into the hallway. "Hey, Kyle."

Ainsley's dark-haired fiancé was wearing a black tux, stimming, shaking his hands, pacing the hall in his shiny black shoes. "Is she ready? We're starting in twenty minutes."

"She just put her dress on," Starla soothed. "She'll be ready on time."

"Is that the last thing she does or the first thing? I'm unfamiliar with the process. I agreed to include Maggie as a bridesmaid, thinking that she could be a source of inside information, but she's been completely useless. She hasn't texted me a single update since 12 p.m.." Starla was fairly sure it was only 12:40 now, but she was clearly not going to convince him that it wasn't an unforgivable sin.

"Putting on the dress is the last thing," she said, trying not to smirk.

"What does the dress look like?" he asked, bouncing on his toes. "No, wait, don't tell me. She wanted it to be a surprise. I should respect that." He took a deep breath and let it out slow. "She's not having second thoughts?"

"Of course not," Starla said gently. "She's very excited to marry you."

"Good," he said, nodding to himself. "That's good. I'm not having second thoughts, either. You can tell her if you want."

"Okay, I will," she agreed with a smile. "Don't forget to keep your opinion about the dress to yourself, if you can."

"She mentioned that at least ten times. I heard her the first ten times." He checked his watch, then started shaking his hands again. "Nineteen minutes now. I haven't seen her in 24 hours. That feels odd. I don't like it."

"Should I have her text you?"

"No, she's done that. I'll feel better when I see her in nineteen minutes."

"Is there anything I can do for you in the meantime?"

"I don't think so. I just need to get started. I just wanted to check on her."

"Okay." She paused. "I should probably go finish getting ready, then?"

His eyes widened and he froze, staring at her. "You're not ready? Go get ready! Why are we standing here talking if you're not ready? You've only got nineteen minutes!"

"Okay," Starla laughed, and before she turned away, she gave Kyle a big hug, pinning both his arms to his sides. "It'll be okay, Kyle. Even if it doesn't go off perfectly. You're still in love. You'll still be married. Okay?"

"Yes. Okay. Please don't wrinkle my tux, I'm taking photos soon." He wriggled out of her grasp and started down the hall, then turned back, tapping his watch. "Eighteen minutes."

Starla was still laughing when she went back into the Sunday school room.

"How is he? Freaking out?" Ainsley called.

"Just a little bit. It'd call it a level seven freak out on a scale of ten. I tried hugging him. It didn't help."

"No, it wouldn't," Ainsley laughed. "He's very paranoid about his tux."

"He also asked me to communicate that he is not having second thoughts," Starla said, sitting down to straighten her hair.

"I should hope not!" Ainsley exclaimed, and her bridesmaids all laughed, even Maggie. Starla had noticed that the girl seemed to feel a bit out of place, so she offered to help with her makeup, which Maggie accepted gratefully.

"I wanted to thank you for helping out my book fairy," she said as she applied a light powder to her nose and cheeks, but Maggie's expression remained blank.

"What's a book fairy?"

Starla folded her arms just above her baby bump. "Drop the act, sister. He ratted you out."

Maggie smiled politely. "No idea what you're talking about. Sorry." The girl should really consider a career in espionage. Her face was impassive, giving away nothing. She was clearly not going to admit to anything without talking to Sawyer first, and Starla had to respect that. He'd already told her she'd refused his offered payment, beyond the new Terry Pratchett he'd ordered for the library.

They were handed their bouquets of sunflowers, white gladiolas, and anemones. They lined up. Starla was escorted in by Daniel. She waved at Emily and Aiden on her way by, who were sitting with Charlie. She couldn't let her gaze rest on Charlie for long; she gritted her teeth and made her smile remain on her face. The fact that he'd been blowing up her phone with texts and questions and pleading for her to come home would not ruin this day.

There were lots of Ainsley's former students in the congregation, and the sanctuary buzzed with their barely-contained energy. Kyle stood woodenly up front, like he was trying not to stim, and her heart went out to him. But he softened as Ainsley arrived at the end of the aisle, craning his neck to see her better. Starla watched his face go from confusion to acceptance to delight when his gaze finally landed on her beaming face.

Despite the tender scene playing out in front of her, out of the corner of her eye, Starla noticed Sawyer. He looked handsome as ever in his black tux; they'd picked the garment up together a few days earlier, but he'd been quiet and he hadn't wanted her to come in with him. She was afraid he was still dwelling on the pants incident; she'd been afraid to bring it up with him too directly, as it seemed to really bother him. But Sawyer wasn't watching Kyle descended the steps to escort Ainsley up, or Ainsley as she kissed her father on the cheek. He was watching her, his gaze heavy as he looked her up and down in her sunny yellow bridesmaid dress. And he didn't stop just because Kyle cleared his throat to speak.

"I don't enjoy speaking in front of large audiences, but I am confident this will be worth my personal discomfort. I have waited approximately thirteen years to make Ainsley mine. She is inestimably precious to me, and I'm extremely happy to be marrying her today. And while we don't need your presence to make it legal, we both appreciate you coming here today as witnesses. So welcome." A little light laughter rippled through the congregation, but it was obviously meant kindly. His mom, Farrah, was already crying. Kyle paused as his gaze fell on her, but she and Evan both gave him a thumbs up, and he went on. "Please silence your cell phones, since this is being recorded for posterity. Children are welcome as long as they won't disrupt the ceremony to the point it cannot be heard. Thank you." He turned back to Ainsley's uncle, who was officiating. "Go ahead."

The ceremony went by quickly. Kyle choked up a little during their vows, and Ainsley offered him her handkerchief. Their unity candle wouldn't light, but they both laughed and rolled with it. And then it was over, and they were recessing. Starla hurried to the bathroom, and she was the first one to reach a stall. A few moments later, she heard two more people enter, taking the stalls on either side of her.

"Is it just my imagination, or did our lovely matron of honor look a little bit . . ."

"Preggers? I thought so, too."

Starla stilled, hardly daring to breathe. She didn't want to hear this. She didn't want stupid town gossip to ruin this lovely day. She didn't want to listen to Gracie Taylor and Patricia Banks say another word; she knew it was them, because they'd been in a play together in high school. Clearly, they were still full of drama.

"Some people just never learn their lesson, I guess," Gracie went on.

"I know, right? You'd have thought someone would've given her the talk by now about birth control."

"I bet it's Sawyer Devereaux's. She's been staying up there on his property."

"The medical school dropout? Well, birds of a feather, I guess . . ." They'd finished their business, and they both exited their stalls as Starla silently fumed. They could say whatever they wanted about her, but thinking badly of Sawyer was a bridge too far. Starla flushed and pushed open the stall door with her head held high.

"I heard he's got a thing for divorcées," she said, as if she'd been part of the conversation the whole time. "Knocks them up and cuts them loose. That's why he never comes into town, he's too busy impregnating women on the rebound." She turned on the water to wash her hands and glanced up into the mirror at their mortified faces. "And speaking of people who don't learn, y'all should know better than to gossip about a pregnant lady in the bathroom. I basically live here." With that, she turned and walked out, still livid. Her shaking legs carried her through the church to find her family, but her mind was officially made up. She was leaving this town and their hurtful speculation about her life behind.

The reception was across town at the VA hall, and it gave her time to calm down as she drove. Charlie had returned Aiden and Emily to her before he went home; he'd tried to talk to her about the baby, but she'd shut him down again. She couldn't deal with this right now. She'd told him to come by the library a week from Monday. She'd have to work out a plan by then. She'd need time to talk to her lawyer, lock down a job, figure out housing . . . there was a lot to do. The VA hall looked beautiful, the height of summer decadence. Twinkle lights lit the inside, hanging from the ceiling like stars. Wildflowers in mismatched vases were tucked onto every table, windowsill and serving table where they could reasonably be placed. Champagne with blueberries was circulating, and Starla wanted one. The cake was gorgeous; she wondered if Kyle would figure out that the ring on it was the one dropped into the lava in Mordor and not a wedding ring.

"Your dance card full?" Sawyer asked, appearing at her table as she tried to get Em and Aiden to eat something healthy before they got their cake.

"Sure you want to be seen with me?" Gracie and Patricia were just two of many who were whispering about her today, she was sure.

"Heck yes, sugar." He held out his hand with a lopsided grin. "It's gonna cement my reputation real good. Come on." He glanced at the kids. "Y'all eat your carrot sticks like good little bunnies, and I'll have your mama back in a few minutes."

The music was up tempo, heavy on the sax, and a man was singing, but she couldn't understand the words. Starla took Sawyer's offered hand tentatively.

"I don't know how to swing dance," she said, letting him pull her toward the dance floor anyway. It was one of Ainsley's favorite things to do, now that she had someone to dance with, but she'd never learned. Charlie had never taken her anywhere, and usually, she was stuck with the kids. Not as often now that they were getting older, but she was about to start that cycle over again with baby number three.

"Ah, it's easy, sugar. Here, give me both your hands." He pulled her in, his left hip touching her right, then gently swung her out and back in on the other side. "And I never thought of it, but it's great for ladies in your condition."

"And what condition would that be?" she asked, smirking.

"Great. Great condition, you're fantastic. We'll skip the lifts and the slides this time," he said, smiling. "Put a little country in your swing." She fumbled her way through the steps he showed her, smiling hard, working up a sweat. When she turned to check on her kids, she saw that her parents had come over to sit with them, and to her surprise, they smiled and waved at her. She waved back, slightly perplexed. They'd been pretty consistently mad at her since the divorce proceedings began. Maybe now that it was over . . . but her mom was pointing at her belly, giving her a thumbs up. *Oh, I get it. They think I got pregnant to get Charlie back. Right.*

"Hold me please," she murmured to Sawyer. It was a slower song, and she pointedly turned her back on her family.

"Hey. What's wrong?" he asked, pulling her close.

She shook her head, not wanting to talk about it, but he'd followed her gaze.

"Your folks are scowling at me pretty hard. I hope they don't hurt themselves."

"Is that possible, doctor? Because I'd be okay with it."

"Sadly, no." He let his forehead rest against hers. "At least we have good company at this shindig, huh?"

"Yeah," she said, closing her eyes. "At least we have that." *At least I have you. At least for now.*

# CHAPTER TWENTY-SEVEN

THE NEXT WEEK WAS FULL of stares, whispers, and even some genuine congratulations, all of which made it tedious. She was late to work every morning, but she didn't care anymore. She was exhausted from staying up late, doing research. Trying to figure out what she'd need, trying to plan this phase better than she had the last. She'd tried to talk to her parents at the wedding; it had not gone well.

"Moving? Where?"

She'd demurred at first, trying to deflect, but her mother wouldn't be put off.

"Arizona? That's over a thousand miles away! You've almost got him back now, why would you give up?"

"I was never trying to get Charlie back, Mom." She'd been too tired and depressed to argue with her. "Would you come and help me when the baby's born? You could see Aunt Rosie. I know it's been a while."

"Of course, I'll help you. But I don't understand this, Starla . . ."

They'd changed the subject then, as Maggie came to get her for her toast. Now it was Monday, the day she'd promised to talk to Charlie about future plans. Ainsley was back from her honeymoon, and she'd come by the library. She'd claimed to be looking to hang out with the kids, probably hoping to change Starla's mind about moving now that she could devote all her time to it, since school was out. She'd walked them over to the school playground, giving them a break from the confines of the library.

Starla tried all morning, but she could not add the book fairy's donations from the previous week to the library's circulation. Not knowing where they came from. Not knowing who'd sent them, who'd sent all the ones before. Every time she tried to pick up the first book, she felt Sawyer's gaze on her again, standing in front of that church. She felt his arms around her when she'd needed holding. She tasted his lips against hers, dismantling her carefully. The closer he got, the more it was going to hurt when she left, but she couldn't bring herself to push him away.

She must have seemed stressed, because Hattie offered to move all the chairs for the Mind Readers herself, and Starla let her. She'd never treated the library patrons so badly in the past; she always had things ready for them. She was dropping so many balls lately. It was all too much.

"Your book fairy make their drop?" Hattie asked as Starla leaned against the big windows, looking out at the front lawn.

"His," Starla corrected, and Hattie's head turned toward her slowly, her smile almost sad.

"You finally caught him? Rats. I was rooting for him. I thought the seizures might ruin it for him, but Maggie was a good solution . . . I've gotta give him credit for that."

"How did you even know?"

"Saw him once when I was going fishing. You always thought he came at night, but he got up early instead. Pretty smart, really, considering how you struggle with punctuality anyway."

"Why didn't you tell me?" Starla whispered, pulling her sweater tighter around her middle.

"What, that he was in love with you? It's as plain as the nose on my face, so I didn't really think I'd have to . . . and it didn't entirely seem like my business."

Starla snorted, wiping her nose on her sleeve. "Like that's ever stopped you."

"Are you accusing me of being a meddler, Ms. Moore?"

"That's right," Starla said, reclaiming some of her composure. "You make the whole town your business."

"My great grandfather founded this town. What would you have me do, abandon it to its own devices? I don't think so." Some of the other members of the Mind Readers approached the circle, and Starla went back to her desk, shaking her head.

When Starla saw Charlie coming up the walk, she tried to jump up and meet him outside, but she wasn't quick enough.

"Hey, babe," he grimaced. "What did you—"

She held out the white envelope to him. He waved it off.

"You don't have to pay me back for anything."

"I'm not. Just open it, please."

Warily, he took the envelope and slid his finger under the flap to break the seal. She'd sealed it on purpose. She was doing this. One way or another. Whatever it took. She'd sealed that envelope with every ounce of determination in her body, even though the act was ultimately meaningless. It didn't feel meaningless.

She saw the moment he started to catch on, his eyebrows snapping together and his mouth turning down in a deep scowl. "What is this?"

"Legal notice. I'm leaving, Charlie. I'm moving to Arizona. Since we have joint custody, I'm obligated to inform you in writing. We can work out a new schedule."

Charlie sat down on a wooden bench in the foyer, and it didn't look intentional. He still hadn't looked at her, his eyes scanning the legalese her cousin/lawyer had drafted.

"This says you need my agreement," he murmured.

"Yes." She took a deep breath before she went on. "But if you don't give it to me, I don't need your agreement to move less than sixty miles away. I've got a nice little town picked out that's 59 miles from here. Either way, I'm out."

He did look up then, and his eyes were glassy. "Did I really hurt you that bad, Star?"

"You're just now figuring that out?" It came out sharp, and she wanted to take the words back as soon as they left her mouth. She had no need to torture him or exact revenge. She just needed to leave.

His eyebrows snapped together. "An hour away would be a lot better than a plane ride away . . ." He set down the paper carefully. "I don't know how I feel about the kids being so far away. I don't know how I feel about you being without any support, about to give birth."

"My mom can fly down for the birth. We've already discussed it. And I'm no longer your concern."

"Star, I'll always love you . . ." he whispered, and one of the tears rolled down his cheek. "I don't know how to stop."

She put a hand on his shoulder and gave it a little squeeze. "Then you need to work harder. Because I am never going to come home. I will never be your wife again. This was not some strange game, some ploy for me to get you to repent. I don't care if you repent. I want to heal. I can't do that with you, Charlie. Maybe you don't mean to, maybe you never meant to, but you just keep hurting me, and I'm not going to let you anymore."

He lunged for her hand, like he could feel her slipping away. "I won't cheat, not ever again, I promise, baby. I mean it, Star. Please, don't do this. Don't take the kids away. Don't walk out of my life for good. Don't leave me here without my . . ." His words slowed from a torrent to a trickle abruptly; he must have seen the stony deter- mination on her face as she pulled her hand away. Because for the first time, his words truly meant nothing to her. She had armor now against his charms. She had too much self-respect to take that crap.

"What about Fourth of July?" he asked quietly.

"What about it?"

"I've got the kids. It's my holiday. If you won't be here . . ."

"Okay. I won't leave until after the Fourth." But she wasn't giving an inch on the actual leaving. Not this time. "But let me go. You owe me, Charlie, for all the shit you put me through. You owe it to me to let me be happy. I need this. I need to start over."

He mumbled something, but the word was so quiet, she missed it.

"What?"

"I said okay. You can go. You can move to Arizona." Charlie buried his face in his hands and sobbed. Starla stood there and stared at him, disbelief preventing her from responding at all. Until today, she'd never seen Charlie cry. Not a manly tear in awe of her beauty at their wedding. Not when their babies were born. Not even when the Seahawks lost the Super Bowl to the Patriots in 2015, though she thought he'd come close then. And now here he was, completely losing it in a public place. She wasn't the only one staring; several library patrons were standing a few feet away, whispering. Mavis came out of the back, gently taking Charlie by the shoulders and guiding him into the back. Starla gave each of the onlookers a hard stare, and when they stared back at her, she yelled, "Show's over!" Snatching her purse from under the desk, she made herself walk out of the library with her head held high, even if she had just broken her ex-husband accidentally. She'd gotten what she wanted; she'd gotten what she needed. So why did she feel so disgusted with herself? The kids were just walking up the sidewalk with Ainsley, who went wide-eyed when she saw Starla's defiant expression.

"Everything okay?"

If this day belonged in the toilet, she might as well flush the rest of it.

"Yes, everything's fine. Guess what, kids? We're moving to Arizona."

They both stared at her, slack-jawed, their breaths shallow, then turned to look at each other, as if hoping for clarification. Finding none, Emily burst into tears, and Aiden immediately started to howl about how he wasn't going, his face red with the shouting. And to her surprise, Ainsley's eyes were filled with tears, too. She couldn't handle this now, any of it; she was *so tired*. She'd hit her limit. Grabbing both kids by the hand, she dragged them to the car, still screaming and crying. Em got in, her face puffy and tear-stained. Aiden, however, planted his feet firmly, arms braced against the opening to the car.

"I'm not going." She didn't know if he was talking about Arizona or home, but either way, the verdict was the same.

"You don't have a choice," she informed him. "Get in the car." He either wasn't reading her tone correctly or he didn't care, because he shook his head slowly, chest heaving. Either way, she was over it. Outwardly, she was calm, but inside, a disturbing ruthlessness had taken hold of her. She was leaving. If he didn't want to get on board, that was his problem. Ainsley was here. Charlie was here. Someone would help him. That's the kind of town this was. They helped their own, unless their own got herself divorced and knocked up. The bitter thought just drove her compassion farther out of reach, and she climbed in and started the car.

"Mom?" Aiden said, and he suddenly sounded uncertain. She huffed out a humorless laugh; why did this family not take her seriously? Charlie's words rang in her ears and made her chest hurt.

"Move back, Aiden," she said, closing the side door with the touch of a button. "I don't want you to get hurt."

"Mom!" He shouted, jumping back to the sidewalk as she backed out of the spot. "Mom! You can't leave me here!"

She rolled down the passenger side window. "I asked you to get into the car. If you want to come with me, get. in. the. car."

Frantically, he shook his head. "I'm not going to Arizona. I'm *not*." Ainsley shifted over and put her hands on his shoulders soothingly, but he shook her off.

"We're not leaving for a few weeks, at least."

"That's not what I mean," he shouted. "I mean, I want to talk about this! You keep dragging me around! You don't even ask me what I want!"

"And who do you think asked me?" she boomed. "You think I wanted to—" She was going to say something stupid, something she'd never admitted to him, about how she'd first felt when she'd gotten pregnant with him. She couldn't do that to him, she didn't want to hurt him like that. She didn't *want* to hurt him at all. But even though she'd dropped this bomb on him the absolute wrong way, he was going to have to learn to obey her, even when he didn't want to. She was about to become his primary parent. There would be no Aunt Ainsley in Arizona, no Dad, no Grandma or Grandpa to go crying to. His eyes widened as she rolled up the window.

"Mom!" he cried again, and she waited one more beat for him to come get in the car, then she put it in drive and accelerated out of the parking lot.

"Mama!" Em shrieked from the back seat. "Don't leave Aiden!"

"He'll be fine, he's with Aunt Ainsley. Daddy's in the library." In her rear view mirror, she saw him launch himself into Ainsley's arms, pressing his face against her chest. Her friend held her son, rubbing his back, and Starla put on her sunglasses. *Enjoy it while it lasts, kid. This won't work in a few weeks.* She had no tears for him right now; if she couldn't even cry for Charlie, for herself, she couldn't be expected to conjure sympathy for her son, even though she could see he was Going Through a Thing. She wasn't even mad; she was numb. Her chest felt hollow where her heart belonged; she actually put her fingers to her neck to make sure she still had a pulse. There was a truck coming down Highway 22 when she looked left at the intersection. She pulled out anyway, pealing her tires, and she could smell the acrid scent of rubber on the road as she accelerated hard. Starla broke out into a cold sweat watching the white semi-truck barreling toward her; reality set in as he blared his horn in retaliation for cutting him off. *What is happening to me? I left my son standing on the sidewalk and just nearly got me and Em killed. And the baby. What am I doing? Have I lost my mind?* When she pulled into the long driveway up at Sawyer's, she got out of the car, leaving the door open and Emily to unbuckle herself. She sat down hard on the wooden porch steps, knowing there were ants and spiders and dirt there. Starla buried her head in her arms, pulled up as tightly around her knees as her bump allowed, and tried to just breathe.

To her left, Sawyer's front door opened, and she heard his voice float to her.

"Yeah, she's here." His boots crunched against the gravel. *He's coming over here. He's going to want an explanation. He's going to want to talk. He's going to think I'm off my rocker. Poor laid-back guy didn't realize what he was getting into with me . . .*

"Okay." He was still talking into the phone, from the sound of it. "All right. I'll tell her. Thanks, Ains. Bye." She felt the step sag under the weight of him. *Oh good,* now *the tears are coming . . .* she waited for the questions. The condemnation. The anger. Instead, she felt a gentle, calloused hand against her back, rubbing big circles, brushing her hair aside. That only made the tears come harder. *Stupid pregnancy hormones.* She turned her head just enough to peek at him with one eye. She caught him wiping a tear from his own face.

"Tears?" she asked.

"For you, always." It was more than a cheesy sentiment; she could tell he meant it. And it was the first time the word 'always' had entered their vocabulary. It helped her settle a little, but she was still hurting.

"I told him. I told him I was leaving," she said, and it suddenly occurred that she hadn't told Sawyer. He was finding out, too.

"Ainsley mentioned that."

"How's Aiden?"

"He's okay. He and Charlie are both with Ainsley. Charlie was apparently in no state to drive, so she took both of them back to her apartment, where they are crashed on the couch, snuggling, eating cookies and watching *Man vs. Wild* reruns."

She let out a heavy sigh and covered her eyes again. *Okay, they're both okay. They're both safe.* She'd go pick them both up later. Maybe they could all go to Annie's or something. After she made some serious apologies for how she'd handled all this. Starla took a few deep breaths, letting the tears slow, wiping her nose.

"Is Mama okay?" Em's small voice seemed even more vulnerable than usual.

"Sure, chickpea. She just had a hard day. Aiden's okay too, he's with your daddy. Aunt Ainsley's taking good care of them. No need to worry. Hey, what do you say you and me get some dinner started?" The man was a natural distractor.

The hope in her voice was palpable. "Tacos?"

The adults both laughed, and Starla lifted her head, swiping at her wet face.

"Of course tacos! What else would a girl want? Let's go get the tortillas started. I'm sure your mama will come inside in a few minutes . . . she just needs a little 'mama time.'" He held out his hand, and Emily skipped over to take it, letting him lead her into the house. "Mamas work real hard when they're growing a baby, you see, so sometimes, it makes them feel real tired, so we have to take extra good care of them."

"Should we make meat, too, then?"

"Definitely. Mamas need meat for sure. What else, do you think?" Their voices became muted as he closed the front door behind the two of them. Starla stared out at the woods, wondering how she could go through with this.

"I have to try," she whispered, and when the wind tossed the tops of the trees mercilessly, she thought maybe the town itself hated the idea of her leaving as much as she did.

# CHAPTER TWENTY-EIGHT

AFTER DINNER, SAWYER washed her dishes. They'd all been quiet at dinner, and the kids crashed out almost immediately after the meal, both exhausted. Starla sat on the counter in the dimly-lit kitchen, watching him, hands braced on either side of her knees, her belly sticking out more than usual. Their thing, it had been casual . . . on the outside, anyway. He'd known it was a possibility that she was leaving before he'd even kissed her, thanks to his nosy cousin. But he was struggling.

"Are you mad at me?" Her voice was meek, and when he turned to look at her, she was staring ardently at her toes. He wiped his hands on his jeans as he went to her, putting his hands on her hips, standing between her legs.

"No, sugar," he whispered, letting his forehead rest against hers. He was just sad. So sad.

"That's not how I was going to tell you," she whispered back. He didn't care about that; it was going to hurt however and whenever he found out. Another question had been nagging at him since Ainsley called.

"Why didn't you talk it over with me?"

She jostled him a little as she shrugged. "I didn't want you to talk me out of it."

He pulled back just enough to look her in the eye. "Star, is this what you need?"

229

"I think so."

"Then why would I talk you out of it?" He leaned forward, pausing, unsure if he was allowed to kiss her now. When she smiled shyly, he kissed her for all he was worth. It was a mistake; not because she pushed him away or in any way resisted; no, he could feel her melting under his fingertips. It was a mistake because the tears he'd been trying to push down all afternoon surfaced suddenly. He'd been able to mostly hold it together in front of the kids, but the kids were in bed now. And he was holding the only woman he'd ever really loved, and he was losing her. But his feelings weren't the big issue.

"You think I don't know what you've been through? I do. And I'm sure I don't know the half of it. So if this is what you need, I want you to take it. Do it, sugar. Grab it with both hands."

Her fingers flexed in his hair and he released a shaky sigh. *I'm not what she needs.* It was self-pitying and pathetic and he hated himself for thinking it. But he knew what it felt like to have a dream stripped away. He couldn't do that to her. Not even if he'd dissolve once she was gone.

"This ain't about me." He had to speak that out loud. He wanted to hear her say it.

"It really isn't," she whispered. "I promise it isn't. You're . . . we're . . . I mean . . ." She kissed him hard, and he felt a deep relief that she wasn't going to hold him at arm's length now.

"Would you . . ." Now she was the one pulling back to stare into his eyes. "Would you come with us?" It touched him that she'd ask. Her face fell when he shook his head.

"For good or bad, I'm a Timberite. You helped me realize that. I think I've judged folks here harder than they ever did me, to be honest. Beyond my own medical condition being no match for the heat, I have my work at the hospital that I've committed to. And I couldn't leave my mama like that. She'd be sick with worry all the time that I'd collapsed at the Piggly Wiggly."

She was wiping her own tears now. "What's a Piggly Wiggly?"

"It's a grocery store," he said, stuffing his hands in his pockets. "Don't know if they have them in Arizona, though."

She bit her lip, and he wished she'd say whatever was on her mind. "I'm not ready to let you go," she whispered, touching his jawline almost reverently. "I know it's not fair to ask, and we haven't really defined what we're doing, but can we just continue as we have been? Is that okay? Can we do that?"

He found himself nodding, and when she kissed him again, he held as tight as he could without hurting her or the baby. Lord, he had no self-preservation whatsoever when it came to her. A smart person would be trying to slow things down, getting some distance, making her departure a little easier. Not him. He was going to rocket right off an emotional cliff, throttle open wide, not even touching the brakes. He was all in. Hopelessly, helplessly, all in.

FOR SAWYER, THE NEXT two weeks went by in a blur of dinners with Starla, dropping the kids off and picking them up, working at the hospital, working on the bikes. She seemed to think she'd given him an out after her horribly-handled moving announcement. If anything, he'd doubled down. He took the kids for hikes and walks; he even hung out with them all day when they didn't want to go to the library. She kept asking him if he wasn't overdoing it, but he just chuckled and kissed her temple. He wasn't going to give up any time with her. Not if he had so little left. She was scheduled to leave on July eighth. Ainsley was going to drive down with her and fly back. He'd never envied his cousin more.

In fact, he'd been cleared to drive at his last doctor's appointment, when he'd gone in to talk about his bladder issues. But he kept letting her drive him around. He relished those quiet times, sans kids, sans anyone else. Her evenings had been devoted to packing lately, so those car rides became all the more precious. He didn't want her to think she had to move; their deal had been driving for housing. That's what he was telling himself, anyway.

On the morning of July fourth, he heard a weird sound outside. He'd decided to take the day off and just chill. *Bang. Bang. Bang.* He peeked between the curtains out front; Starla was back from dropping off her kids for their weekend with their dad. And apparently, a cardboard box that had once held peaches had somehow wronged her, because she was kicking it across the driveway toward the dumpster.

He slipped on shoes and came out onto the front porch. "Everything all right?"

"Fine! Fabulous, why wouldn't it be?" she snapped.

"Oh, I don't know. Seems like you might be upset."

"Whatever gave you that impression?" she barked, giving the box another giant kick, sending it flying four feet.

"Good. This is good. It's good to get your feelings out." He yanked the ax out of the log. "Now, let's teach you how to chop wood."

"I don't want to chop wood!" she yelled, and it was like fighting with Tinkerbell. There was nothing intimidating about her whatsoever.

"Look, getting your feelings out is a good start, but you need to *do* something. Get your feelings out of your body, not just out of your head." He handed her the tool, praying she wouldn't decide to use it as a weapon and lock herself in the house to get that alone time she was wanting.

She pushed her hair out of her face with her wrist, trying not to get her face dirty, but she left a wide muddy streak across her forehead that she was apparently unaware of. He'd make sure she showered before she went into town again. If his plan worked, she'd be sweaty and need one anyway before too much longer.

"That actually makes sense." She marched over to him, her hand out for the ax. He didn't let go when she clamped onto the handle.

"You're gonna need a bit of instruction, sweetheart . . ."

She stepped closer so they were toe-to-toe. "Been camping with my father since I was knee-high to a grasshopper, pal. I know how to split a round. Now pass it over."

"My apologies . . ." he murmured, trying hard not to grin. He released the handle and she had to take a step sideways to accommodate the weight of the tool or lose her balance. *Having a burgeoning baby belly will do that to one's balance, I suppose.*

She muttered something about mansplaining being unattractive, and then he did chuckle. To her credit, she braced her feet apart and anchored her left hand at the end. She even slid them together when she brought the ax head over her shoulder like a pro. "There!" she cried. "There's nothing sweet about that, is there?" He wished she could see herself through his eyes. Her focus, her drive, her careful way with something as pointless as firewood. Her absolute certainty that she was a badass. It wouldn't surprise him if she was giving him tooth decay, she was so sweet. Starla turned and set another log on the stump, carefully balancing it on its end before she brought the ax down on it like she was taking someone's head off.

"No, you're right," he assured her seriously. "You're clearly a menace to society with a tool like that in your hands, Tinkerbell."

"Tinkerbell? I am not a flighty, stupid fairy." She jutted her chin out. "And as for being a menace, I *am*. I could be, if properly motivated."

"And are you? Motivated?"

"I am today."

"Why, what are you so mad about?"

"Everything!" she yelled. She brought the ax down on the unsuspecting log and split it cleanly in half. "I'm mad that Charlie won't leave us alone. I'm mad that my kids miss him so effing much." She set up another log and bisected it the same way. "I'm mad that I miss him, even though he lied to me constantly. I'm mad that I had to leave my own house, because there's boxes everywhere and I can't find anything now. I'm mad that I have to move, even though I know it's what I need." The ax slipped from her grasp, and her eyes were shining. "I knew the first holiday without them would be hard, I just . . ." Her voice dropped to a whisper. "I shouldn't miss them so much when it's just two nights." *She's going to cry.* He wouldn't tell her not to, even if he hated seeing it. He'd been teased too much about it growing up.

"That sounds real tough." He hoped she didn't hear the catch in his voice. Sawyer felt a lump in his own throat. He'd always been an easy crier. Couldn't get through half of the Disney movies he'd seen as a kid without his 'allergies' acting up. But a mild panic kept the tears at bay, because he had no idea what she expected of him right now.

"It is." Her lower lip was quivering, and he felt the hot tears gathering in the corners of his eyes as she sat down hard on the empty stump. "It's really hard. But everyone in town just keeps asking if I don't feel better now that we're apart. As if being brave made everything all right. They want to hear that it's all better, when the truth is that I've never been closer to falling apart." Seeing his tears, she got up slowly. She raised her hand and wiped the tears from his cheeks with her finger, one by one.

"Thank you," she whispered.

"For what?"

"For letting me chop your wood." It was nice of her not to mention the tears, though she seemed to view them as a show of solidarity and not a sign of weakness.

"I'm going to the Fourth celebration at the falls. Come with me tonight." The words out of his own mouth were news to him; true, he'd told Aunt Nancy he might come weeks ago, but he hadn't thought much about it since. Until now.

She let her hand fall away, and he kept his gaze on her face. Her gaze was laced with indecision and doubt.

"Don't overthink it. Just come be with people you like. You can drink. I'll drive."

"I can't drink and you can't drive, remember?" She sniffled. "And *thank you so much* for reminding me. I love sangria, and Ainsley has an amazing recipe."

"Actually, I got my license back a couple days ago," he mumbled.

Her hands went to her hips in irritation. "And when were you going to mention this?"

"Soon, probably. Maybe never."

The fear in her eyes was a huge surprise. "Sawyer, if you can drive again, does that mean you want . . . I can't pay you rent, I don't have the—"

He stopped her anxious speech with one finger to her lips. "And that's why I didn't say anything. I find your company exceptionally tolerable, sugar. I don't want you to leave."

"This thing tonight . . . people are going to know it's a date, right?" she said, her voice wavering.

"Is that what it is? I was wondering."

She snickered, but then paused. "But I'm leaving."

"All the more reason to make the most of our time together."

She bit her lip, then seemed to decide. "Do I need to make something?"

"Nah. Aunt Nancy always makes enough food for an army." He slung an arm over her shoulder. "Come on, menace. Let's go get cleaned up."

While she was in the shower, he managed to find a big blue cooler and some drinks, so he figured that was good enough for their contribution. She came back in the cutest blue and white polka dot dress he'd ever seen, a red bandana tied around her ponytail, and he suddenly felt like a slob. It even accented her growing belly, and he couldn't find it in himself to dislike that, either. That'd crank the rumor mill up full tilt, showing up in that dress on the Fourth of July. But that wasn't the only reason he was smiling.

"Can we take your bike?" she asked shyly. He shoved the cooler farther behind the kitchen counter with his foot as subtly as he could.

"Are you sure that's wise?" *Please say yes.* He'd wanted to put her on that bike for the longest time, and he hadn't thought he would ever get to.

"Maybe we could go slow," she said. "It's only five minutes on the highway."

"I know a back way," he said, already corralling her toward the garage excitedly. He'd take care of the melted ice when he got home, whatever time it was. "We won't even need to hit the highway. We'll take the BMW." It had an electronic suspension and anti-lock brakes; he was taking no chances with her being bumped around too much. It took a few minutes to find her the right gear; she was swimming in the jacket, but the helmet was good. He got on first in order to stabilize it while she climbed on behind him. It was in his mind to tell her to scoot forward, to wrap her arms around him, to hold the bike with her legs, but she apparently solved whatever skirt problem she was having, and he felt her do all those things. And it just felt . . . right. His soul sighed in contentment, and he told it to forget it, that this was a one-time thing. Not something to get used to.

"You good?" he asked through the sound system in the helmets, and she thrust forward her hand, giving him a thumbs up, which made him smile. He was relieved that she'd recovered some of her usual good humor. He hated to see her down. If going to a town thing would help cheer her up, he'd go. Maybe they'd leave early, but he'd go.

# CHAPTER TWENTY-NINE

THE LOOK ON HIS MAMA'S face when they approached the picnic blanket was priceless: utter shock and delight. She said something he couldn't hear to Aunt Nancy, who looked up with the same expression.

"Hey, y'all. You remember Starla." He held her hand, and she trailed behind him a little, almost hiding. She waved shyly.

"Sorry to show up like this, unannounced . . ."

"Oh, honey, we are just tickled to see you whenever you want to come around. Paige, make room," Rhea said, jumping to her feet and picking her way over to them past picnic baskets and open drinks. Sawyer rolled his eyes. As always, his mom took his face in her hands and examined him. "Your doctor approved you riding the motorcycle again?"

He nodded. "And just in time, too. Starla's leaving for Arizona on Wednesday." No sense in getting their hopes up that this was a thing. But of course, they pretended not to hear him. *They're as deep in denial as I am, apparently.*

"Well, sit down, both of you. You hungry? Nancy made a feast. I think we've got root beer, Starla, if you'd like some. Gary and Kyle were just trying to challenge some of us to four-hand canasta."

That had his attention. It wasn't as good as Boggle, but he'd still enjoy it. He was the reigning family champ by a long shot in most games.

"I'm still learning the mechanics of the game," Kyle said. "I could use the practice."

*A novice? Excellent.* "I'm in." He pulled Starla down onto the green Army blanket with him. "What's the buy in?"

"Look out, y'all," Rhea called from the other side of the circle. "When Sawyer starts gambling, you should only bet what you can afford to lose."

"Ooh, is that a challenge? I'll play," Starla said, scooting closer to him. "I didn't bring any money, though."

"I think I'm the only one who'll accept kisses as currency," he teased quietly in her ear, and she giggled. When he looked up, Paige, Nancy, Ainsley and his mama were all beaming at them, and he sighed. Did they not hear him before?

"I'll stake you," Kyle offered, and she thanked him. The trash talking started before Uncle Gary even dealt the cards.

"Is this going to be a repeat of the Wallowa Lake incident?"

"Outlier, Uncle Gary. I'd had a lot to drink."

"Uh-huh," Gary grunted with a grin. "What'll your excuse be tonight? Showing Starla the ropes?"

"Oh, I don't need anyone to show me the ropes," she said, re-ordering her cards in her hand. "Ainsley and I play all the time."

"She's terrible," Kyle offered. "She doesn't understand the nuance of the game. Gary's much better."

"Well then," Starla said, sounding sincere, "I look forward to learning something tonight."

She'd already melded and drawn two red threes by the time Sawyer laid down his first cards. It seemed that the universe was eager to make up for all her bad luck in the last year with some extra fortune now. *Unlucky in cards, lucky in love.* That'd explain why he was losing. He kept stealing sidelong glances at her; she was even cuter when she was trouncing three men who thought they knew what they were doing. When she paid Kyle back, Sawyer thought he might give up. But all three of them stayed in, losing round after round to her, until the ladies made them take a break to eat. As he'd predicted, there was more than enough for them . . . but not much of it was keto. He'd just have to suffer through and eat what was available, fried chicken and all. It didn't feel like a hardship. The younger crowd gravitated toward a couple blankets laid out together, and the older people formed their own circle. Random people he'd known in high school kept stopping by, and he shook the hand of more than one person who thanked him for his work at the hospital. How they even knew was beyond him . . . maybe the good news ran as fast around here as the bad. It felt nice, though. It just confirmed what he'd told her; a lot of the criticism he'd imagined was just a lie. He'd thought if he never came into town, he never had to feel their rejection. But by not coming into town, he gave them no chance to embrace him, either.

The longer they talked, the more Starla was yawning.

"Here," he said, crossing his legs at the ankle and patting his jeans. "Pillow."

"Just for a minute," she said, curling up next to him. The sun was finally going down, like it didn't want to leave the party. Hundreds of people had shown up to the park, and he saw more still circling the parking lot, looking for a spot.

"Hey, you think my bike is safe where we left it?" Sawyer looked down. She was out. He wanted to rake his fingers gently through her dark, thick locks. They were always coming loose, and it was like they were just making themselves available to be touched. Someone next to him cleared her throat, and he looked up to see his mama offering him a piece of cherry pie. She was beaming again.

"Would y'all cool it with the starry-eyed looks?" She grinned at him, but did not, in fact, cool it. He mollified himself by listening to his family tell old jokes and stories, underpinned by Starla's steady breathing and the sound of the falls in the distance. He waved mosquitoes away from her face and pulled her jacket up over her shoulders to ward off the cold. Not that it was cold. He made the mistake of catching his cousin's gaze.

"Is this a date?" Ainsley mouthed to him from where she reclined against Kyle's chest, gesturing insistently at Starla's sleeping form. It was finally good and dark, but he could still see her lips fine in the light of a Coleman lantern someone had thoughtfully brought.

"No," he mouthed back. *I told you, she's leaving.*

"Yeah, it is," she mouthed again, grinning from ear to ear. "Is she staying?"

Sawyer shook his head. He expected to see the hope drain from her expression, but it didn't. She clearly didn't believe him.

"Talk at the expected volume, please," Kyle said, demonstrating what he meant, and Starla stirred. Instinctively, Sawyer put his hand on her shoulder, and she relaxed again, melting into him, and he let his fingers comb her hair the way they always wanted to. It all felt too good. Maybe he should've let her wake, taken her home. Back to the lodge, he should say; it wasn't home. It wasn't *her* home. The first starburst of white popped above the tree line and everyone started to cheer, settling back onto their elbows to watch, blowing out their lanterns.

"Starla," he murmured, shaking her shoulder gently. "It's starting, sugar." It was futile; neither his prodding nor the explosions overhead could wake her. Sawyer gazed down at her, her skin glowing in reds and blues, her beautiful face a better attraction than any firework ever could be. Temporary. She was temporary, just like the pyrotechnics. A burst of light and color that brightened his life, just for a moment. And then she'd be gone.

And it was too late. He should've resolved harder not to love her, not to fall for her. He should've put his heart in a steel box and dropped it in Detroit Lake. She never would've found it there. She never could've taken it with her when she left.

# CHAPTER THIRTY

"YOU'RE NOT GONNA FALL asleep on the way home, are you? Because that could get disastrous real quick." His accent was thicker, and his voice was quieter than usual, spoken into her ear as he gathered the coat around her shoulders, helping her into it.

"No," she said, sniffing. She lied to herself and said it was grass allergies, but inside, some part of her was wounded, weeping, at the thought of not being here for the Fourth next year. It was the first of the Lasts: the last holiday here. And there were a lot more coming. He helped her onto the bike behind him, and then he started it up, the purr of it soothing.

"I ain't kidding," he said through the microphone. "You fall asleep and fall off, I'll kill you."

She just wrapped her arms around his middle and let her eyes close again.

"Talk to me, sweetheart, so I know you're awake."

"What should I say?" she yawned. "I'm too tired to think."

"What was the best part of tonight?"

"Kicking your butt at canasta."

"Which reminds me: I want a rematch. You fell asleep before I could reclaim my title as Canasta Champ."

"All right," she said, yawning again, giving his middle a squeeze. "But you're not getting your money back."

"Was it hard being apart from your babies tonight?"

"No, it was okay, actually." Even though she hadn't had her kids, she'd still had a wonderful time with Sawyer and Ainsley and their family. The games, the food, the laughter, it was all nearly perfect. Even though she missed her babies, she hadn't felt like she was missing out, and she was thankful to Sawyer for suggesting they come.

"That's a surprise," he said.

"I don't know what to tell you, your family's pretty great."

"Yeah, you're not wrong there," he said, his voice a little more growly than usual, and she didn't know if maybe he was having feelings about it, too.

"What was your best part?"

"Aunt Nancy's cherry pie."

"Mmm, it was so good. I want the recipe."

"Sorry, it's some kind of family secret."

"You ask then," she mumbled, then she shook her head, trying to force herself back to consciousness. "Did you celebrate the Fourth with your dad, ever?" It was safe to bring that up now, when he couldn't get away from her.

"Nope. He was always on the road a lot in the summertime."

"I like holidays," she babbled, yawning again. "Only . . ."

"Only what?"

"I always peek at my Christmas presents. I hate the suspense."

"Wow, you just cannot abide a mystery, can you?"

"No matter where my mother hid them, I'd always find them. I didn't always know which ones were for me and which were for my siblings, but I didn't have to wonder at it anymore."

"You wouldn't find them if I hid them."

"Yes, I would."

"No, you wouldn't," he said firmly. "I'm the king of hiding things." It was adorable that he thought so, especially considering how he wore his heart so readily on his sleeve.

"We'll add it to your title: Former Canasta Champ, King of Hiding Things, Chief Tortilla Maker . . ."

She fell quiet again, not meaning to, her eyes closing on their own again as the roar of the engine had sleep tugging at her, pulling her down. She jumped when he reached back and squeezed her leg with one hand, his gloved hand still warm against her bare leg. "Wake up, sweetheart."

"I'm awake," she slurred, "I'm . . ."

Sawyer pulled over into the gravel shoulder, and at the feeling of the uneven ground and tires sliding disconcertingly, she sat up straighter.

"What are you doing?"

"Get off."

"What? No, drive. Take me home."

"Starla, get off. Sit your sweet backside on that log, and I'll come back with the truck in ten minutes flat. Promise."

"What? No, Sawyer, I'm awake. I swear I am . . ." She had to pause for another yawn to overwhelm her, and he just shook his head. She took off her helmet so he could see her face better. "I'm awake! See? Just drive. It'll be fine."

"And how will I explain to your babies that I treated their mother so badly? I should've anticipated this, I know you're not a night person . . ."

She got off, taking off her coat, too, lest it impede her demonstration. "Here, watch." She pretended to walk a sobriety line in the grass, and he chuckled.

"Well, you better not be drunk, that's for damn sure." He got off the bike, and she watched him warily as he shucked off his jacket and helmet. "Jumping jacks. Come on."

Starla groaned. "No, doctor. Not at 11 o'clock at night. I don't even do jumping jacks when it's daytime and definitely not while pregnant. My poor abs can't take it."

"Come on," he prodded, capturing her arms and moving them in wide arcs up and down. "Do it. It'll get your blood moving." His face came closer to hers every time her arms went up, and he still smelled like cherry pie and lemonade. "Come on, honey. Up, down. Up, down. I can't let anything bad happen to you."

"Why?" she asked, staring up at him, framed by a sky thick with stars, stars like so many grains of salt scattered.

He stopped moving her like a marionette, letting her arms fall to her sides, not letting go of her. "Why what?"

"Why can you not let anything bad happen to me?" It was undoubtedly the most grammatically incorrect sentence she'd ever uttered, but she was too tired to care.

"Because . . . because . . ." Sawyer cursed softly under his breath, his hands slowly moving up and down her bare arms, then he pulled her against his chest. "My dad stopped by the other day."

"Oh?" Her brain was fuzzy with fatigue. She didn't see how that related, but she held him and felt him nodding slowly.

"I expected to feel something powerful. Hate or love or contempt. You know what I felt?"

She shook her head.

"Nothing. I didn't really know the man. He let his MS rule his life, break his relationships."

"Do you wish you knew him?"

He shrugged. "He's a stranger. I could try to change that, but . . . I don't know if I want to."

"It might be healthy," she said softly. *He'd still be a great dad*. She didn't know where that thought had come from . . . Lord, she was tired. "What does he have to do with me falling off a motorcycle, though?" she said, slipping her hands under his jacket to rub his back.

"He just got me thinking. I came close to making the same mistake he did."

"You haven't done what he did, though. You have us. You have your mom and Paige."

"I almost did. But you . . . you were worth trying for. That's why nothing bad can happen to you. Because I love you, sugar. Love you enough to take that risk."

She tried to understand what he was talking about. Hadn't he said he loved her when he'd shown up on her porch? And yet, deep down, she knew what he meant. He'd meant infatuation before, attraction. It was something more now. The kind of 'all-in' feeling that made you want to trade rings, buy a piece of dirt together, get matching tattoos.

"I love you, too," she whispered, pressing into him. Now that she'd said it out loud, she felt the enormity of what she was giving up, leaving behind. Because she was still leaving. Plans were in motion. She'd already quit her job. She'd already put down a deposit on an apartment near the community college that had hired her. She couldn't see his expression, but she felt his exasperation in the way he held her head against his chest, listening to his heart pound, singing to her. She was taking her own risks, and she knew he understood that.

"Star, look up." She obeyed, just in time to see the meteor streak across the sky. He turned to hold her from behind, and they watched the stars put on a show for them as they held on tight to something that was slipping away too quickly.

# CHAPTER THIRTY-ONE

SAWYER HEARD CHARLIE'S Tahoe pull up on Monday morning, and he checked his watch. Charlie always opened the dealership early. It was nice to see him doing his part to run the kids around. He'd better not be here to try to mess with Starla again . . . He moved his stool to the door of the garage, just to keep an eye on them. Charlie walked the kids to the front door, carrying their bags for them. He spoke briefly with Starla, his head bowed, and her posture said that the conversation was okay. When Charlie started back down the steps toward his car, Sawyer pushed his stool back toward the Harley he'd been working on.

"Can I talk to you?" Charlie stood in the doorway, backlit. Sawyer stifled the desire to correct his grammar.

"Sure."

"I know I made some mistakes with Starla," he started, and Sawyer laughed. Charlie narrowed his gaze, widening his stance, but Sawyer just shook his head.

"I'm sorry, man, but that's the understatement of the century."

"You were right, okay? I toyed with her. I didn't treat her right. I just never thought she'd . . . leave." He looked heartbroken, and Sawyer prayed he wouldn't cry. He'd rather cry with war criminals than cry with Starla's ex. He cursed his empathetic nature for the thousandth time.

"But she likes you," Charlie went on. "She'd stay if you asked her to."

Sawyer sighed. He couldn't believe he was doing this. He gestured for Charlie to follow him, and he led them to his cabin for a little privacy and a more comfortable place for him to sit. "You want something to drink?"

"No, thanks." Charlie stood in the living room, shifting his weight, looking around like he was waiting for something to fall on his head. Sawyer sat down in his favorite chair, his forearms on his knees, his hands folded.

"I could ask her to stay. But all I'd accomplish is pissing her off and deepening her resolve. We were friends before I fell in love with her. I'd like to stay friends once she's gone."

"Do you think . . ." Charlie's lower lip trembled. "Do you think there's anything I can do to make it up to her?"

"I don't rightly know. Maybe you should ask her. I think giving her your blessing to go was a good start, actually. Strange as it sounds."

Charlie sat down on the couch. "I don't want her to hate me."

"I don't think she does. I think that's what makes it harder." Sawyer raked a hand through his hair, thinking back to her wood-chopping yelling. "I think she still cares about you and she's all torn up over leaving. But she's tired of the games."

Charlie dropped his chin to his chest, massaging his temples. "I handled this so badly."

"Agreed. Have you thought about seeing a counselor?"

Charlie glowered at him and took a breath to reply, but Sawyer cut him off. "You're the one who said you wanted to fix things."

The man's anger wavered, mirage-like, then evaporated. "I do. I know she'll never take me back, but I'd like to at least be friends again. But I don't know if that's even possible."

"Time apart might be a good thing. Give you time to work on your issues. We've all got issues, man."

The two men sat in silence. Finally, Charlie stood up and offered Sawyer his right hand. He stared at it for a hot moment, but his hatred for the man was starting to morph into merely intense dislike. He could even see mild distaste in their future perhaps. A truce wasn't a bad thing, especially if he had any hope of having a good relationship with Aiden and Emily and the baby. Sawyer shook Charlie's hand, but he still glared at him, just to let him know that it was tenuous peace and he'd still kick him off his property if he tried anything stupid. Charlie nodded like he understood, then turned to leave, pausing at the front door. He shook his head with a smirk.

"I can't believe she left me for a sensitive lumberjack."

"That's sensitive *forest hermit*, thank you very much. And I'm not why she left you."

Charlie's smile faded into something sadder. "Yeah. I know."

# CHAPTER THIRTY-TWO

"DID YOU GET THE BLUE backpack from upstairs?" Starla called to Aiden, and he pivoted and went running back into the house. They'd been loading all morning. He'd been bringing out bags and boxes, but he didn't think he could stomach any more of it. Letting her go was one thing; helping her go was another. But it was important. And not just because she was pregnant.

"I think that's it," she said, dusting off her hands. "Everyone hit the bathroom, please. We're not stopping until we cross the Nevada border." Then she turned toward the car, muttering, "Oh, who am I kidding? We'll probably be stopping in Burns."

Sawyer just leaned against the car, trying to get through the next five minutes without breaking down. The kids came down the stairs with considerably less enthusiasm than he'd ever seen from them, closing the front door. He should go over and clean, get it ready for renters again. But not tonight.

"All right," she said, clapping her hands. "Everybody say goodbye." Then she turned toward him and really looked at him for the first time all morning, and he saw the pain she was in.

"I'd do it, you know. If you asked me to."

She looked up at him with big eyes. "You'd do what?" she asked softly. He couldn't look at her. It felt more right to stare at the canopy of trees above his head as he bared his soul.

"All of it. I'd learn how to French braid. Read her those dumb pony books. Eat tacos every night. Walk your sleepless baby girl around the living room at one in the morning. Build pointless stuff with Aiden. Watch Star Wars over and over. Hold you when you're crying. Defend you when folks are cruel. Dance with you at every wedding. Have one of our own. Hell, I'd even let you win our sprayer battles or Canasta occasionally, if that would make you stay. If you'd let me keep loving you."

She was crying silently, tears streaming down her face. With her mouth covered it, he was having a hard time reading her expression.

"Sweetheart?" When her hands fell away, trembling, he could read it clear as day.

"I'm sorry," she whispered. "I'm so sorry. But I have to do this, I have to go. I have to try."

He rubbed her shoulders, giving them a squeeze. "I know you do. I'm not trying to make you stay, I just . . . I'm sorry. I just had to tell you." He felt his own tears coming, and he didn't bother to wipe them away.

"Okay," she whispered. "You know that it's not that I don't want you, right? This is just what I need. And it isn't goodbye, really. We're going to stay in touch."

"Yeah, I know, sugar." He kissed her forehead, knowing it was probably the last time. His pulverized heart wasn't a surprise; he knew she'd still go. But the force of how much he already missed her was crushing him; he felt his heart was literally being smashed inside his chest with the weight of it.

Her kids were quiet for once; normally, they'd be hollering at her, ready to get going. Instead, they were both standing by the car, giving him big, wet eyes. Sawyer strode over to them, kneeling despite the gravel.

"You taking off, chickpea?" he asked Emily, and she nodded, tears escaping. She wrapped her arms around his neck and he squeezed her back. "You listen to your mama, okay? Both of you. And don't eat too many tacos. Spaghetti has its merits." Emily laughed a little, wiping her face as she stood up again. Sawyer could tell Aiden was fighting tears, too, so he motioned him in for a hug, too, but the boy just held out a fist. Sawyer bumped it with his own, giving Aiden what he hoped was a meaningful nod.

"Y'all take care of each other. What's my number?"

"503-555-2637," they both recited dutifully, even though Aiden rolled his eyes. He'd wanted to make sure they'd had it, just in case, even though he didn't know what he could do for them from 1,228 miles away. He'd looked it up: it was a nineteen hour drive. The thought terrified him. He turned back to a red-eyed Starla.

"No heavy lifting, you hear? There's gotta be some broke college kid you can pay to move stuff for you. And let Ainsley drive when you get tired. And text me when you get to the hotel tonight. Please."

"I will," she promised. "Thank you. For everything."

"Believe me when I say it was entirely my pleasure. Drive safe. I'll see y'all at Christmas."

"Yes, Christmas," she echoed. Then she turned and got into the car, as if she was worried she'd change her mind if she stood there any longer. He watched the red SUV pull down the driveway, signal its turn onto the forest service road, and disappear into the trees. And he stood there a long time, simply trying to figure out what had just happened. Why she wasn't turning around, calling all this off. How he'd lost her.

AT 9:15 THAT NIGHT, there was a knock on Sawyer's front door. He paused *Rogue One*. He didn't know why he was watching it past

bedtime, anyway; Starla and Ainsley had both already texted him that they were safely at the Holiday Inn Express in Winnemucca. And what was it with people showing up on his porch lately, anyway? He tried not to be annoyed as he peered outside, then opened the door wide.

"Paige?" He was more than a little surprised, especially since he was scheduled to have dinner with her and their mama on Sunday.

She held up a bottle of amber liquid. "Thought you might want to drown your sorrows a little. Bourbon is keto, right?"

He snorted a little, then stepped aside to let his sister in. "You come straight from work?"

She nodded and took her hair out of a sloppy bun as she sat down on the couch. "I'm beat. I've been on my feet since seven a.m.."

"Wow. Long day." He brought two glasses from the kitchen and set them on the end table between them.

"How was the hospital?"

"I told them I couldn't go in today. I knew I wouldn't be in any state, after saying goodbye . . ."

She nodded, then poured them both two fingers.

"Why'd you let her go?"

That ignited his temper. "Let her go? What am I, her warden? What makes you think my permission was sought?"

"You know what I mean. You could've gone with them. Moved your business down there."

He shook his head. "The heat isn't good for my MS. And I just started at Santiam."

Paige leaned forward. "Who are you?"

"I don't know what you mean," he muttered into his glass as he took a sip.

"Just what I said, dummy."

"There's no need to be belligerent, Paige."

"My big brother, he's had a ten-year plan since he was six. He worked his backside off to get into Emory. Got such good grades, Mama didn't just put them on the fridge, she *framed them*. Set his sights on helping people who needed it and didn't let anything get in his way. So I say again: who are you? Because you can't be my brother."

Sawyer just glowered at her. Of course she didn't understand; she'd never tried anything beyond working at Riverside Coffee. She'd never lost anything of consequence.

"Do you want her?" Paige pressed.

"Of course I want her."

"Then make a ten-year plan. Get off your caboose and be a Devereaux. If I had a love like that, I'd never throw it away."

"I'm not throwing it away," he snapped. "I'm letting her go *because* I love her. I told her so before she left. I encouraged her to go because that's what she needs."

"What about what you need?"

"I can't have it. Haven't in years." *Now that I have medicine back, all I need is her.* He threw his head back and finished the amber liquid, relishing its burn down his throat. "And when you do find a love like this—and I hope you do—you'll understand that giving them what they need can still give you life, even when it's killing you. I know it sounds like it makes no sense, but it's true. That kind of sacrifice isn't fun and it isn't free, but it's worth it. I swear it's true." Feeling restless, he surged to his feet and lost his balance, knocking his knee painfully into the end table before he caught himself.

"I'm sorry, Bubba. Sit down. I didn't mean to upset you . . ." Paige looked distressed, her voice laced heavily with guilt.

"Stop it!" he shouted. "Stop treating me like I'm fragile. I'm *fine*. I tipped over, all right? It's not anyone's fault, it just happens. I hate it when you wring your hands over me."

"Okay, okay," Paige said, standing up quickly, holding up her hands, but she looked like she had tears at the corners of her eyes.

He shuffled over to her, deflated. "I'm sorry. I shouldn't have shouted at you."

"I just hate to see you lose this," she sniffled, wiping her nose on the back of her hand. "You've come so far with her. I just hate it."

"Yeah," he muttered, gathering her into a hug. "Me too, sis." He held her for a long while, then cleared his throat. "Dad stopped by." He was sometimes a sore subject for Paige, who'd gotten even less of their father than Sawyer had.

"He came by the café, too. I haven't heard from him since. I'm still not sure what he wanted. I was working, and I couldn't exactly pause to talk to him."

"I know. It was weird, right?" He let her go and gave them both modest refills. "He told me he's got MS."

"Did you tell him you've got it, too?"

"Honestly, I was in kind of a weird mood when he came by. So I didn't, but now I wonder if maybe I should've. He seemed like he was trying to warn me or something."

Paige gave a slow nod, spinning her glass between her palms. "That's worth something, but it doesn't make up for taking off on us."

"True." He paused again. "Would you want to see him again, if he came back? If I invited him?"

"Sure." She smirked. "Couldn't be worse than drinking with you, Debbie Downer."

Sawyer laughed for the first time all day.

ON THURSDAY, HE GOT a selfie of the four of them, crashed on the living room floor of the apartment with the words, "Made it."

**Sawyer:** And how is it?
**Starla:** Hot. AC doesn't work.

*Ugh, no AC in July down there? Brutal.*

**Sawyer:** Make sure y'all are drinking enough water, all right?
**Starla:** Yes, doctor.
**Sawyer:** Sweet dreams, Star.
**Starla:** You, too.

ON FRIDAY, HE GOT ANOTHER text.

**Starla:** Hi this is Aiden can you cee if I lef my hedfones in my old room thanks

**Sawyer:** Hi, Aiden! I don't see them here, sorry. How's Arizona?

**Starla:** Ok I gess. I have to sher a room with Em. Can you send me a piktur of a motorcycle your working on?

Sawyer chuckled. He couldn't spell 'share,' but he could spell 'motorcycle?' *Yeah, that sounds about right.* He did him one better: he propped up his phone on the stool and made a video of exactly how he was replacing the muffler on this fine machine. What he got back was underwhelming, but he'd take it.

**Starla:** Cool thanx

He got nothing else from them the rest of the weekend, and it was hard not to feel mopey about it. They probably had a lot to do, connecting the utilities and buying beds and such. Then Monday rolled around. He didn't get much mail, but on a whim, he checked the mailbox on his way home from work. It looked like junk mail at first: it was a postcard from South Mountain Community College . . . in Phoenix. He turned it over.

*There is no Piggly Wiggly here. I feel cheated.*
*Love,*
*Star*

He traced the word 'love' with his finger before carefully putting it on the fridge with the magnet he'd gotten from the library. He hadn't been down there since she left. It wasn't the same. And she was right, they did have e-books if he wanted them. But what he wanted was teasing glances over her glasses and banter about his choices and speculation about who was blessing her doorstep with new releases every week. And that wasn't in the online catalog. He stared at the postcard; it was funny. It had made him smile. He had her address now; he could write her back. But he'd need something first: propaganda. Sawyer grabbed the keys to his truck. This couldn't wait until Thursday.

# CHAPTER THIRTY-THREE

STARLA HAD SPENT ALL day in the records room. It smelled lightly of mold and old paper, and it did not have a single window to open. No one talked to her except to complain that she didn't have the resource they wanted. She ate lunch alone outside and sweated through her dark blouse. Inside, she still needed a cardigan . . . at least one thing hadn't changed. She balled up the paper bag she'd brought her lunch in, then on second thought, she smoothed it out, folded it, and carefully put it back in her bag. It'd still work for tomorrow. She didn't get paid until the end of the month, and she hadn't heard from Charlie since she left Oregon. After a long afternoon of sorting and organizing a pile of microfiche that someone had dumped on her desk, Starla went and picked up her kids from their daycare, which they hated. They fought in the back seat all the way home and went immediately for their tablets when they walked in the front door. Strangely enough, she did miss actually getting to interact with her own kids. Sometimes.

Lord, it was hot here. It didn't help that she had her own personal space heater living inside her; she rubbed her belly affectionately as she walked down the sidewalk, and her baby girl kicked back. Someone had planted aloe near the large metal neighborhood mailbox in the midst of a blanket of white rocks, and Starla stared at it for a minute as she collected her bills. "How do you live here?" she asked the plant. It wasn't rhetorical, but the plant said nothing. It was well into afternoon, and the sun's burning gaze was still heating her exposed skin. It probably wasn't a bad thing that her job kept her inside a lot. There were no more walks to the cafe at break time; no money for that at the moment. She pulled her mail out of the keyed mailbox . . . was that necessary? Were people going to try to steal her identity? The closest they usually came to identity theft in Timber Falls was when husbands and wives tried to share library cards. She'd been shocked to come out to her car the other day to find her radio missing. What kind of place was this? Water bill (high); electricity bill (oof, sky high; she really needed to remember to turn down that air conditioning at night); medical bill (prenatal appointments were covered, but not her blood pressure medication?); postcard. *Postcard?* She squinted at it, letting go of her keys in the mailbox lock. It was a picture of the red brick library in Timber Falls. *What?* She turned it over, feeling raw at seeing this place that had meant so much to her.

*There is no Starla here. I feel cheated.*
*Love,*
*Sawyer*

Tears sprung to her eyes, even as she laughed, and she wiped them away. He must have gotten hers. Man, what she wouldn't give for one of his hugs right now; she squeezed the mail tightly to her chest. At least he wasn't too mad at her, if he could still joke with her. It felt like more than she deserved, keeping his love after she'd turned him down flat. She didn't know any place you could get a postcard of the library in town; he must've printed it himself. Riverside had tourist stuff, but even they wouldn't have that. She scrutinized it all the way back to their apartment door, fumbling for the door handle because she didn't know this place well yet, and she couldn't rip her eyes away from that little piece of home, that little piece of cardstock he'd written on with his slanted script; he had the right handwriting for a doctor, after all. The kids were on screens, so they didn't notice her come back in. She'd let them play until dinner was ready, then she'd make them for go a walk with her after dinner. Maybe it'd have cooled off a degree or two by then. She stuck the postcard in her left back pocket and pulled her phone out of her right back pocket.

**Starla:** Thanks for the postcard.
**Sawyer:** Thanks for yours. Having a good day?
**Starla:** Yeah. You?

It wasn't a lie. Not anymore, anyway.

**Sawyer:** Yeah. Have you eaten anything green today?
**Starla:** Yeah, I ate some of those sour apple gummi worms earlier.
**Sawyer:** Do we need to video chat so you can see me scowling?
**Starla:** Fine, I also ate a salad.

*But only because it was starting to go bad and I didn't want to throw it away. So bitter.* There was not enough ranch dressing in the world to make it palatable, but she was supposed to eat more vegetables to help with the blood pressure situation. Not that she'd mentioned that to Sawyer.

**Sawyer:** Your baby will thank you.

**Starla:** Shows what you know about babies. What'd you work on today?

**Sawyer:** I drove to Salem and picked up some parts. Screwed around with a Goldwing, changed the oil on my Honda. Posted on Instagram.

**Starla:** Oh?

**Sawyer:** Yeah, you should go check it out.

**Starla:** I'll do that.

"Mom," Aiden called. "I'm hungry."

"Hi Hungry, I'm Mom," she replied absently, tabbing over to Instagram. "Nice to meet you."

She didn't need to look up to know that her son was rolling his eyes.

"What's for dinner?"

"Tacos."

"Again?"

Ainsley had posted a picture of the new Legolas figurine Kyle had bought her, apparently protecting the candy stash in her desk. Martina posted a picture of her kissing Carter on the cheek after they'd gone running together. Little bits of care. Little bits of love. Bite-sized, and yet she felt they were taking a bite out of her. No one did her dishes here; no one took care of her at all. She took care of herself now, because that's how she'd wanted it. Starla kept scrolling, past bookstagram accounts with their beautiful rainbow stacks of books and cute flatlays featuring the newest romance she could no longer afford. Then there he was, clad in a gray T-shirt and his Atlanta hat, grinning into the camera, and her insides clanged with momentary jealousy wondering who'd taken it, who he'd been grinning at like that. Then she saw his arm, coming down to the camera; it was a selfie. Man, she needed to get her ridiculous heart under control. His mom was in the picture, shyly smiling, and she was holding a white sign in front of her chest. Her breath caught, and her hand flew to her lips as she silently read the text.

*Apologies to all who've followed this account for pictures of motorcycles and care tips for your machines, but I'm a man on a mission. See, there was this woman . . . it's a cliché, I know, but she got under my skin, in a good way. She's got my whole heart, but she's gone and taken it with her to Arizona. So I'm gonna borrow this platform for a bit, in case she's feeling lonesome down there in the desert, wondering if she means anything to the people here, and my sweet mama agreed to help me out. You'll notice her sign says #timberfallsmissesyoustarla; that's because this woman was precious to this whole town, and we feel the loss of her acutely. So we're gonna show her. #timberfallsstrong*

Her hands were shaking so badly, she could hardly navigate back to her text messages. She didn't even think to switch to a free messaging platform instead of paying for the text. There was just one word burning a hole in her brain, aching to be asked.

**Starla:** Why?
**Sawyer:** You know why, sweetheart.
**Sawyer:** Did you get my package?

Starla looked around, trying to peek out the front door without letting too much hot air inside. "Did you guys see anything on the front step?"

"Oh yeah," Aiden said, looking up. "It was heavy. I put it on your desk."

"Thanks," she said, dodging boxes, scrambling over to her pathetic table/desk.

"Why?" he asked, getting to his feet, his curiosity apparently piqued. "What'd you get?"

"I don't know yet, it's from Sawyer."

That had Emily's head lifting, too. "Mr. Devereaux? Did he send me something, too?"

"Let's find out . . ." She rummaged around until she found the scissors, carefully scoring the top strip of tape. Apparently, Powell's delivered anywhere, because it was full of books . . . three new historical romances for her, *CatStronauts* for Emily, a couple of old-school Superman comics for Aiden. The kids were babbling and getting grabby hands, flipping open their new presents, so they didn't see the note on the bottom of the invoice.

*They were never really for the library. They were always only for you.*

*Love,*

*Sawyer*

Her heart was mushier than the pinto beans she was about to take out of the slow cooker. She crushed the books to her chest, hurrying down the hall to put them away before someone spilled something on them, only stopping briefly to let herself feel the way his actions were tugging at her heart. He hadn't asked her to come home; not in so many words. He hadn't pressured her, even though she was sure he wanted to. A few more of these romantic gestures, and she just might go home anyway. *Things will get easier in a year or two. You'll settle in here, make friends, find a new dry cleaner, learn where the farmer's markets are . . .* but that felt so far away.

> **Starla:** Yes, we did. Thank you.
> **Sawyer:** You're welcome. Let me know if y'all have a wish list.
> **Starla:** You really don't have to send anything . . .
> **Sawyer:** I want to.
> **Sawyer:** Miss you, sweetheart.
> **Starla:** I miss you, too.

It was true, after all. Why shouldn't she say it? She looked around the apartment and wondered for the five hundredth time why she was here.

"Mom! I'm *really* hungry . . ."

Starla sighed. Taco time. With an affectionate pat to her new books, she trudged back to the kitchen to make dinner. But not before she sent one more message.

**Starla:** I'll take that video chat tomorrow, if you've got time.
**Sawyer:** Yes. Just tell me when.

# CHAPTER THIRTY-FOUR

STARLA HAD EVERYTHING she needed for her nightly call with Sawyer: a glass of water (because it was hot), a bowl of popcorn (because Always Hungry), and kids in beds (because she didn't want to be interrupted). On weekends, she'd been calling him when they were around, just so they could say hi. Aiden especially was quick to steal the phone and go out onto their pitiful balcony—"to be *alone*"—to get Sawyer all to himself for a few minutes. She had no idea what they talked about, but she wasn't worried.

She curled up in bed and pressed call. At first, she'd been out on the couch, but it was truly a piece of junk (and since she'd gotten it for free, that made sense) and not comfortable at all. If the intimacy of talking to her in her bed bothered him, he'd never mentioned it.

Hmm. No answer. That was strange. He should've been home by now . . . he'd sent her his hospital schedule unprompted, and she appreciated knowing when it would be convenient to call. It wasn't anything more than that, or so she kept telling herself. She took the opportunity to search her hashtag . . . there was another new post. Timberites had taken it up with relish once he started the movement. Today even surly Pavel had gotten in on it, posting a picture of himself in front of the broken photocopy machine with a sign that said, "Starla could've fixed It. #timberfallsmissesstarla #pavelmissesstarla." It was true. She'd always had a special relationship with that copier. The outpouring of love had been really . . . un-expected. And appreciated.

The fact that her first video call with Sawyer had spiraled into every night . . . well, she'd wean herself off him eventually. She'd miss his sweet southern accent less and less as time went on, surely . . . she hadn't started to yet, but soon, probably. The problem was that Sawyer was fun. He liked to play as much as she did . . . board games, card games, even their stupid sink sprayer battles. He'd start-ed a Words with Friends game with her, and her win/loss record was decent. Maybe she could find an online video game they could play together for Christmas . . . it was only three months away. Had she re-ally been here two months already? Her due date was fast approach-ing, too: only 42 days to go, in theory. Babies did tend to have a mind of their own, though.

Her phone rang, and she smiled when his face popped up on the screen.

"Hi, sugar." She loved that he still called her that . . . maybe more than she should. There were clicks and beeps in the background, and she squinted at the screen.

"Where are you?"

"Leaving work. I just knew you were waitin' for me. Didn't want you to fall asleep on me. I gotta get my daily dose of Starla. It's medi-cinal, you know."

"Mmm, a new side hustle for me, maybe. Gracing people with my presence for money." She stretched and sighed as he smiled.

"I'd buy it all up. How was your day?"

They made small talk as he walked out to his truck. He propped her up on the dash as he left the parking lot and made his way to Highway 22. She liked hearing about the new ways he devised to tor-ture his students: today's had included suturing a banana peel to his satisfaction.

"It was black, and I mean *black*, by the time she finally got it done, but she did it. She's no quitter, Dr. Udawatte."

"Why didn't she just buy a new banana?" Starla mused, rolling onto her back and holding the phone above her face. "That's what I would've done."

"Oh, I think my—*shit*—" She heard the sound of screeching tires against asphalt, and his face disappeared suddenly. The app asked her to rate her call. Starla sat bolt upright in bed. *What the . . .* she tried redialing, frowning. No answer. Hands shaking, she called his phone number. No answer. Did he have a seizure? Hit a deer? Should she call the sheriff—maybe Lizzie Painter would go check on him for her. Or Ainsley? Or his mom? She tried calling him again, her lower lip trembling. No answer.

Helplessness rolled into fear, and she tried his number over and over, her panic snowballing, her whole body tense as she paced, not knowing what to do. A bright pain in her abdomen had Starla doubling over, gasping. Blubbering from the combination of the pain and the fear in equal measure, she dialed Ainsley.

"I think he . . ." she sobbed. "I think he was in an accident."

"Slow down, Star. Who was?"

"Sawyer, he was talking to me on his way home, and then he just . . . he just . . . gone, he was gone."

"Okay," Ainsley said, and she could hear the jingle of keys. "I'm going to go drive toward his route. I'll let you know when I find him, okay?"

"He might've had another seizure," Starla cried. "Just find him, please find him, Ains."

"I'm going. I'm going right now. Don't panic, okay? I'll find him."

It was too late. Another stabbing pain in her abdomen had her crying out.

Kyle's voice came on. "Starla, what's happening?"

"I don't know. I think maybe I'm . . ." She rubbed her belly, the muscles still tense. "I think maybe I'm having contractions."

"I want you to get some water and lie down on your left side."

"No," Starla cried. "I can't. Not until I know if he's okay."

"Preterm labor is very serious and can be brought on by severe emotional stress. If they don't stop soon, you need to get an IV and magnesium sulfate immediately." The phone in her hand vibrated—she was getting a call.

"Kyle, I'll call you right back." She swiped away from before he could say another word. "Hello?"

"Sorry about that, sugar," Sawyer said. "My battery was dying, and then a damn raccoon ran right out in front of me. But I'm back now. I don't know why she didn't just buy another banana, maybe I'll ask her."

Starla sank to the thin carpet in relief, tears still coursing down her cheeks.

"Hello? You there?"

"I'm here," she choked out. "I thought you had . . . I thought . . ."

"Whoa, whoa. What's going on? Are you crying?"

She heard him pull off onto the shoulder, pulling the e-brake.

"Talk to me, Star. What's wrong?"

"I thought you'd had a seizure, I thought you'd crashed . . ."

"Oh, sweetheart." His voice was all sympathy, and he let his head tip forward and rest on the steering wheel. "I'm so sorry. I'm all right, I swear. I just used my phone a lot at work today. I'm all right. Don't cry, honey. Not when I can't hold you."

She couldn't stop, though. If she'd lost him, even this feeble, weak way that she had him now, it would wreck her. Another strong pain ripped through her abdomen, and she curled in on herself, a moan leaking out of her.

"Starla?" Now Sawyer was the one who sounded scared. "What's happening?"

"Nothing, I'm fine. I'll be fine."

"That is not fine, sugar—are you having contractions?"

She wiped her wet cheeks on her shoulders and didn't answer. She suddenly felt exhausted. She just wanted to sleep. Starla heaved herself off the floor and crawled back onto her bed.

"Starla, answer me." He was desperate, not firm. "Are you having contractions?"

"I don't know, I might be."

"I want you to drink some water for me. Can you do that?"

She drained the glass on the bedside table while he watched, his face pinched and tight with worry.

"Now another one."

"No, I just want to sleep," she murmured, laying down on the bed. "I'll call you tomorrow."

"No, do not hang up. Stay with me, Star." She heard slamming doors in the background.

"Are you all right?" Ainsley asked him, and they had a short conversation, the point of which seemed to be that Starla was not all right. She heard her friend spilling the beans about her high blood pressure, which had the two doctors feeling all kinds of upset.

"Kyle told you to lie down and you hung up on him? Are you kidding me, Star? Lie down. And you need to start timing them to see how far apart they are." Now he sounded kind of mad . . . but that wasn't fair. She'd only hung up on Kyle because he'd called her back.

"Maybe it'll stop on its own . . ." she said meekly, resting her head on her arm as a pillow.

"Fine. You have fifteen minutes to see if they stop. If not, you're going to get up, wake up your babies and go to the hospital. Or call an ambulance. Please. For me. You cannot mess around with high blood pressure. It's dangerous for you and your girl."

She sighed. "All right."

He stayed on the line with her—she could hear him pacing the gravel shoulder— but her body seemed to be adamant that this was happening, much to everyone's dismay.

"I'm getting up," she sighed. "I'm finding my purse."

"Good. Text me when you're in the car. I'll be there soon." Then he hung up. She looked at the phone in confusion. Did he just say he'd be here soon? That couldn't be right. She must be more tired than she realized, she thought, as she headed into the kids' room to wake them up.

# CHAPTER THIRTY-FIVE

STARLA WAS JUST SCRAPING the last of her chocolate pudding out of the bowl when Sawyer walked in. He was a mess: his hair was greasy, his dress shirt was pit-stained, and some kind of baggage tag was stuck to his charcoal pants. He'd never looked better to her.

"You were serious?" she whispered. "I thought I imagined that."

Sawyer dropped his bag and took her face in his hands. "Are you all right?"

"Never better," she chirped. "First time I've gotten to lie around all morning in years."

As the tears filled his blue eyes, she knew that was the wrong thing to say. Starla pulled him in for a kiss despite what were possibly un-brushed teeth, then wiped his tears with the edge of her sheets.

"I'm sorry," she whispered. "They said I was super dehydrated. I guess I'm not used to Arizona weather. Paired with being afraid you were dead and the high blood pressure, it was too much."

"You should be sorry," he whispered back. "I was worried sick about you. I couldn't get here fast enough. I didn't even change after work, I couldn't sleep at all in the airport, I just paced in the terminal until . . ." He buried his face in her shoulder, and she rubbed his back, trying to be soothing. She was really just so happy to see him. The smell of him, slightly rank though it was, was like coming home. "Did they stop your labor?"

"Yes, they did."

He straightened up enough to see her better and pressed a hand to her forehead. "You're all flushed."

"It's just the magnesium, they said. I had a headache, too, but they gave me something for it."

Sawyer nodded, then pinched the bridge of his nose. "Where are the kids?"

"With Aunt Rosie. Sit down, honey. We need to talk."

He looked down at her, his eyes wide.

"Sit down, Sawyer," she repeated, gesturing insistently at the chair across the room. Not taking his eyes off her, he pulled it over next to her bed and did as she asked.

"I've been thinking," she started. Starla let out a shaky sigh. "Man, I'm so nervous."

"Why?" he asked, taking her hand.

"Well, for one thing, I wasn't planning to make this speech until I showed up in your driveway in Timber Falls with a U-Haul behind my car . . ." She swallowed hard, but seeing the way his face flickered with momentary hope, she plowed forward.

"Sawyer Abbott Devereaux," she said, and his eyes somehow widened even more. "I had to text your mom to find out your middle name, and I guess that's partly why I'm nervous. I don't really know you that well, in some ways . . . but I know your heart. I know that I trust you and I've missed you terribly and . . ." She coughed to clear her throat, still a bit dry from being dehydrated. "Did you mean what you said, before I left? About how you'd learn to be part of our lives?"

"Every word," he said, his voice gravelly with emotion.

She nodded. "I've thought about that every day since I got here. And then last night, when I thought I could've lost you . . . I decided to go home and take you up on your offer." She took a deep breath and wiped a tear from the corner of her eye with one finger. "I know I broke your heart, and I'm sorry. I know I'm supposed to stop apologizing so much, but there's times when you need to, and this is one of them. I thought I was doing what was right for me, and I hate that I hurt you. I thought I had to come here to find myself, to figure out how to listen to my gut, to know my own mind. But there wasn't anything in Arizona that I needed. It turns out I'd already become the person I wanted to be. Only I didn't have anyone to share myself with." She rubbed her belly, almost absentmindedly. "Plus, the weather *sucks*."

Sawyer snorted out a laugh, wiping at his eyes. It was completely pointless; tears were running down his face so hard, she could see them wetting his beard.

"So that being the case," she said shyly, "I thought maybe I could come live there with you." She stared up at him, silently pleading with him to say something. He pulled her into his arms awkwardly, leaning over the bed.

"You're coming home?" he choked out. "You're coming home for me?"

"Well," she said into his dress shirt, "you said you couldn't come to Arizona. Did I mention the weather sucked? Plus, your mama said it best: I gambled with my heart, and I lost it to you."

He laughed, pulling her into a sloppy kiss like he couldn't help himself. "Loving you was never a game, Star. I promise it wasn't."

"Is that a yes?" she laughed, kissing him back, and he nodded as he peppered her face with a thousand kisses.

"You'd better not need to go anywhere any time soon, because I'm not letting you out of my sight for a long time."

"I might have to hyphenate my name," she breathed between frantic kisses. "My kids won't understand if . . ."

"I don't care about that," he growled. "He can have your name. Everything else is mine." He plundered her mouth; Sawyer kissed her like he was trying to possess her soul. Like she was the sweetest thing he'd ever tasted, and he needed just one more taste. Her whole body buzzed with happiness.

"Starla," he murmured. "Tell me I'm not dreaming."

"You're not dreaming, honey."

"Call me honey again."

"Okay, sweetheart."

He cursed. "Lord, you're contrary. That's even better. Keep talking."

"Hard to talk when you're kissing me . . ."

"Not planning to stop any time soon." He did pause then, though. "What about Charlie?"

"I think he finally gets it; he sent me a letter, apologizing for a lot of things. I think he'll give me more space this time around. I know he's been miserable without the kids. And the whole town is suffering without me there to fix the photocopier, so . . ."

"But no one more than me, sweetheart," he murmured as he captured her lips again.

# CHAPTER THIRTY-SIX

*CRYING. DAUGHTER.* Sawyer opened one eye to glare at the clock: 1:31 a.m.. Ugh. At least he didn't have to work tomorrow. He rolled away from his sleeping wife and his feet hit the floor, the February cold making him shudder. He really did mean to look into getting heated floors in the lodge somehow. He'd put them in the cabin already, and it was constantly booked; people really loved warm toes. He shuffled down the hall in his plaid boxers and gray T-shirt and into the room the girls shared. Emily was out cold like her mama, oblivious to her sister's unhappiness.

Sawyer picked her up, cradling her in the crook of one arm, the way that made Starla crazy. He could almost hear her yelling over the child's cries, *two hands, two hands, Devereaux!* As if he'd ever drop her. Ridiculous. He moved her up to his shoulder and thought he might regret it, putting her closer to his ear like that. But Dahlia quieted immediately, and he smiled. He was starting to figure her out. She liked to look around. It was like she was afraid she'd miss out on something Emily and Aiden were doing.

"The big ones are sleepin' right now, pumpkin," he cooed. "So let's follow suit, what do you say?" He knew it was just poor balance, but the way she knocked into his neck and stayed there, snuggled against him, almost made him believe she understood.

He and Charlie had both been present at her birth; he'd thought it was going to be awkward, but it was one of the most peaceful things he'd ever experienced. Say what you want about Starla, but the woman was good under pressure. A lifetime of tough experiences would do that to a person. Charlie seemed to know that he was only welcome as long as he didn't make snide remarks, and Sawyer made sure to keep himself far away from stirring up trouble as well.

They'd done rock, paper, scissors to decide who got to hold her first, but she'd turned in Charlie's arms toward the sound of Sawyer's voice, which of course, made him choke up.

"Dude," Charlie had admonished, "is there anything you won't cry over?"

"Haven't found anything yet," he'd murmured back, gently stroking Dahlia's fine light brown hair. He'd looked at Charlie, who was beaming down at his daughter. "Does it ever get old? Meeting these new little people?"

"Hasn't gotten old yet," Charlie had replied softly, twisting his words. "You guys gonna have one of your own?"

"Nah," he'd said, wiping his running nose. "I think we're good." Lots of people with MS had kids, though it was harder on women with MS than men, so it really had nothing to do with the illness itself. He'd just never felt an instinctual desire to procreate; he didn't daydream about kids that looked like him. He liked kids well enough, but he just didn't need to make them himself to love them. Whenever he said as much, Starla just rolled her eyes and gave him permission to change his mind, which he appreciated. This baby, this beautiful little girl, would be like him in other ways: she'd know how to change the oil in a Ducati, she'd know how to dissect a frog she caught down by the creek, she'd know how to grow tomatoes. Maybe it was small, but he knew he'd have influence in her life, no matter their genetic differences. Whatever amount of Charlie was mixed into her didn't matter to him. Starla's ex-husband must have seen the turn his mind had taken, because he turned his body to face him.

"Ready?" Charlie said, and Sawyer had put his arms out to receive her, careful to cradle her soft head. "Got her?"

"Yup." Emotion made his voice rumble. He'd tucked the blanket tighter around her with his other hand, and she yawned, showing her gums. She was so light . . . how could someone who meant so much to him weigh so little? "Hey, pumpkin. How's my girl?" He understood now, what his mom had been trying to tell him when he said she'd be fine without him, as he'd laid on her couch, recovering from his seizure. Because the love in his heart, the absolute adoration for this little girl, already threatened to overwhelm him. There was nothing he wouldn't do for her.

"I thought I was your girl?" Starla had teased from the hospital bed, and Sawyer had smiled at her as he slid over to her side.

"No, you're my woman. This is my girl." He'd leaned down and gave her sweaty head a kiss. He paused, aware that he needed to tread lightly regarding this subject. "Does my girl have a name yet?"

Starla and Charlie were watching each other, having some kind of silent conversation, then Charlie nodded, as if he'd decided something.

"Well, whatever it is, it should sound good with Devereaux."

"What?" He was so surprised, he almost dropped her. He started shaking his head, even before he could formulate any words in response to that announcement.

"I'm leaning toward a floral name," Charlie went on, "but I'll consider other options."

"Charlie . . ." Emotion was clogging his throat, and he tried to clear it. "She's *your* daughter. I know that," he ground out. "I was just being a goof, I don't expect . . . you don't have to . . ." He cursed. What he wouldn't give to be able to articulate himself right now. Staring down at Starla's baby girl, feeling Starla and Charlie's eyes on him as he struggled, was not helping. Especially since Charlie was such a smooth talker. And what's worse, he *had* thought about it. What he'd name the baby. And now he felt outed somehow, that they'd known he'd been secretly saving up ideas for her.

"Her mama will be a Devereaux," Charlie said, running a hand through his hair. He'd needed a shower as bad as Starla did. Maybe worse. "She'll live with you. It makes sense this way. I don't mind."

"Starla, tell him we don't—"

She'd held up her hands in surrender. "This was his idea, not mine. And I think we both know I'm crap at telling people things."

"Except when you left me," Sawyer had pointed out. "And him. And moved out of the state."

"Outliers," she said, letting her head flop back onto the pillow with a big yawn. "So tired."

Sawyer had handed the baby back to Charlie carefully, so he could take care of his fiancée . . . and honestly, he just needed a minute to try to get his head together. "Dahlia," he'd muttered.

"Pardon?" Starla had asked, yawning again, and he'd waved her question away as he started to gather up their stuff, not ready to come clean just yet.

Now, bottle warmed, he carried Dahlia Devereaux Miller back upstairs and settled into the rocking chair in the corner of their bedroom. The baby fussed at not getting the milk out fast enough, and Starla rolled over.

"Sorry, sugar."

"No, don't be," she yawned. "That's hot."

He chuckled. "What, me feeding a baby?"

"Yes. Hot. I don't want to miss this."

"Well, it is technically Valentine's Day, so I'm glad I could do something sexy for you."

"I can think of a few more things, but I don't want to say them in front of Dahlia . . ."

"You're a good mama, Starla Devereaux."

"And you're a good papa," she said, snuggling deeper under the covers. "I'll show my appreciation properly when the sun is up."

"I'm gonna hold you to that," he said, smiling, and he watched both of them as they fell back asleep, feeling like the luckiest person alive. He had two jobs he really enjoyed. He'd gained three great kids. But most of all, he'd lost Starla and found her again. There was no greater gift than that.

# EPILOGUE

STARLA WALKED THROUGH the sliding double doors of Santiam Hospital at 6:05 on a Friday night in search of her husband. *His phone must be dead again*, she thought, as she peered down a few different hallways.

"There you are," Starla said, smiling down at him, shifting Dahlia to her other hip. "Ready to go?"

"Almost," Sawyer said, frowning at a chart. He pivoted in his wheelchair with one hand. "Dr. Keynes, can you run an ESR and a C-reactive protein test? I don't like the swelling around the incision site; it doesn't look quite right."

"Ride?" Dahlia asked, squirming to get down. "Papa, ride? Ride?"

Sawyer grinned, passing off the clipboard to reach for her. He settled her on his lap, and Starla watched her daughter white-knuckle the arms of the wheelchair like she was about to go upside down on a roller coaster.

"Not too fast," Starla reminded them. "You remember last time."

Sawyer scoffed. "She was just being sensitive. I'm sure we didn't actually run over her toe. Did we, chickpea?"

Dahlia shook her head vehemently, and Starla rolled her eyes as he began to crank the wheels, picking up speed down the long, straight hallway toward the front doors, Dahlia squealing her delight.

"Faster, Papa!"

"Mama said we gotta be good, chickpea," she heard him reply, and she chuckled, lengthening her strides to catch up with them. That is, until she spotted Winnie Durand trying to corral her own daughter, Kendall, back into the nursing station.

"Hey Winnie. Hey Kendall." The little girl's white blonde curls bobbed as she scowled at a stethoscope that just wasn't doing what she wanted it to do.

"Hey Starla," Winnie smiled. "Here for pick up?"

"Trying," she said, leaning on the counter, in order to stay out of Sawyer's way as he made another circle around the floor with Dahlia. She lowered her voice. "How's he doing?"

Winnie shrugged. "He seems to know his own limits. And he has a wonderful rapport with the interns, to hear my mother tell it. She's delighted to have him more days."

*So am I,* thought Starla, and she called out, "Last circuit, you two. We gotta get to the restaurant." She tried not to ogle Sawyer's biceps as they went by; they'd become truly drool-worthy now that he was using the wheelchair more often.

"Oh, that's right, it's Aiden's birthday, isn't it?" Winnie asked.

Starla nodded. He was turning twelve, God help her, and he'd picked Annie's for dinner, then he and his friends were going to play paintball in the woods around the house. The parents had all agreed that they could crash in the cabin. Sawyer had put a filter on the internet a while back; it should be fine. Charlie was going to play with them, too. Her phone rang. *Speak of the devil . . .*

"What's taking so long? I thought we were supposed to be here at six . . ."

"Just finishing a wheelchair ride," she assured him. *Devil* wasn't fair; he'd made impressive strides in the last few years. And it was a lot easier to be friends with him now that his problems weren't hers. He'd even come to their wedding . . . he'd gotten drunk and embarrassed himself on the dance floor, but he'd come. "Dahlia, Daddy's waiting for us." If it struck Dahlia as odd that she had both a Daddy and a Papa, she'd never mentioned it.

"Dawson and Rhea been here even longer than I have," Charlie added.

Starla moved the phone away from her mouth. "And Mimi and Grampy's there, too."

The little girl's eyes lit. "Grampy? Go see Grampy?" Dahlia had embraced Dawson Devereaux with the most gusto, but the other two kids were warming up to him. Getting an invite to Aiden's birthday had been a big deal. The expensive presents he lavished on them didn't hurt; he seemed to have no qualms about them not being Sawyer's biological kids.

Sawyer pulled up to a stop by the front doors, set the little girl on her feet, and he got out of the borrowed wheelchair smoothly. An elderly couple gaped at them as he passed by.

"This is a great place," he said to them with a grin. "Miracle workers." They awkwardly returned his smile, and he winked at Starla. She couldn't help but laugh.

"What's so funny, sugar?"

"You and your shock value antics, that's what."

"Just doing my part to combat ableism like you taught me," he drawled, leaning over to kiss her. "I should be able to use my device when I want to and not when I don't."

"Fair point," she said, kissing him back. "Also, your girl's getting away."

Sawyer cursed quietly under his breath as he hustled to catch up with the toddler, who was exiting on her own via the automatic sliding glass doors. "Hang on there, sunshine. Hang on. Wait for Papa."

Starla grinned after them. If she'd been asked to guess on that lonely Valentine's Day what the next few years would hold, she'd have never come up with this scenario in a million years. Obi-Wan was right: there was no such thing as luck. She'd made choices that brought her here, and given the chance to do it all over? No hesitation. She'd gotten more than she'd bargained for, and she wouldn't give it up for anything.

This was where she belonged.

# Don't miss a moment of Timber Falls fun!

*Could Be Something Good* (Daniel and Winnie)
*Must be a Mistake* (Kyle and Ainsley)
*Right Back Where We Started* (Martina and Crash)

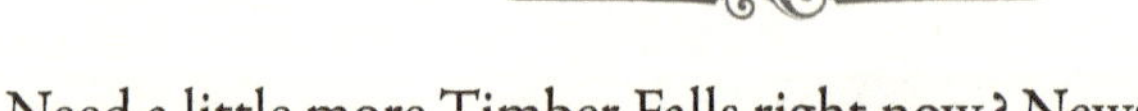

# Coming Winter 2020...

*More Than We Bargained For* (Starla and Sawyer)
*Never Say Never* (Lizzie and Chase)
*Don't Push Your Luck* (Christopher and Paige)

Need a little more Timber Falls right now? Newsletter subscribers get two bonus short stories, *When All This is Over*, a quarantine barbeque with all the main characters, and *Good To Know*, a steamy honeymoon epilogue featuring Kyle and Ainsley.
Sign up now at https://www.subscribepage.com/timberfalls.

# Connect with Fiona!

Thanks so much for taking the time to sample my work. I hope you enjoyed reading it even more than I enjoyed writing it, though I doubt that's possible. Being an author is a dream come true, and getting to share my books with delightful, thoughtful readers like you just adds to the sweetness. Like many indie authors, I love talking to fans! Here's where you can find me:

On Twitter as @FionaWestAuthor[1]

On Facebook as @authorfionawest[2]

On Instagram as fionawestauthor[3]

On Goodreads as Fiona West[4]

Or email me at fiona@fionawest.net.

---

1. https://twitter.com/FionaWestAuthor

2. https://web.facebook.com/authorfionawest/

3. https://www.instagram.com/fionawestauthor/

4. https://www.goodreads.com/author/show/18433825.Fiona_West